BOOKS BY THE AUTHOR

Justice Beyond Law
Justice Without Mercy
Shades of Justice
The Justice Trilogy

To follow the author's view on contemporary events
sign up for his blog,

EIGHT DECADES OF INSIGHTS

It can be found at
www.factsandfictions.com,
on his author's page at Amazon, or
Barry Kelly's Facebook page.

Blogs are published several times a month.

RUN TO FREEDOM

BARRY KELLY

PP
PROSEPRESS
www.prosepress.biz

Run to Freedom

Comments: davidbarrykelly@hotmail.com
or visit the author's website and blog at
www.factsandfictions.com.

Find the author on Facebook at www.facebook.
com/factsandfictions or follow him on Twitter at
factsandfictions80.

ISBN: 978-1-941069-02-8

This material has been reviewed by the CIA to prevent the
disclosure of classified information.

Run to Freedom is a fictional novel. Any reference to real
people or historical events or places is coincidental. All
places are used fictitiously and the author's imagination
has shaped them to fit the story.

Published by Prose Press
Pawleys Island, South Carolina
www.ProsePress.biz

Cover design by OBD
Contact: prose-cons@outlook.com

This book is dedicated to the brave young men who were sent to Siberia just after WWI to fight a war no one even remembers today.
They fought and some died or went missing in the frozen wastes along the Trans-Siberian Railroad for a cause they never knew.

ACKNOWLEDGEMENTS

People who I may have forgotten and those I have worked for and with have left a legacy in my mind, upon which I rely to write stories. Most of them would not want to be named. I thank them for showing me a path through the many minefields of our shared past.

Many thanks to Linda Ketron, who encouraged me at a very low point when I was despairing of ever seeing my first book in print. She has edited all of my novels despite a work schedule that would have killed most people. Bob O'Brien, my publisher and friend, has used his writing and artistic talents to work magic on the cover artwork and publishing preparations.

Without loyal readers, no author could muster up the discipline to keep writing. Reader comments have fueled me many times when I was avoiding the keyboard. I'm deeply indebted to those who read and comment on my stories.

Caroline Evans, a very talented young woman whose skill with designing web pages and maneuvering through social media networks to promote my books, has been my go-to person. Her skills as a sales manager have freed me to write my novels and blogs. She is an outstanding editor. Where my writing looks good, Caroline's hand shows.

My brother, Jack Kelly, brings his career experience as a Marine Officer, university professor, and all-around best friend to use in helping me with my novels. He believes after reading the first 50 or so pages that this is my best work so far. My friend and colleague, John Nugent, also a college professor and astute business analyst, read the opening of *Run to Freedom* and encouraged me to keep writing.

My wife and fellow intelligence operative, an outstanding writer herself, has taken on many chores that her husband neglects to devote time to his blogs and novels. She is and always has been an inspiration. She never sets the bar too low.

PREFACE

It occurred to me while musing over my first three novels featuring Jack Brandon and his team that the story of Jack's father, Peter, had been neglected. Here was a man who was a fast-track KGB officer who escaped from his masters and re-established the Brandon family in America. How did he manage to flee the KGB? How did he come to live in the U.S.? What was his life like in the Soviet Union? Who was Jack's mother? What was she like? Where did the name Brandon come from?

Run to Freedom is the beginning of the Brandon family story.

Has anyone ever written a fiction novel that was 100 percent fiction? I doubt it. Some truth always makes its way onto the pages the readers see. My characters are a combination of truth and imagination. None are actual people.

My novels contain a lot of detail. In the worlds of espionage, detail is king. Without it, any operations plan is useless. You may have to ignore pieces of the plan to deal with reality but scrambling from a plan is better than no plan at all. Detail also is necessary when devising and using aliases. Knowing when to change an alias is a learned skill. Bear with me as my hero changes identities multiple times over his journey.

For the intelligence operative, changing identities often requires a matching change in behavior. It is not easy to keep all this change straight. I've personally used many identities. Some lasted only a few hours, others months. The longer you use an alias, the more you slide into being someone else and the greater the impact on the real you.

I try to take few deviations from the truth when dealing with geography, distance, travel time, and various hardware items. Weapons used by the Brandon team and their capabilities are real. Distance shooting scenes are probable. Hand-to-hand combat is from my own training in Hapkido and the choreography of those scenes is correct. The firefights are plausible. Serving with CIA in I Corps Vietnam in 1968 and '69 gave me some experience with small-scale firefights.

The operational planning is real as is the casing of targets. The execution is based upon first-hand knowledge with a varying amount of fiction. Knowledge of the KGB is from study and two years in Moscow as the CIA Station Chief. The KGB is a worthy opponent and I added to my lore of tradecraft by that experience. Whatever skills I have in planning operations, I owe to excellent training by the CIA.

I want my readers to follow along with Peter Brandon as he tries to escape the KGB and feel they too are in the action. There are no superhuman actions. Many of you with the proper training could turn the clock back and face the same challenges.

My knowledge of the Irish Republic Army is slight. I hope I haven't used too much imagination and too little fact in writing about it as it existed in the 1970s.

I hope my readers will enjoy the story of the early Brandons as much as they like reading about Jack and Kathy. Buckle your seat belt and enjoy the action!

"When the time comes, the way will be clear."
Barry Kelly

PROLOGUE

November 1919

*A*s a kid in St. Cloud, Minnesota, Johnny Brandon *loved riding trains. He loved everything about trains. Their windows opened a vista beyond the structured world of school, church, family, and neighborhood. He loved looking out the window of a moving train and listening to the clickety-clack of the wheels as they sped over rails that narrowed to nothingness behind and opened to the future as it moved forward to new adventures. It was as near to time travel as you could find in 1910 in the Midwest.*

Now, nine years later, he would be glad to travel back to the certainty of a life he could count on. Lieutenant John Brandon stared through the clear circle he had rubbed in the frosted window. Outside, the bleak, frozen, forested land of Siberia swept by as the train from Vladivostok, laden with supplies for the White Russian Army of General Kolchak, moved closer to Irkutsk. In another hour they would be there.

Lieutenant Brandon knew the area around Irkutsk was especially dangerous and he was making sure his platoon was ready for action. The platoon had drawn train-guarding duty for the last three months. Once back in Vladivostok, they were scheduled for a change in duty assignments.

Lieutenant Brandon had volunteered for train-guarding duty. Big mistake. Endless cold, bad food, and long periods of boredom broken by sudden and deadly firefights when bands of Red Army Communist soldiers managed to tear up sections of the track and stop the train. His platoon and other units of the Polar Bears managed to fight off all the attacks and the trains eventually got through but not without costs to the Polar Bears, a self-appointed nickname for the regiment. Most of the men were from Wisconsin and Michigan with a small percentage from Minnesota. Some of them could speak some Russian, German, or Polish. Many had been too young to have served in France, but when President Wilson decided to support the democratic Kerensky revolutionaries in their struggle against the Bolshevik party of Lenin, John Brandon and thousands of others found themselves on troop ships going to fight an unknown war in a frigid environment they were not prepared to fight in.

Their mission from President Wilson was to protect and recover the significant amount of war materials the United States had sent to Russia when they were fighting on the Allied side against the Germans. Now that Russia, under Lenin, had withdrawn from the First World War, Allied soldiers from Britain, France and America were sent to prevent war supplies from America from falling into the hands of the Red Army or the Japanese. American sympathies were with the democratic Kerensky Russian White Army of General

Kolchak. To protect the supplies they had to fight off the Red Army and keep the Trans Siberian Railroad open.

Most of the men in Brandon's platoon felt they were being treated unfairly. The war they had been fighting was over. They had expected to go home, not to Siberia. Not even the field grade officers could explain why they were riding trains across Siberia's frozen landscape. Their hearts and minds were not in this backwash of questionable American interests.

Lieutenant Brandon was halfway through checking his platoon of train guards when the engineers sounded the alarm and applied the emergency brakes. Brandon knew it would take a half-mile to bring this train to a full stop. By that time, they would hit whatever caused the engineers to try and bring the speeding train to a stop.

"Hang on, men!" he yelled. "Get ready for action!" Nothing could be seen outside. The blowing snow and the late-afternoon darkness made it impossible to see.

Lieutenant Brandon felt the train derail. He estimated they were moving at least 40 miles an hour. At that speed, several cars behind the two locomotives would leave the track and overturn. The car carrying his platoon was two cars behind the coal tender.

Even before the car overturned he heard an explosion, followed by raking small-arms fire.

At least half of the members of the platoon were struggling to their feet and moving toward both ends of the car to get out and set up firing positions to protect the platoon first and then the train. Lieutenant Brandon and his platoon sergeant, Sam Reilly, managed to get firing points set up. Nearly all the platoon was in action.

Only a few were too severely injured in the crash to make their way out. The railroad embankment provided good cover for the riflemen and the machine gunner. The overturning of the car might save all our lives, Brandon thought. Most of the firing is coming from the rear of train where the valuable equipment is carried.

The attackers were mounted and racing up and down the right-of-way. The Polar Bear riflemen were armed with bolt-action 1903 rifles and the boys from the Midwest could shoot. The Springfields were the best rifles they had ever been issued.

Several horses were down. In the light of the flares fired from the train, Lieutenant Brandon saw a mass of infantry emerge from the forest. He realized the cavalry was only a probing attack. "Reilly," he yelled to his sergeant, pointing to the emerging infantry. "Bring up your men!" He wasn't going to lose his entire platoon in a fight to the death over an overturned rail car. When the platoon was together, he moved them back into the forest.

The accurate fire from the platoon's rifles from the cover of the forest turned back two waves of mass attacks. Lieutenant Brandon gave the order to fire one more magazine on the next attack and fall back into the forest and evade west down the tracks to Irkutsk. The next attack came after a new barrage from some horse-drawn field artillery. The wedge of attacking infantry broke through the thin line of Polar Bears. Only a few members of the platoon were able to fall back and escape to the west as a sudden heavy snowfall masked the battle area. Lieutenant Brandon saw Sergeant Reilly

4

go down with a fatal wound. He turned to move deeper into the cover of the forest when he was knocked down by a blow to his right thigh. Scrambling on all fours, he managed to find a dead fall of two down trees and crawled under cover. The fight for the train was over. Surviving was the next mission.

It was now snowing so hard he couldn't see anything. The wind strengthened to a gale force. The whole battle area was obscured by a swirling, white cover. Lieutenant Brandon, lying between the two fallen trees, could hear the shouts of Red Army soldiers and an occasional gunshot and explosion. They will kill all the prisoners, wounded or not, *he thought,* I've got to lie still. I don't think my leg is broken or any major arteries were severed. If the bleeding stops and I don't freeze to death, I can live through this. I'm already covered with snow. My tracks and blood trail must also be under snow cover. The Red Army officers will call off the attack and use the soldiers to load up the supplies they want. There must be a trail or road close by for tractors and horses to pull wagonloads of supplies away from the ambush site. I won't freeze. It's 20 degrees Fahrenheit. My winter gear and this snow cover will keep the worst of the cold out.

Brandon was dozing when he was awakened by something moving in the snow near his hiding place. He lay still. Listening, he heard a snuffling sound and Russian voices, then he felt the snow being brushed away. He reached for his .45 Colt but couldn't manage to get it out. As he struggled he heard a Russian voice saying, "Over here. This one is alive."

Strong hands pulled him out of his snow-covered hiding place. He tried to stand but his leg wouldn't hold him, and he sagged against the person who had pulled him out of the snow. He felt his .45 being taken away. He slowly raised a hand and brushed the snow from his face and eyes. The first thing he saw was a huge white dog sitting in the snow, watching him. He saw several armed figures bundled in fur clothing gathered around him. After a few tries he managed to say he was an American and pointed to the patch on his uniform.

One of the smaller fur-covered figures said, "We know that. We can tell by your weapons and uniform. You are a lieutenant."

Brandon, using his limited Russian, said, "Speak slowly. I understand and can speak a little Russian."

"Good," said the small figure in a female voice. "I speak some English. Better than your Russian. Now in English tell me about your injuries."

"I was shot in the right leg last night. The leg is not broken and the bleeding has stopped. I feel weak and don't believe I can walk on this leg. Who are you?"

"My name is Katrina. You don't need to know any more now. Just do what you are told. We are bringing a sled up to carry you. The trip will be hard. We will reach a safe place with heat and food sometime late tonight, if we have no trouble. We can't do anything with your wound now. If it starts to bleed again, tell someone. Not everyone will want to take you with us. They believe you will slow us down and they want to carry supplies on what sleds we have, not wounded soldiers. Do not worry. I will convince them to put you on a sled."

One

July 1921

John Brandon, now called Yevgeny Roskovski, was dressed completely in animal skins and furs on a trapping and hunting trip deep in the forest 300 kilometers northeast of Irkutsk, still carrying his beloved .30-40 Krag. He liked the Krag and when the platoon was issued Springfields, he had kept it. Enough ammunition had been carried on the sled with him to last for years if he was careful. His leg wound had finally healed and now caused very little pain. The people of the village, themselves outcasts from the civil war, had convinced Lieutenant Brandon two years ago that there was no going back. The Reds were still hunting down and executing anyone who had helped the Whites in any way. His status as an American soldier would not mean anything except a quick execution. If he was captured and the Communists discovered his real identity, the entire village would be wiped out.

During his convalescence, Katrina coached him constantly on the details of his new life. Brandon was now speaking Russian well enough to pass in the linguistic polyglot of languages spoken in the village. Katrina became his wife shortly before their daughter

Maya was born. With the help of a few of the villagers, Brandon had built a sturdy, three-room log cabin. He was a skilled woodsman, hunter, and fisherman when he was living in Minnesota and those skills came in very handy here. He was by far the best supplier of meat for the village. Some of the villagers joked about the treasure they had found under the snow at the battle for the train. To Brandon, that event seemed like ancient history. He loved Katrina and Maya. He would love to take them back to Minnesota and often found himself dreaming of ways they could get back to America. He was the last of the Brandon line. His parents depended on him to continue the family's bloodline.

Instead, the Brandon line was beginning in Siberia. The village became John's world. He now could think in Russian. He was Yevgeny Roskovski. When a son was born, he would be Peter Roskovski. As long as the Roskovskis remained in their remote village, they had as much freedom as people anywhere. Only very occasionally did any officials of the Communist Party travel anywhere near his village. There was no money and no tax collectors. The census takers didn't care. It was easier to estimate a census from offices in Irkutsk. Occasionally, furs were sold for cash money but most transactions within the village used a well-understood barter system.

Lieutenant John Brandon became a very small shadow that occasionally emerged only to be chased away by the needs and risks of living in a subsistence economy at the mercy of the weather. A cold or dry summer and the land failed to yield its meager return for the village's labor. A warmer than usual winter and the furs were substandard, and the river ice was not firm enough to allow trappers much time to service their traps along the river banks.

Late February, 1923

It was just such a winter. Yevgeny was ranging far north of his normal trapping territory. Maya needed some costly medicine and he had to find good, quality furs. His cache of furs was nearly large enough. He judged he had a 40-kilo pack. Today he had added five very nice fox pelts. A few more runs and he would start for home. Yevgeny had noticed the tracks of other trappers the last several days and didn't want to run into any other hunters or trappers. *No wonder though*, he thought. *This is a great area to trap.* He might have to come back next year.

As he pulled up his last trap, three fur-clad men stepped out from behind a growth of scrub fir trees along the game trail. One of them pointed a rifle at Yevgeny and in a dialect he could barely understand, told him to hand over his pelts and rifle.

"Who are you?" Yevgeny asked in Russian.

"Never mind," said the man who was pointing the rifle at Yevgeny. "Just do as you're told."

The other men had knives out but were not acting like they knew the difference between killing an animal or an armed warrior. Yevgeny knew after killing him they would search for his hide and the rest of the pelts.

Yevgeny dropped his pelts and began to hand over

his rifle, which had a round chambered and the safety off, as he always carried it when he sensed danger. The increasing appearance of tracks along his route had raised his preparedness.

As the armed trapper smiled and reached for the rifle, Yevgeny flipped the Krag up under his right arm and shot him in the chest. Two more quick moves with the bolt action and all three were down and dying. He knew there wasn't enough time to hide the bodies. The men weren't carrying packs. They must live close and people would be looking for them. People who knew this country better than he did. He decided his best option was to travel fast, pick up his furs, and put as much distance between himself and any pursuers. He was twelve days' travel from the safety of his village. He had 15 rounds of ammunition left. Not enough to keep several armed men at bay.

On the morning of the third day, he was beginning to believe he had escaped. Then he faintly heard dogs howling. Yevgeny picked up his pace, still carrying his pelts. Maya needed the medicine so he needed the pelts. With the rifle, traps, supplies, food, and pack of pelts, he was carrying more than 100 pounds. There was no way he could keep ahead of the dogs carrying that much weight. By the sound, he figured his pursuers were three or four miles back. He was within an hour of the next river crossing.

There was sure to be some open water along the riverbank, Yevgeny thought, planning. *A good place to hide the traps and maybe find a way to separate the men from the dogs. Dogs would go out on the ice. Men would not. Too much risk.* When Yevgeny made his way down the ridge and got to the river, there were several places he could leave his traps.

Picking a spot marked by a light-colored boulder, he dropped his traps in the water. No one would find them under the shallow, murky water along the riverbank. The pursuers were now above him on the ridge. He couldn't go back up. The only option was to continue southeast along the bank and find a place to cross the river.

The ice hadn't broken into fast-moving floes yet but it looked weak. He knew ice from years of ice fishing in Minnesota lakes and the Mississippi River. With his pelts and gear, he still weighed nearly 300 pounds, even without the traps. He traveled due south down the river until he found a wide sweep where the current eased off. Without wasting any time, he struck out across the ice. He avoided snow-covered portions and dragged his pack and pelts behind him to spread out the weight. The river was a good 75 yards across and the ice was mostly firm. As soon as he detected any sponginess, he moved laterally until the ice felt firm again.

Yevgeny breathed easier when he reached solid land. This was a good place to make a stand. He dropped his load of pelts and gear behind a large, fallen log on the edge of the tree line, checked his rifle, the light, and wind. By now, his hunters would only be minutes from reaching the place where he crossed the river.

The dogs appeared first. The men came out of the forest, held the dogs in check near the bank while they discussed their next move. Yevgeny's tracks were in plain view.

From his hidden position he could clearly see his hunters. They were all dressed the same. They gathered around the man Yevgeny assumed was in charge. The men were all carrying rifles and packs. *Must be army or police. This is getting more and more serious,* Yevgeny thought as he lined up his sights. *That's why the pursuit was so swift and well organized. These are experienced trackers. They may even have others coming behind them.*

While he watched, the men leashed the dogs and started across the ice at intervals of 15 feet. When his hunters were all out on the river and the lead man was, he judged, more than halfway across, he fired, aiming at the ice in front of the lead pursuer. The man immediately stretched out on the ice and began to fire at the edge of the tree line. As Yevgeny had hoped, the others closed up with the dogs until the whole group was within a fifty-foot circle.

Leaving his heavy packs, Yevgeny moved down the river while staying within the edge of the forest. The men on the upper part of the group no longer had a good line of fire and moved down to form a new firing position. Now the men, dogs, and packs were all concentrated in a much smaller area.

Yevgeny picked a good line of fire with protection and fired his five-round magazine within 20 seconds. Now he was shooting to kill. He hit one man and caused the whole group to move and shift. Yevgeny dumped five more rounds into the magazine and fired one more round, hitting a second man, who had been moving and now fell to the ice. He went through the ice and the entire section of river ice began to break up.

The three uninjured men tried to run back across the river, but it was too late. With their heavy clothing, boots, weapons, and packs, all sunk under the surface after a brief struggle. One of the dogs made it to the riverbank but couldn't get up the bank. Yevgeny ran up and reached down the bank and grabbed the leash to haul the heavy husky up on the bank.

The dog was exhausted after his time in the freezing river water and lay panting. Yevgeny rubbed him down with dry, powdery snow and wrapped the shivering dog in a blanket. "We both need to warm up and get some food," he said aloud to the dog. The dog perked his ears and lifted his head up to look at Yevgeny. The dog watched as he built a hot but nearly smokeless fire and warmed some smoked meat.

"You know, maybe we can be good friends. Let's call you Smoke," Yevgeny said, offering the dog some meat. Smoke licked his hand then gently took the meat. "Someone has taken good care of you. You're some version of a husky. Before your coat freezes, I'll get you a bit drier. We have to move out, but not too fast. I'm tired, too."

During the nine-day trip back to his home village, Yevgeny and Smoke bonded. It was almost as if the big husky mix constantly understood what his new partner wanted and tried his best to give it to him. He and Smoke avoided any trails that looked like they may lead to inhabited areas. At night, Yevgeny was able to relax and sleep for he trusted Smoke to watch over the campsite. In the morning at first light they were under way, leaving the campsite looking like no one had been there.

Yevgeny thought they would reach his village shortly before they had to camp again. The ground was still snow-covered and three light snows had fallen that covered any trail they left. Yevgeny was sure no one would be able to follow his trail. He had slowed the pace since his race against the men hunting him, and he no longer was carrying his load of steel traps. He knew he had to be careful. The word would be out. You don't kill five government law enforcement officers and three trappers without expecting the search to continue.

By the time the few lantern lights of the tiny village showed in the cold stillness of the night, both man and dog were ready for warm food and a roof overhead.

Yevgeny knocked on the heavy plank door and called softly to Katrina. She swept the door open and ran into his arms. Tears were streaming down her cheeks. "I was so worried. You were gone so long."

Smoke thrust his muzzle into her hand. Katrina looked down. "And who's this big furry thing? A friend of yours?"

Yevgeny laughed. "This big furry thing is Smoke. He helped me get back here."

"In that case, both of you can come in and get a decent meal. Smoke, you and I are going to be good friends." Smoke licked her hand and brushed against her leg as he walked into the house.

Yevgeny went in to look at Maya. Katrina joined him. "She is doing better. She may not need that expensive medicine. She has no fever and is eating and sleeping much better."

While Yevgeny and Katrina were watching over their first child, Smoke searched the room and lay down by the fireplace. He was sound asleep before Katrina was halfway finished putting a meal together. While she worked, Yevgeny told her the story of his trapping expedition and escape from the police pursuing him.

Katrina stopped cooking and took Yevgeny in her arms. "My love, you don't understand Russian police. They will never give up. They will follow every little clue no matter the costs in money or time. They answer to no one. You cannot ever go back there again."

"My Katrina, I must go back one more time. My traps are hidden nine days to the northeast."

"If they find your traps they will wait for you to return. The police know how important traps are to everyone out here. And you cannot buy more, even if we could afford to. They will investigate every purchase of enough new traps to run a trap line. Your traps were all marked. If they find your traps, I think they will put up a reward for anyone who can tell them whose mark is on the traps.

"You cannot sell any furs unique to that area in our local fur market. The police will be looking for any stranger selling furs where you were trapping or anyone selling furs from outside their local area. My father traded in furs and he could instantly identify unusual quality and where the furs came from. He could even recognize the skinning skills of the trappers."

"There is even more," Yevgeny said. "The cops may find those thieving villagers were killed with a .30-40

Krag rifle. It is not unique here, but it's not common, either. Ammunition is getting hard to find and our supply is getting low."

"I know we've been happy here," Katrina said. "But it is time to leave. I want Maya to have some decent schooling and a different choice of lives than she will have if we stay here."

"Okay, but we don't have to move right away."

"Yes, we do. I have a fear and an appreciation of the tenacity of the police you will never understand. It comes with generations of living in a country where there is law but no justice. Where the accused are guilty before, during, and after trial. The sentence doesn't matter. I know several people who have been sent to the prison camps. I know no one who has ever come back.

"Tomorrow we begin our planning. In thirty days we begin our move closer to Irkutsk and the services our children will need to survive in this society. You see, I believe things will get very much worse in the next ten years. The Bolsheviks will stop at nothing in their zeal to transform Russian society. The little people, like us, will pay the price. So accept there is urgency in our need to move."

"But how will we live? Here I earn enough by hunting and trapping for our needs. What will I do in civilization?"

"We'll become low-level party members and workers. I already have some of the documents we will need. Thousands of records have been destroyed in the war. With some forged documents and a few new ones from the government, we can establish ourselves with new identities. We must be careful to never stand out. Never be exceptional. Strive constantly to be a part of the masses. No one must be envious of us or our position. It is the Russian way to achieve equality by pulling people down. Not by everyone improving."

"This is your country. I'll follow your lead."

"You must think, my husband, that this is also your country or your attitude will bring us all down."

"Katrina! You have been planning this for some time."

"Yes, I knew at some time we would have to disappear and emerge as different people. Your language is now good enough and the danger to us if we stay here in the village is real. Now, think hard. I need your advice. Parts of my plan you will not like, but let me finish before you comment. Agree?"

Yevgeny nodded and Katrina started to lay out her plan. "Thirty days is not an estimate. It is real. I will take Maya and Smoke and find a place to live near or in Irkutsk."

Seeing Yevgeny getting ready to say something, Katrina held up her finger and stopped him. "Maya and I will change our names in this move. I'm taking Smoke because I don't want him arriving with you a month later. A man arriving from the wilderness with a big white dog is too much of an identifier. No one will think twice about a woman and a child traveling with a dog.

"You will arrive wearing poor urban clothes like a migrant worker who is looking for construction work would wear. Your past as a trapper, hunter, and woodsman will not come with you. If the authorities come here looking for the trapper who killed five policemen, the villagers would eventually identify you and describe the dog as your constant companion. A trapper traveling with a big white dog is too easy to find. Smoke would give you away. I know you well enough to know you would not kill him as most men in your position would. I respect you for that but I will not let Smoke endanger Maya or you. So he comes with us."

"And where does that leave me?"

"You, my love, disappear. In ten days you go on your last trapping run of the season. You find a well-hidden campsite, maybe in one of the many caves in the area, and wait two months before coming to find me. At noon every Sunday and Wednesday in the Irkutsk central train station I'll be drinking a cup of tea."

"So after two months I leave my hunting and trapping equipment behind and join you and Maya?"

"Yes. Leave everything behind, including your furs and rifle. An old Siberian saying is, 'Leave everything behind except a trail.'"

"How long can you live on the money we have?"

"Many months. I've hoarded the money you had in your pockets at the train wreck and some more I got from other dead soldiers. Gold and silver coins are good anywhere. But you must be careful where you use them. The corrupt officials and thieves are always on the lookout for gold. You always earned enough money from hunting and trapping for us to live on without using my hoard. Even when Maya was sick I didn't want to expose our treasure for her medicine. If she got worse I would've but I was sure you would bring in enough furs."

"I'm convinced. What will my name be?"

"When you meet me at the train station I'll give you your documents. I'm not even going to tell you what name Maya and I will use. It's better you don't know. If you are captured, they will make you talk before they kill you."

Two

March 1923

Ten days later, just before first light a sad Yevgeny left a tearful wife and a sleeping daughter as he slipped away into the night. Smoke wanted to come with him but seemed to understand when Yevgeny dropped to his knees, hugged the big shaggy dog, and told him he had to stay and guard the family. He took a southeast heading to take him into the mountainous region north of Irkutsk. He had hunted in the area but did not know it well.

Yevgeny carefully covered his trail until he was several miles from the village. He had seen some caves with grown over entrances. He planned to set up a camp in one of them. He would do just enough hunting and fishing for his food. The less travel in and out of his cave, the fewer tracks he would have to worry about.

For the next three days, Yevgeny moved like a ghost through the rolling, rough country north and east of Irkutsk. He kept off the wider trails used by villagers along streams and rivers and chose the numerous game trails in the higher, rough terrain. He seldom saw anyone. His fires were nearly smokeless and small. The snow and ice were melting. With his sheet of oiled canvass and bearskin, he could keep warm and dry. He still carried the beautiful furs Katrina wanted him to destroy. He just couldn't do it. He had taken great risks to get the furs and carry them back to the village. Who knows, he might be able to sell them somewhere.

On the fourth day he judged he was within two days of Irkutsk. There was no use moving any closer to populated areas. He had nearly two months to live alone and stay out of sight. He wouldn't even be able to pass the time hunting and trapping.

Yevgeny had passed several suitable caves in the last few days. He hoped he could find another one now that he was close enough to Irkutsk to wait. It was nearing dusk when he noticed a thicket where two pine-covered slopes came together in a near fold, forming a narrow passage that he only saw when he was preparing to set up his camp for the night. Stopping his search for dry firewood, he crawled under the tangled scrub growth for a closer look. As he pushed his way through, he saw a small clearing ahead. Once in the clearing he stood up, using his rifle barrel to part the remaining branches. Yevgeny saw a very old, narrow trail leading through the passageway between two adjoining cliff faces.

Going back and returning with his pack, he carefully moved through the screen of scrub fir trees. Moving along the twisting path, Yevgeny found a cluster of caves. Slipping his pack and checking his rifle, he went into the second cave of the five he could see. Inside he made a small fire. As the flickering light drove the shadows back, he saw signs that the cave had once been

21

occupied. A series of elegant, primitive painted figures covered one wall of the cave. The cave roof was several feet over his highest reach.

He cut enough pine boughs to make a bed, being careful to hide the fresh cut marks. For the first time since leaving the cabin and Katrina, he slept soundly.

The next morning after a breakfast of smoked meat and tea, he explored the other nearby caves. All the caves had been occupied at one time, but very long ago. He could find no evidence that anyone had used the caves since the primitive people who drew figures in all the caves left. One cave smelled like a bear had used it but he couldn't tell how long ago. The droppings he found were dried hard. He figured this was as good a place to hole up as he would find.

The only drawback was the lack of water. Now that the snow was nearly all melted due to the warm winter, he had to leave the small hidden canyon to get water. His goatskin bag would only hold two gallons. Every two days he had to make the two-hour round trip to a meandering stream to fill his water bag. He hated to keep going back to the same area but without venturing an additional unknown distance, he had no choice.

In the fourth week of waiting in the cave, he saw footprints along the small stream where he came for water. The tracks were all made with the same type of boot. *These footprints were left by some kind of government unit. Maybe there are still small units of the remnants of the White Army subsisting in the forest.* Moving carefully back into cover, Yevgeny studied the tracks. It looked to him that the tracks were left by men who came to get water and made a search of the area. Maybe in one of his many visits to the stream he had left some kind of a trail. He could see the men had searched both banks of the stream. They had to have seen something. If they were good trackers and really interested, they would eventually find his trail. A tracking dog could find him with no trouble.

The next week, Yevgeny stayed within the walls of his hidden canyon. He explored the narrow, winding trail until he ran into a blank wall that would take a major effort to climb carrying a heavy pack and rifle. At the base of the wall he found a small catchment basin filled with water from the melted snow fifteen feet above the canyon floor. At least that was something. He was at most two miles from his cave camp.

Feeling more secure than he had since leaving the cabin, he moved slowly back to his camp, day dreaming about his reunion with Katrina and Maya. Yevgeny was nearly back to his cave site when he smelled cigarette smoke that lingered on the light breeze blowing in his face. He edged around the last corner of the trail and could now see the opening to his cave. There was no sight of any movement or any sound but the smell of cigarette smoke was stronger. He edged closer to the hidden opening to the canyon. Now he could hear voices. With his back to the wall, Yevgeny slowly moved closer to the thicket that concealed the entrance to the hidden canyon. The voices were Russian and he was close enough to understand what was being said. Yevgeny stiffened when he heard the dominant speaker saying, "I'm telling you, there is someone out here. There are still enemies of the Revolution and deserters living in the forest."

A second voice said, "Sergeant, we've been out here looking for ten days and have only found one partial footprint on the stream bank."

A third voice said, "That's true but there are few sources of water in this area now that the snow is gone. Anyone hiding out here has to get water from that stream. All we have to do is wait a few days."

Yevgeny could identify the sergeant's voice when he spoke again. "I've been hunting men in this forest for the last two years. I know someone is hiding near here. No one is trapping now and there is almost no game for hunters in this portion of the forest. Anyone here is hiding from something. Remember, just ten days northeast of here five local policemen disappeared with no trace. The body of one of them was found two weeks ago with a bullet hole.

"The police believe the killer is well armed and a highly skilled woodsman. It is also believed he killed three local trappers who were armed. Now tell me, would an innocent man get water from a stream and leave almost no sign anyone was there and no tracks leading anywhere? No, the man who left the partial footprint is skilled in the ways of the forest and is not innocent. We will stay here until we find him. I don't believe he is more than few hours from right here."

"Sergeant," one of the earlier speakers said, "I know this part of the forest. For more than 20 years I've hunted here. A few years ago one of the elders in the village told me there are stories about a primitive settlement in a small hidden place in the hills with ancient paintings on the walls of several caves. He said the last person to see the caves died many years ago. But he swore the story was true."

"He might be right," the sergeant said. "Remember when you told me you smelled smoke a week ago? I wasn't sure then but that was before we found the footprint. I believe now you did smell smoke. We need to search in the rougher country. The way these hills and ridges fold together, there may be hidden caves all around us. Look at the way those two ridges come together, not 25 meters from our fire. Drink your tea and let's begin right here to search for a way to look between those two ridges."

Yevgeny felt trapped. He could feel the trickle of sweat running down his back. He couldn't hold them at the entrance. He only had 15 rounds left for his .30-40 Krag, not enough to engage three well-armed men. Also he didn't know if there were more men nearby. He judged he could only count on having 15 minutes before they found the entrance. They were practically drinking tea in the entranceway.

No matter how much he tried to erase all signs of having lived for weeks in the cave, it wouldn't be enough. The smell of his now dead campfire, or a few scattered green pine needles, his human smell, marks in the dust, his latrine, and food smells would give him away. Maybe if he had several hours he could sterilize his campsite but not in less than 15 minutes. No, his only chance was to travel light and try to climb out of the canyon where the steep cliff made this a dead-end canyon. Taking his rifle, water bag, food, and the city clothes he would need, Yevgeny concealed his tracks as he left the cave using his distance running gait down the canyon.

He hoped when the searchers found his cave, they would take time searching it and deciding what to do. They would not be able to tell if he was outside the canyon or inside. They would have to cover both possibilities. Probably post two men at the entranceway, as they would most likely decide he was outside the canyon. They couldn't know the canyon was a blind canyon. One man would either be sent to explore the canyon or to go for more men.

The furs he left behind would tell them he had moved there from two weeks' travel to the northeast. If the smart sergeant put the story together, he would know he was on the trail of a skilled killer and decide to move slowly and send for more men. Yevgeny hoped so, and that was the best he could hope for. But now as he looked up at the nearly sheer wall, he knew his biggest challenge was to get out of the dead-end canyon.

The canyon wall extended for at least 50 meters. He examined one end of the wall and then ran to see the other end. He saw a chance of climbing the wall where it joined the sidewall at a slightly obtuse angle. Fifty feet up he saw a narrow ledge where he could rest and maybe even hide. Here and there on this corner of the canyon wall stunted, wind-bent trees had found purchase in the poor, loose soil.

Yevgeny adjusted his pack, wiped out any tracks he made leading up to the climbing point, jammed his boot into a small crevice, and started up the wall. He had some rock climbing experience and found handholds, some risky, but he had no choice. He knew he had to reach the ledge before anyone came.

Looking back down the cliff to the canyon floor, Yevgeny could see the eroded handholds he used had been cut there by someone else, probably the ones who lived in the cave settlement. Looking up the cliff face he saw without rock climbing equipment he could go no further. The narrow ledge led behind the steep wall blocking the canyon to a small concealed opening. He had to crawl, pushing his pack ahead of him to get through the opening. After crawling several more feet, he found he could stand. He was in a large, gloomy cavern. There was enough light coming through the crawl space for him to make out the outline of the cavern. It didn't look as if the cavern went anywhere but it was large enough to hold many people.

Yevgeny moved to the back wall and built a small fire from the makings in his pack. In the light from the small fire, he saw primitive art as high as 15 feet up the wall. Yevgeny stayed in the cavern for two days. On the second day, he heard voices and crawled to the mouth of the cave. Yevgeny heard four distinct voices and it sounded as if more men were walking along the base of the cliff.

"Only a bird could get out of this canyon," Yevgeny heard one man say.

The sergeant said, "Don't underestimate this man. He may have rigged a rope to help him escape from here. Did we find any tracks near the entrance or in the area of the entrance in the light dusting snow we got last night? No! He is either still in this canyon or he got out just before we arrived. Saw us and took off, leaving the stuff in the cave behind. No man would have left those beautiful fox furs without a very good reason. So keep looking. I think he is in this canyon laughing at us."

The sergeant is a wise hunter, Yevgeny thought. *If I killed him, the others wouldn't know what to do next. If anyone climbs up here, they will find this cave. Still, maybe waiting is best. I have enough food to get by for another few days. There's enough water in the trickle in the back of the cave to keep several people alive. This cavern is immense. I need to explore it all. Maybe there's another way out or at least a place to hide if they climb up to the ledge and find the entrance.*

Yevgeny sat down near his small fire. As he looked back up at the cavern walls, he noticed the smoke from his small fire drifted up and toward the back of the cavern. *There has to be at least an opening to the outside somewhere.* As he was making a torch out of a piece of clothing dipped in the small can of cooking fat he always carried, he heard shouts and noise outside. Hurrying to the entrance, he heard the sounds of something moving along the narrow ledge. The light coming in the entrance dimmed and he could see a moving shadow from the bit of sunlight entering the tunnel at this time of day.

Yevgeny stood to the right side of the entrance. When a man's head appeared he struck him on the back of his neck with the butt of his rifle. The man groaned and stretched out face down. Minutes later, voices called "Alexandrov" repeatedly, followed by the sergeant demanding he answer. *If they don't hear anything and Alexandrov doesn't return, the sergeant may not find any more volunteers.* Yevgeny checked the down man's pulse. He was dead. *Tonight I'll drop him off the ledge to add more problems for the sergeant. After the 50-foot fall it may be difficult to tell what killed him. They won't know for sure that I'm up here. I can outwait them. They won't stay for more than a week, probably be gone in three days. That sergeant may set up a guard at the entrance. I'll worry about that later.*

Yevgeny waited until several hours after dark before slowly dragging the body out through the cavern entrance and part way along the ledge. It was tempting to keep the man's rifle and ammo but that would have removed the mystery. He smelled smoke as soon as he was through the tunnel entrance. There was a dying fire 100 meters up from the canyon face, just where the canyon narrowed. A strong wind muffled the sounds he made in dropping the body head first down the wall. He heard the thump when the body hit the canyon floor. He watched. No sign of men moving. He sat on the ledge until the darkness began to fade and crawled back through the tunnel. It was good to be out in the fresh air.

Shortly after dawn, Yevgeny heard loud voices and men shouting. He crept to the entrance so he could hear some of the conversation. He could make out the sergeant's voice.

"Yes, I know it looks like Alexandrov fell, but he didn't. That bastard is here. I can feel him. Alexandrov didn't fall headfirst off the ledge. Yes, I know he has all of his equipment and even his weapon. But where did he disappear to? He was talking to us and then silence for almost ten hours then he shows up here below the ledge dead. How do you dummies explain that?

"Okay. You can't. I want someone to go up there and find out what happened. What, no volunteers? Okay, you'll all draw straws. The short straw goes up on the ledge. But first, four of you go cut two 20-foot trees and some cross branches so we can make a ladder. The first 20 feet of the climb looks to be the hardest. Be back here in two hours. Then I'll decide who volunteers."

Yevgeny heard noises outside the cavern but couldn't make out what was happening. He was sure someone was climbing the wall but the sounds didn't fit in. There was no effort to be quiet. The noise stopped and he crawled to the entrance. There were no voices. The scraping sounds had stopped.

On the floor of the canyon 25 meters from the end wall, the sergeant was briefing his men. "Here is the plan. Our best climber, that would be you, Vasily, will climb the wall carrying our rope. Once you are on the ledge, Georgi and Ivan will climb the ladder one at a time. When they get to the top of the ladder, Vasily will lower the rope and help you join him on the ledge.

"There must be a cave, a hiding place or maybe even a way out of the canyon. People lived here in very ancient times. Who knows what could be here or what Alexandrov saw. This time there will be no periods of silence. If he is there, he knows we are here. No need to try tricks. Just kill him. He will not be captured. Shoot on sight. Now go get him. Remember Alexandrov."

Using most of his homemade candles, Yevgeny went

deeper into the cavern. He explored three short side tunnels that narrowed until they were impassable. He found three skulls in one of the tunnels and put one in his pack. There was no question people had lived here in primitive times. The smoke from his candle drifted away from him, down the main part of the cavern. He sensed the cavern continued on for some distance but with his light supply limited, he had to start back. He doubted his ability to make his way back in total darkness.

Yevgeny's timing wasn't perfect. Fortunately, he had put out his candle as soon as he could see a glimmer of light from the entrance tunnel. Unfortunately, he could see three men silhouetted in the dim light by the entranceway. They couldn't see him with the darkness of the cavern cloaking his movements. He brought the .30-40 Krag to his shoulder and shot the man who was closest to the entrance tunnel. The second man was down before he could fire a shot. The third had dropped to the floor at the sound of the first shot and returned fire at the flash of Yevgeny's second shot. His snap shot hit Yevgeny in his side just above his hip. He recovered, moved to his right, and fired the remaining three rounds in his magazine.

One of Yevgeny's shots ricocheted off the stone floor just inches from Georgi's head and hit him in the side of the neck, rupturing the carotid artery.

I'm in serious trouble, Yevgeny thought, dropping his rifle. *This wound may not be fatal but it is very dangerous. I've seen abdominal wounds and recovery is rare, even in the field hospitals. I need to check the downed men. I don't want to get shot again. My ammunition is almost gone, food for only two more meager meals.* He cut a piece of soft leather from his shirt and forced it in the wound. There was not a lot of external bleeding.

Yevgeny cautiously approached his hunters. He found no pulse, but he did find enough food for a few more days and weapons with plenty of ammunition. Exploring his wound, he discovered the bullet went through and through, but he was bleeding more from the exit wound. He cut another piece of soft leather and strapped it over the wound. He took things he could use for bandages from the bodies. Each man was also carrying a few candle stubs.

Before moving deeper into the cavern, Yevgeny placed the skull in his pack in the center of the entrance tunnel. He was feeling weaker and struggled to get back to one of the side tunnels where he had found a perfect hiding place. He checked constantly to make sure he wasn't leaving a blood trail. Yevgeny knew the sergeant would never give up. More men would appear tomorrow or within a week, depending on how many men were close.

He crawled into the small offshoot of the tunnel that was just big enough for one man to stretch out and obviously had been used before. Inside the small opening was a carefully placed boulder that could be rolled to hide the opening. He had plenty of water, a safe place to rest, and now enough food for a week. Using all the strength in his good leg, he pushed the boulder into place, totally blocking the small entry. He noticed the boulder rolled easily after he got it started. *If this damn hole in me will heal, I have a chance to get back to Katrina.*

Three

Yevgeny never heard any sounds from the extensive search a dozen men made of the chamber. He was awake on and off for the first two days and then, with a growing fever, he lost consciousness. The next day he awoke with no awareness that he had been out for another day. He drank deeply of his water supply and later ate some dried smoked meat. He was very weak and his shirt was sticking to his skin over the wounds. He heard no sounds. After resting, he tried to move the boulder blocking off his hidden space. No matter how hard he pushed and pulled at the boulder, it did not move.

He rested again and managed to move the boulder a few inches by using his rifle barrel as a lever. He was drenched with sweat and fell asleep again. Waking hours later, he drank more water and ate again. After a while he felt stronger. His shirt pulled away from his wounds and he could feel that the bleeding had stopped. Inserting the rifle barrel into the small opening he had made earlier, he pulled as hard as he could and the boulder moved enough for him to ease out into the side tunnel that led back to the main cavern.

Moving slowly and using the rifle as a cane, he made

his way to the cavern entrance in the flickering light of a candle stub. *It must be night. There is no light coming through the entrance.* Yevgeny could see the blood spots on the floor but no bodies. *They came here and searched for me.*

Walking up to entrance tunnel, he squatted and put the candle inside the tunnel. The tunnel was filled with broken rocks.

They must have blown the entrance. God knows how many tons of rock collapsed into the entrance tunnel. More than I'll ever move as weak as I am and without any tools. Unless I can find another way out of here, I'm trapped. I may never be found in this cave. Johnny Brandon from St. Cloud, Minnesota, you are in a very strange crypt. I'll rest and then try to find another way out. Don't panic. At least no one can now make me tell them about Katrina and Maya.

****

Katrina could hardly wait. It was the first Sunday she and Maya were going to the central train station to meet Yevgeny. She knew if it were possible Yevgeny would be there at noon today. She and Maya would be in the canteen drinking tea. Katrina hadn't told Maya they were going to meet her daddy. She didn't even want to look as if she were waiting for someone. She fit in well. There were many mothers raising children without a father. The war and party campaigns to prune away all vestiges of dissent had made eligible young men scarce.

Katrina waited an hour, sipping her tea while

chatting with Maya, who was acting like a little lady enjoying her tea and cookie. She had settled well into a private school that Katrina could afford now that she had a job interpreting for the Irkutsk Department of the Trans-Siberian Railroad. She could speak Russian, some Siberian dialects, English, French, and Polish, at least well enough to handle most situations. Maya was proficient in English, French, and Russian. At 1:00 PM Katrina paid her bill and left.

For the next month she took her tea every Sunday and Wednesday at noon. Then, afraid she was becoming a local story by her regular tea schedule, she only went to the railroad station on Sundays. By this time it was obvious to all she was carrying a baby. In her heart Katrina knew something had happened to Yevgeny. He was never going to show. Her Johnny Brandon. Katrina always thought of him as Johnny, the young American they had pulled out of the snow after the Red Army ambushed the train his platoon was guarding. She knew she was carrying his son and that gave her great comfort. She would bring another Brandon into her life. Maybe someday he or his offspring would get back to America. Katrina said a silent prayer for her husband, put her cup down, and merged into a crowd of tired, arriving passengers moving slowly toward the exit.

Four

Katrina never forgot the emptiness she felt as she left the terminal that last Sunday all those years ago and all hope of ever seeing her husband again. She was quite old now but she still went for her daily walk along the streets of Leningrad. Katrina had moved from Irkutsk to Leningrad in 1939 with her two children, Maya, when she was just turning 19 and Peter 17. Those early years had been hard even though she had a good position as an interpreter-translator. Life was better now.

Both children had received good educations. Maya was the better scholar of the two. She had been working on her graduate degree in Russian languages and the history of the Revolution at the University when she fell in love with a young math professor. Katrina liked the young man and gave her blessings. Maya and Mikael Orlov were married shortly before Hitler's panzers roared across the German and Polish borders. Neither of them survived the siege of Leningrad.

Katrina's son, Peter, volunteered for service and was trained as sniper. He had always excelled in anything that required physical skill and coordination. While still in training he met Anna, a young Russian woman, who was the best shot in their sniper group. Peter sent

Katrina a photo of the both of them in uniform before the Nazi siege cut off Leningrad from the world.

When they were assigned to the Stalingrad front, Anna knew she was pregnant but told no one. She and Peter were a team and she was not going to abandon him. Soon they were recognized as the best sniper team on the Stalingrad front. When the two of them singlehandedly stopped an entire German company from advancing, they were given the highest medals for bravery and assigned to train other snipers in the tactics they had developed. It was more coaching than training, as they never left the front area and were constantly engaged in fighting for every foot of Russian soil.

In 1943 the tide had turned on the Stalingrad front. The German supply lines were cut by the Red Army and the German troops fighting in Stalingrad were surrounded with no way out. Peter was killed in the last of the German artillery barrages. Anna helped bury him and then made her way east to get away from the fighting. She knew her baby would be coming soon and she had to find a safe place.

Their sergeant told her to seek a place to have her baby and marked her as killed in action. Anna left her uniform and rifle in the ruins of Stalingrad but kept her sidearm and medals. She scavenged a dress, though it was two sizes too big for her, and a full-length coat. Her condition was obvious and she used it to get a ride with a female truck driver who took her to the nearest hospital and helped her get admitted. She gave birth to a son late the next day. Anna paid the midwife to give them a room until she could gather her strength and be sure the baby could travel.

****

Six months later, she made her way to the address of Peter's grandmother. He had made her memorize the address and promise to go there if anything happened to him. It was almost dusk when Anna knocked on the weathered door of her destination.

Katrina opened the door and saw the young woman carrying a baby. Before she could say anything, the woman said, "I'm Anna and this is your grandson, Peter." Katrina pulled Anna inside and tears ran down her cheeks as she hugged both of them. Anna handed her grandson to her. It had been a long time since Katrina had felt such happiness.

Anna and Katrina talked and drank weak tea until dawn and Peter wanted fed. For nearly a week, Katrina's small house was alive with activity. Even at six months Katrina could see her son in the young infant's face and actions. As the weeks passed, Katrina noticed her daughter-in-law looking sad when Katrina happily talked about future plans. "Anna, what's wrong? You look so unhappy."

"The war is not over and I must rejoin my old unit. I'm planning on leaving the day after tomorrow. You must take care of Peter. I'll be back as soon as I can. For the first time since he was born, I feel he is safe."

Katrina never saw Anna again. She was killed in the final assault on Berlin.

****

The years passed and Peter blossomed. He was first in his class and a star soccer player. He grew up with his grandmother interchanging languages. She knew English, French, and Polish as well as Russian and a few Siberian dialects. Peter's English had a natural American accent.

By the time he was in his tenth year of education in the Russian system he was known for his ability to speak and read several languages. Peter had the kind of a mind that could remember great amounts of detail and recall it when he needed it. Following his grandmother's guidance, he focused on language courses and worked very hard in each of them.

With his language skills and being the son of two Leningrad war heroes, it was natural for the KGB to recognize his potential and put him in their special schools that trained spies to infiltrate the West after several years of training.

Before his Nana died, she made him promise to escape from the Soviet Union at the first opportunity and establish their bloodline in a free country. She told him that their true family name was that of her husband, his grandfather, the American soldier who had come from America to fight against the Communists.

His name was John Brandon. She left nothing out and finished by saying his grandfather dreamed about taking them all back to America. Peter, his grandson, now had to make that dream real. She wanted the bloodline of her beloved warrior husband to be taken back to America to defend freedom, a freedom that would never come to Russia. From that revelation on, Peter thought about nothing but escaping from the deadly, boring rule of the Communist Party.

The KGB school for spies, or intelligence operatives as the students preferred, required constant focus. Failing was not an option. This was the path to the world Peter now dreamed of since he sat with his grandmother and listened to her stories of the family's true history.

Ray, Peter's English language instructor, was from Pittsburgh and would never be able to leave Russia. Ray was entrapped in Moscow ten years ago. He now had a Russian wife and family who lived in a special compound near the school. The KGB kept all their language instructors from enemy nations under tight control. They had seen too many undercover KGB officers to ever be allowed to leave Russia. They were lucky to get permission to visit Moscow or Leningrad.

Russian was never heard or seen in Peter's part of the training facility. It was set up like a University with specialty training in different buildings. No one used their true names and cameras were not allowed other than in the areas for photography training. The restaurants, shops, exercise and medical facilities, entertainment, and even barbershops were all designed after their western counterparts.

Practical training in living under different identities was constant. Peter was now studying under the name Ivan Kalin. He disliked the name Ivan and preferred to be called Kalin. Peter was a whiz at languages and a straight 'A' student. He was now at home in the total immersion training in American English and culture. He knew he would soon be getting an assignment.

****

Kalin didn't have to wait long. His KGB handler and mentor came to him and told him to get ready, as he would be leaving the school for further preparation for his upcoming assignment. Making friends with other students was not encouraged, but Kalin had a few people he liked to drink beer with and talk about the world outside the school. One of his friends was a young KGB officer who taught the course on terrorism. Over a beer in the canteen, Yuri Kolenko lectured him to pay more attention to the theory of terrorism.

"You will soon be getting your assignment somewhere in America, and you need to impress your handlers with your knowledge of terrorist tactics and theory. Now I'm going to give you something to impress them. Memorize as much as you can."

He then passed Kalin a paper he had written. Yuri added, "I'm going to tell you something this school never passes on. The use of aliases over a long period of time can have an effect on your thinking and behavior. All identity changes require a change in behavior. To be effective you must act out and live each role. To cope with that you must devise an anchor for who you are. I always chose an alias starting with the English letter 'H.' My favorite is Harris. I've done my best work under that name. As long as there isn't any clear security problem, I'll use the name Harris. That simple thing is my anchor to maintain who I really am behind the façade of an alias and cover story. I trust you not to ever mention what I've just told you."

Back in his cubicle room, Kalin propped his feet up and read Yuri's notes.

"The goal of terrorism is to create in the Target State an atmosphere of chaos that will cause the State's reaction to result in an even higher level of chaos. The Target State will lose its internal cohesiveness and will gradually move toward vulnerability to either external military action or political attacks from within. Carefully managed terrorism could successfully destroy an enemy, an enemy that was previously thought to be invincible. It is not as most terrorists and their supporters think that the individual terrorist acts have to be sensational in order to be successful. In fact, many sensational terrorist operations end up making the target state's resolve stronger and its internal security procedures more effective. Average citizens expect that important people and large landmark structures are the targets of terrorists from time to time. What is far more effective is to have people from all classes lose confidence in the ability of the government to protect their lives and property. The western media will act as the carrier of this political disease and focus on the failure of the security services to protect people from terrorists.

"In the past, terrorism has been limited to attacks against targets with high political impacts. After a time the terrorist incident will disappear from the front page only to reappear if someone is caught and put on trial. It is too hard for terrorists to continually hit high-profile targets. The detailed planning and logistical effort required to hit high-impact targets cannot be sustained. If, however, the new terrorists concentrate on soft or unprotected targets, they can continue a drum beat of assassinations and sabotage. Then local governments are unable to cope and begin to break down. The media demands action. Citizens lose confidence and no longer trust the authorities to protect them. Proving once again that the greatest freedom is freedom from fear.

"It is in the actions taken by States to protect themselves from terrorism that the real payoff for terrorism occurs. As States put into effect more and more protective measures, the very nature of democracies like the United States begin to change from a government that emphasized individual freedom and initiative to one that seeks to control and track its citizens with a growing security apparatus. A security apparatus that can easily, if unchecked, form the core of an emerging police state that will eventually enrage the populace.

"Small forces should not attack high-impact targets that by their very nature will be protected. The terrorist leader of today must count upon the media to frighten the nation much in the way media focus on a serial killer can paralyze a local area. Timing and selection of targets must be carefully managed to develop and maintain momentum."

****

Three days later, Kalin was called out of his class on American fashion. The senior KGB officer in charge of his preparation said, "With all the turmoil now in the United States because of the war in Vietnam, my superiors decided the opportunity to infiltrate agents into the United States, often through Canada and Mexico, is now ideal. This is a new program. In the West it would be called a 'pilot program.' Seldom do we send KGB officers into this kind of a program. An exception was made in your case. No one except your instructors knows of your affiliation with the KGB, and they will never leave the Soviet Union.

"Your American English and academic knowledge of the U.S. and Canada is comprehensive. It was decided to infiltrate you into Canada as a refugee immigrant from Poland. A young man traveling alone presents a higher profile of risk to the Canadian counter-intelligence, so you will be provided with a wife. The KGB is a resourceful organization and you should never underestimate our abilities and tenacity. Within three months you will be married to a twenty-year-old Polish woman whose parents are committed Communists and under the control of the KGB. The woman is an excellent student, speaks English, and was selected as a volunteer candidate for training by the Polish Intelligence Service. She is a very beautiful young woman. I told my superiors in Moscow you would carry out your assignment as planned. Am I right about that?"

"Yes sir, I'm ready to serve my country."

"Good! Get your stuff together. We are leaving for another place tonight. Meet me in front of the Admin building in two hours. Do not tell anyone you are leaving. You will be leaving the name Ivan Kalin here."

Five

Outfitted with new clothes made in Poland, new identity documents, quite a bit of Polish money, and emergency re-contact procedures in case he had any trouble before reaching Canada, Ivan Kalin – now Stephen Closki – made his way via Aeroflot to Warsaw. When his bride-to-be met him at the airport, Stephen was surprised. *The KGB certainly has an eye for beautiful women,* he thought. *In American English this woman is a knockout. I'm already in love.*

Marie Karmosi was tall, with hair that was almost black and contrasted strikingly with her fair skin. Her posture was erect and her full-figured body showed beneath the light trench coat. Stephen guessed they had both been instructed on how to act at this first meeting. Undoubtedly, both intelligence services were watching and recording the meeting.

Her father was a high-ranking Party official. The civil marriage service was elaborate and the following reception was large, featuring a huge sit-down dinner and flowing vodka. The noise and celebrations rose with the non-stop serving of vodka. Only the Catholic Church was missing. Marie whispered to her husband as they left the celebration to begin their honeymoon that she would have preferred a church wedding.

Armed with KGB-provided papers that gave them new Polish identities as Marie and Georgi Wasneski and with all the necessary documentation, including University student identity cards from Warsaw University, drivers' licenses, a military status card for Georgi, medical records, and a collection of pocket litter that breathes authenticity into cover stories, they made their way across Poland and Czechoslovakia into Austria, where they joined with other refugees in the endless processing. Eventually, they got their Canadian immigrant visas and arrived in Canada. The journey was not hard. The KGB had planned well and was always watching in case they needed assistance. The papers were perfect.

Georgi had money for small bribes and telephone numbers committed to memory so that he could initiate emergency meetings with KGB operatives along the way. The trip from Poland to Canada was the easiest part of the whole journey.

Spring of 1969

After a few weeks of processing, the Catholic Church helped them get settled in a small town near Ottawa. Much to her husband's surprise, Marie had been fascinated by the Christian church and enjoyed the irony of acting out her cover role by attending church several times a week. Georgi occasionally went along but was never able to match her interest in religion.

All this time they had to hide their English language skills. There were a few Polish families in the general area, but the KGB had made it clear they were to avoid personal relationships with "other" Polish immigrants.

Marie's dream was that someday they could return to Poland. She needed that dream and Georgi let her keep it. Her growing belief in Christianity was slowly eroding her zeal for Communism and the importance of the mission. He found work as a carpenter's helper and, with the help of the church and Canadian social services, they lived modestly.

Georgi's KGB mission was to make his way into the United States and eventually settle within thirty miles of Washington, D.C. He would be given control of an illegal network and a list of important Americans to neutralize just prior to the start of an attack on the U.S.

The intent was to confuse the American political and military chain of command prior to the initiation of a hot war. He would have a secondary mission of creating chaos in the civilian sector by spreading bacteriological agents, placing bombs in designated key areas, starting rumors, and sabotaging select targets. But first they had to establish themselves in Canada, improve their social and economic standing, and practice communicating with the KGB. It was a lifelong mission.

Georgi went to school nights and Anna attended a daytime English course run by the church, and within two years they had acquired an explanation for their ability to speak and read the English language. Of course, their teachers never knew that the only thing difficult about their study of English was the necessity to conceal their already proficient ability to read, write, and speak nearly native English. Marie especially got a kick out of pretending not to understand some people in everyday life. In the process of studying and living in Canada for two years, Georgi, and Marie to a lesser extent, acquired a slight Canadian accent that influenced their KGB handlers to make the Great Lakes area the couple's first stopping point in the U.S. on the way to D.C.

The two years in Canada passed uneventfully. They purchased a used Toyota, rented a nice home in the countryside, and looked to the neighbors as an immigrant couple that was fitting into the working-class life. Unfortunately, from the inside they were struggling. Marie grew increasingly resentful of their immigrant status in Canada. She missed Poland, the privileges granted to her family as members of the Communist Party, and most of all she resented her subservient role in the planning and carrying out of the mission. Georgi tried to get her to share his sense of adventure, but it was not enough and some strains began to replace what had been passion and enthusiasm.

Marie began to drink more than she should, and it caused many unpleasant arguments between them. The drinking gradually affected her ability to focus on their mission.

Marie was afraid KGB watchers would find out if she sought help for her drinking problem. She never told anyone about their illegal status and Georgi was sure she never would, but he hadn't mentioned her drinking problem to the local KGB handler.

Georgi had known for years that if he ever got a chance to get out of the Soviet Union, he would never go back. His Nana, Katrina, despised the cruelty and arrogance of the Communist Party members and had instilled Georgi with the same feelings. She was certain that one day the Russian people would rise up against the regimes that one after the other had brought them hardship without hope. The threat of the camps and the omnipotence of the KGB sapped the courage of even the bravest and wrung the light and gaiety out of people wherever the Hammer and Sickle flew on its field of red.

Alex, their KGB handler, knew nothing of Georgi's true feelings, and neither did Marie. Georgi was afraid to give Marie even a hint of his dream. He believed her dedication to her family and Poland wouldn't allow her to take such a risk.

Georgi's problem was how to get them into the United States and, once there, break away from KGB control, with or without Marie's help. Once she saw that she could never return to Poland because of her role in his traitorous act, he hoped Marie would recognize that she had no real choice but to go along with his plan. He knew they could not stay in Canada. There were not enough places to hide or cities large enough to absorb a family on the run from the KGB.

At the next meeting, Alex said, "Get ready to move. The Center has decided to push up your timetable. Once in the U.S. your contact will be limited to infrequent clandestine radio contact. So if you're unclear about anything, now is the time to ask."

"No. I understand the mission and am ready to leave Canada."

"Good. Now pay attention. No notes are allowed. Be ready to move within the next few weeks. I'll give you new identity documents and infiltration information. You will find a rental place in St. Cloud, Minnesota. Both of you are expected to attend college and acquire a BA or BS to further your cover and improve your social mobility in America.

"You will cross the border into the U.S. with $200,000 in cash, nothing larger than a hundred-dollar bill. If the project works out, more KGB officers trained in the American and Canadian language, culture, and history will be infiltrated into the United States. Perhaps even more importantly, several KGB careers will benefit from project 'FALCON,' including mine. Now you have to listen to my version of the mission in the United States."

Georgi grinned and poured a fresh cup of strong black coffee as Alex began his required briefing. "The counter-intelligence forces in the U.S. are rapidly improving. Personal contacts between KGB controllers assigned to Soviet embassies and consulates, and illegals or deep-cover agents are becoming more and more dangerous. This old method of contact has to be changed.

"Many promising KGB cases have been compromised by Western counter-intelligence forces following suspect KGB officers from their Embassies or homes to meetings with illegals and foreign agents. KGB officers who will live as illegals must be the network controllers of the future. Communications between the illegal controllers like you and the Moscow Center will primarily be through short-and long-range clandestine radio links. Georgi, you are the first to be selected to test this concept. You have had all the training required.

"You will be given all the financial resources you need to keep your network viable. You will have ample funds to improve the social status of key members of your network, recruit American agents, and acquire real estate and other material assets required for the mission."

While he was listening to Alex, Georgi thought about the capabilities and procedures of the KGB. *They would never give up hunting for a turncoat who had brought disgrace upon the whole organization. Marie and I will be on the run for a year or more, until we find a place that could provide us with both sanctuary and an opportunity to live normal lives. We need money, a lot of it. The money will come from the ample funds Alex is talking about that is stored in safety deposit boxes in banks across America.*

We can't go to the Americans for help. Once we walk in as defectors or volunteers to any counter-intelligence organization, we wouldn't be able to walk out. For the rest of our life we would be in their hands. They would never fully trust us nor allow us to live our lives by following our own choices. I don't trust the Americans to keep us safe from a vengeful KGB.

While some people will keep their word, all governments break their word as soon as it is expedient to do so. From now on, I want to be in control of my life and to give my future children the opportunity to live their own lives.

He swore then and there that once he achieved security, he would try to protect the Americans from the KGB cancer that was growing within their wonderful but naïve country.

Six

Two weeks after the briefing, with all their permitted belongings crammed into three backpacks, Alex drove them down close to the border between Canada and Minnesota. Only the vast boundary waters separated the two nations. They had been well briefed. Alex's role ended when he dropped them off beside a dark green Ford pickup truck towing a large canoe.

As soon as Georgi got their backpacks out of the trunk, Alex made a three-point turn and was gone. When he put the backpacks in the bed of the truck, Georgi noticed a man waiting there with his back against the cab.

The driver gave them no name and did not want to talk beyond giving them instructions. "In less than an hour, I will put the canoe in the water. You will put your backpacks in the canoe. My friend in the back will paddle the canoe. Do exactly what he says when he says it. He knows these waters. As the crow flies you will have only about six miles to your landing point across the border, but it will take several hours to Black Bay and another hour or so until you meet me again on Route 53 in the Rabetogama State Forest. I am going to give you

54

a compass in case you need to be on foot after getting out of the canoe. When you reach the hard surface road, that will be Route 53. Wait on the edge of the forest until you hear my horn. I have legitimate papers to cross the border in this vehicle. Then come out quickly and get in the truck. I will drive you to the city of St. Cloud in Minnesota. Then I will leave and you will never see me again." Georgi and Marie nodded.

The young man seated Georgi in the front and Marie in the center of the canoe. He told Marie to sit still and Georgi to paddle the canoe. "And no talking because there are park rangers as well as customs and immigration boats patrolling."

He pushed off and nimbly jumped into the back. Georgi didn't even think he got his foot wet. The sun had gone down and the light was fading fast. Their canoeist showed no hesitation. Only once he whispered for Georgi to stop paddling and they drifted silently for a number of minutes. Finally, Georgi heard slight engine sounds in the darkness ahead of them.

They both had passports and proper papers to use until they got to St. Cloud. Once there, Georgi had been told to destroy those papers and to use the second set in the waterproof packet in his backpack. From there on security would be his concern and he could expect no help.

After three hours of steady paddling, Georgi was told to stop paddling, and get ready to jump out and beach the canoe. "We all need to stretch and empty bladders. This small island never had any campers. You can talk in low tones and this is your last chance to ask any questions about meeting with the pickup truck on Route 53. It's taking at least three or four hours longer because I want our arrival in Black Bay to look like we are coming from the American side."

"It is so beautiful and quiet," Marie said. "The water is clearer than I have ever seen. And what is that mournful sound?"

The transporter laughed softly. "That is a loon."

Marie looked puzzled. "What is a loon?"

"It's duck-like waterfowl that can be seen in the Boundary Waters. They are very territorial. Usually only one to a lake. Okay folks, let's move on. I want to be in Black Bay just after first light. If you need a drink you can drink right out of the lake."

While he was paddling Georgi thought, *So far so good. Marie hasn't even touched her scotch flask all day. The first time in months. I hope she can stop drinking. The odds are against us already. If I have to deal with her drinking, we won't have a chance. She doesn't know yet what's in store for us.*

I'll be glad to drop this dumb name. I don't feel like a Georgi. Changing names frequently is hard psychologically, especially if the name doesn't sit right. I can't wait to take my old family name permanently as soon as we make a clean break. Thank God for Nana and her efforts to keep the Brandon name alive. I wish I had picture of my grandfather. He was a great warrior and my grandmother was incredibly tough. They must have made a formidable couple. I love the stories she told me about life in the Siberian tundra in the 1920s. It is really strange that the KGB is sending me first to the city my grandfather lived in before WWI. I'm sure some trace of the Brandons is still there. Probably even some gravesites.

Georgi's musing was interrupted as the canoe reached the shore and they jumped out with their packs, leaving the canoeist behind without a word. The border crossing had gone just as the KGB planned. It was only a short hike from the canoe beaching to Route 53. Marie was strong and carried her share of the load. The driver was there waiting for them but never said a word on the trip to St. Cloud. On the outskirts of the city, he pulled up next to a dark green Ford station wagon with Illinois license plates and gave Georgi the keys. When they loaded their backpacks in the wagon, he drove off.

The first thing Georgi did when they got in the wagon was to gather all their old identity papers and put them in a plastic bag. "That is the end of Marie and Georgi. I never liked that name."

"I didn't mind my name except Marie drank too much," Marie said with a sigh.

"Are you going to stop?" Georgi looked at her and couldn't help the hopeful tone in his voice.

"Of course," Marie said, holding her head up. "Sue doesn't drink. I feel we have a fresh start and for the first time in my life I feel free. In control of my life. In Canada, I felt we were always being watched by the KGB."

"Well, we are now the Olsens, Richard and Susan."

Susan took her new documents and looked them over. "Since Susan doesn't drink, she is starving. Find her something to eat."

"Richard sounds so formal. People with the name Richard often are called Dick. Until our next change, call me Dick. We'll be Dick and Sue Olsen, the American couple from Chicago."

"I like that, but Sue is hungry. Do something."

"You're on. Get ready for an American farm country breakfast." Dick drove toward the downtown section of St. Cloud and pulled into an almost full parking lot of a diner serving breakfast.

After breakfast of poached eggs, biscuits, ham, and home fries with a carafe of strong black coffee, Sue said, "Okay, husband, I've been fed. Now where do we sleep?"

"We passed a row of cheap motels on the way in. When we leave here, you can pick one and we'll get set up. Tomorrow we rent a house. Today after we rest I just want to cruise the town and read local papers. There will be a local Chamber of Commerce. We can pick up some information there, and I want to visit the local university."

"Sounds good," Sue said, settling back into the comfy booth and taking another sip of the coffee. "The future looks ... hopeful."

Seven

The next day, Dick and Sue Olsen contacted a real estate office and got a list of rental houses on the outskirts of St. Cloud. After a morning of driving around and looking at neighborhoods, they picked a two-bedroom, one-bath bungalow in Pantown. The house had a nice lot, a nearby park, and easy commuting to St. Cloud State University. Neither of them had any experience in buying furniture so it took them a week to get enough furniture in the house and arranged to Sue's satisfaction. Finally they moved in and Dick carried his bride over the threshold of their first house in America.

Sue took courses in English literature and European history. She attended church services at St. Mary's Cathedral and began enjoying her life in America. She found freedom was real, something she could feel. It expanded her way of thinking. The load of fear of doing something the authorities could punish her for was replaced by the effort to take control of her life and build toward a future with many options, different even than Canada that was much closer to the European way of life.

Dick didn't have the luxury of becoming a part-time student. He had a network of spies to manage. Running

59

his network took up all of his time. He had to travel to meet each agent and give them directions. He used all of his KGB training in contacting his network. If the FBI caught him now, he would never be able to convince them that he was planning on escaping from his KGB masters. Even if he cooperated with the FBI or CIA, he would always be in their control and would never be able to live the dream passed down from his American grandfather.

At the end of their first full year in St. Cloud, 1972, Sue presented him with a baby boy they named Jack. She spent more time at home with the new baby, but Dick kept up his busy year by re-locating his entire network of six illegal agents to a city or town within 40 miles of Washington, D.C. He also gave each agent contact instructions and $200,000 to make the move and acquire housing. The contact instructions were all activated by a personal ad in the local paper.

During his travels throughout the year, Dick visited all five banks where the KGB had rented safety deposit boxes. The large boxes were full of money, gold, and diamonds. His best estimate was they collectively held in excess of ten million dollars. Each box also contained a handgun and two sets of identity documents, which included social security cards, driver's licenses, credit cards, and lesser cards like library cards, club memberships, highway rescue services like AAA, proof of insurance, and even discharge cards from military service.

Dick knew none of these would help him. The KGB had good records and would look for him under all the aliases provided in these boxes. He had to get some new documents to support a few different identities on his own.

Sue was pregnant again in January 1974 and they started getting ready for a second child. Dick didn't want to wait much longer and planned to make their break for freedom from the KGB when the baby was old enough to handle the fast travel required.

They would have to be on the run for at least a few years. The KGB would never give up the chase, but if he could fool them long enough to wipe out all the ways of picking up his trail, they would almost be home free. When they left St. Cloud no trail could be left. New identities, a different car, and changed covers. He would have to move fast. As soon as the baby was ready to travel, he would tell Sue she had to get used to yet another name.

With his network finally taken care of after nearly four years of travel across the country, Dick was able to spend time searching microfilm at the local library and visiting St. Cloud cemeteries looking for information about his American family, the Brandons. On the second day of his microfilm search, he found two Brandon obituaries from the early 1950s. A Mr. Paul Brandon and his wife Teresa Brandon were buried in the North Star Cemetery in St. Cloud. In the obituary, he read a son, John Brandon, was still listed as missing in action against the Communist Army in Siberia in 1919. Lt. Brandon had been a member of the Polar Bear Expeditionary Force sent to Russia.

Microfilm records only went back as far as 1965.

Dick got up and found a librarian. "Excuse me, ma'am. Do you have copies of the newspapers extending back to World War I?"

"Yes, but they are in the basement and not very well stored. Almost no one ever uses them."

"I'm doing some research for a book I plan to write, could you show me where they're kept?"

"Sure. Hang around for ten more minutes. I'll be on my lunch break and someone will be here to cover the library. Not many people come here during the day."

Once downstairs, Dick went right to the stack marked 1918. Nearly every edition had an article about young men enlisting or being inducted into the armed forces. After an hour of scanning for articles about inductees from the St. Cloud area, he found an article and a picture of Lt. John Brandon. Using his pocket knife, he cut the picture and article out of the paper.

Sitting in the library parking lot and looking closely at the picture of Lt. Brandon in the clear light streaming through his windshield, he gasped at the similarity between the picture and his own image. Leaving the library, he drove directly to the North Star Cemetery. From the obituary information and the plot information from the cemetery, he found the Brandon family plot surrounded by mature pine trees. One granite marker was engraved "John M. Brandon, missing in action in Siberia 1919. A good son and fine soldier."

He was nearly overwhelmed with feeling. His American ancestors lay before him. His grandfather's body had never been found. *Too bad he couldn't be here to see me and his great-grandson. How strange that the grandson of John Brandon is standing here as a KGB officer, gathering information to reclaim his Brandon name as soon as he is free of the KGB.*

Dick knelt beside the granite marker. "As soon as our next child is old enough to travel, I will tell my wife that we are going to run from the KGB and become Americans," he said out loud to his grandfather. "We will never to return to the Soviet Union. We will restore the Brandon name to its American heritage. I promise."

He stood up and dusted his pants off. He knew Sue's family would suffer persecution for his defection, but it was a risk he was willing to take. He would not tell Sue the name of his American ancestors. If she ended up getting captured by the KGB, they would make her talk. He knew the principle was that people couldn't tell what they did not know.

Eight

February 1975

Their second child, a healthy little girl Sue named Christina, was now four months old. Old enough to travel. Dick felt the time was right and got the teenager next door to baby sit so he could take Sue out for dinner at a popular roadside café. The winter snow made the landscape look like Leningrad.

The Southern Italian food was excellent and, after the last course as they were finishing the bottle of Chianti, Dick cleared his throat. "I want to tell you something, and I want you to let me finish before you respond."

His wife nodded, poured the last of the Chianti into her glass and said, "I'll try. You know patience is not one of my best points."

He took her hand and began. "I have been planning for years, my whole life really, to get out of Russia and come to America. I never told anyone this story. My grandmother was married to an American Army officer who was wounded in the fighting around Irkutsk in 1919. He was never able to get back to his country. He changed his name, learned Russian, and lived in Siberia with my grandmother and their two kids. Katrina, my grandmother, made the decision to move to Irkutsk from their isolated village. She believed they could blend in more safely in a large city. Their daughter was about three. My father would be born some months later in Irkutsk after grandmother had found a very good job with the city government. My grandfather, who was an excellent trapper, hunter, and all-around woodsman, was supposed to meet her in the Irkutsk train station. For months, my grandmother showed up at the meeting place, waiting for him. She knew, if he was alive and free, he would come. After several months, she gave him up for dead or imprisoned. Years later, she saved enough money to move her daughter and son, who her husband never got to meet, to St. Petersburg.

"She told me my grandfather always was looking for a way to escape with his family to America. He wanted his wife and children to live free in a free country. After hearing her stories, I grew up with the desire to move to America. Now I, we, have that chance because the KGB doesn't know anything about my true heritage due to my grandmother's excellent planning and ability to meld with the rest of Russian society. I have a very good plan. Will you join me?"

"I like it here. Everyone lives better here than people in Poland. I'm truly terrified of the KGB. The Polish secret police may not care too much but you know the KGB will never give up. My parents will suffer, but freedom for our family is worth fighting for. I always thought someday we would have to go back or be jailed by the Americans. Do you really believe we can get away?"

"Honestly, I'm not 100 percent sure, but I believe we have a better than 75 percent chance. We have money and I have new documents the KGB doesn't know about. We will need some good luck and more importantly, no bad luck. But yes! If I didn't think so, I could not expose you and the children to such a risk. The only two good things the KGB has done for me is selecting you to be my wife and giving us the opportunity to live free by sending us to America."

"As they say here, count me in!"

Dick smiled and squeezed his wife's hand. "Tomorrow we start getting ready. We must leave no clues behind. I'll leave $400 with our realtor to take care of the remaining month on our lease. All our bills are paid. We can take only essentials and won't leave a forwarding address. Pack whatever you need to take care of the kids for a few days. We will be traveling by car and moving fast. The KGB will be able to track us by the banks I visit to get our money.

"There are five banks I must visit in the next week. There will be long hours in the car. Where we can, I'll leave you all in a motel, while I take what we need from the safety deposit boxes. When we have been to all the banks, we have to think through every move. The first six to eight months will be the most dangerous.

"You're good at reading maps. When we pick up our escape car, you can start planning our routes. We'll change cars in Minneapolis, and I'll visit the bank and then on to Chicago."

March 1975

Three days later, the Olsens pulled into the
Minneapolis Airport in their three-year-old Dodge
sedan early in the morning. *This is the last of the Olsens,*
Dick thought. *When we get back in the car, we will be
a different family. We will be Frank and Alice Kincaid
and children Jack and Christina. I don't want to confuse
Jack with constantly changing his name. Christina is
too young to notice. Switching identities adds stress to
all our lives. I'm looking forward to the time we can all
be Brandons. In the next two years we'll have to deal
with identity changes and all its complications.*

Dick let his wife and two children off at the departure
gate for Northwest Airlines, so they would look like they
were catching a leaving flight. Sue took the children
through the interior of the airport then moved up to the
arrival gate area where they would wait for Dick to pick
them up and assume their new identities. Two weeks
earlier Dick had parked a year-old Ford station wagon
in the long-term lot. There was an empty space beside
the station wagon, and Dick pulled the Dodge in the
empty space. It took only a few minutes to transfer the
baggage and do a final check of the Dodge's interior for
anything he might have missed earlier. The Ford station
wagon started up despite its wait in the cold weather.

He pulled to the curb at the Northwest arrival gate
and Sue, now Alice, who had been watching for the grey
Ford wagon, came out with the still bundled-up children.
Jack was lifted into the backseat and strapped into a
child's car seat. Alice held Christina on her lap. The

chill of the car's interior had given way to the powerful car heater. She leaned over and gave her husband a kiss. "This is an improvement, Mr. Frank Kincaid. Much more space. If we had to we could sleep in the car."

"I'll try to do as well on the next change. The Ford dealer was happy to make a cash deal. This is a good car. Equipped with tires to handle bad weather. I think it is supposed to snow later today. I hope we are in Chicago before the roads get icy. You and the kids will have to stay in the car while I go in the bank here. I want to find street parking within a few blocks of the bank. It shouldn't take me more than 30 minutes. As soon as I come out, we'll leave for Chicago. We can have lunch at a McDonald's. Okay?"

"Yes, and I can feed the baby while we're waiting for you. I have crackers and chocolate milk for Jack. We'll be okay. Go and make us rich. Never thought I would be married to a bank robber."

"Hey, it's our money. I'm just withdrawing it a bit early."

"Somehow, I don't think the KGB will accept that explanation."

He had cased the bank thoroughly and been inside one time a few years ago when he was setting up his network. A parking space opened up on South Sixth Street, and he maneuvered the station wagon smoothly into the space. He was within two blocks of the bank. He kissed Alice and walked up to the bank with his briefcase. Each safety deposit box had two names on the access card, Mr. Charles P. Brown and Mr. Robert Garrett. In this bank, he was Mr. Garrett and had all the identification papers he would need.

Changing names and keeping them straight required focus. The penalty for failure was so high, it wasn't difficult to maintain the discipline required to slip in and out of the different roles. It was the short-term aliases that were the hardest. He had checked his documents before he left the car. He left his Kincaid identity in the glove compartment. It was against protocol to carry more than one identity at a time. No cover story would help if he got caught with two or more identity documents. The Garrett identity was only for this bank. The other name on the access card was so the KGB could check the box and add or subtract contents whenever they wanted. He wasn't sure but believed whoever Mr. Charles P. Brown was would get notified regarding Garrett's access to the box. Frank hoped that would take at least three days.

He walked in the front entrance, passed the bored guard, and crossed the highly polished floor to an open teller window near the safety deposit box vault. He told the teller he wanted his safety deposit box and showed her the key. The woman teller signaled and an attendant hurried up. He showed his I.D., a Minnesota driver's license, and was escorted down to the vault. Once inside, the attendant inserted both keys and pulled the large box out and carried it to small private cubicle.

When the attendant left, he opened the box and began transferring the packets of dollar bills, in denominations of twenties and hundreds and thousands, to his briefcase. His previous count of $300,000 he was sure was still correct, but he wasn't going to count it again. The small cloth bag of several ounces of diamonds went in his briefcase next. He had no idea of their value. The same was true for the twenty small gold bars. The last items to go in the briefcase were two sets of identity documents and a Browning nine-millimeter handgun with two loaded magazines. He remembered the Browning magazines held 13 rounds. To cover the difference in weight, he took a cloth-wrapped red brick from his briefcase and a heavy wrench and put them in the box. The difference in the weight of the box would probably not be noticed by the attendant.

He called the attendant and when the box slid into space 214, used his key to lock the box in slot. He thanked the attendant and left. He was in the bank less than 15 minutes and was on his way to being a wealthy man, thanks to the generosity of the KGB.

An hour later the Kincaids pulled into a McDonald's parking lot for lunch on the outskirts of the city. Sue left to change the baby while Dick ordered cheeseburgers, fries, and Cokes. Christina had been breast fed while Dick was in the bank.

The Kincaids arrived in Chicago too late to visit the Chase Bank, just off North State Street, near W. Kinzie Street, so Frank picked a mid-priced motel just outside the city. A stiff wind was blowing and the temperature was forecast to drop to 30 degrees before morning. If he could get out of the Chicago bank by 10:30 a.m., they could make Cleveland before the banks closed for business. He hoped for decent driving weather tomorrow. He couldn't push the speed limit. Their credentials, while good, would not hold up to an in-depth police inquiry.

He had heard a few senior officers at the KGB School talk about how much complexity was added to an operation if any family members were included. *They were right,* he thought. *I'll need a lot of luck to pull off this escape. The KGB will never stop hunting for me. This is a very large country with scores of cities large enough to hide in. It is also a country full of immigrants. The sensitivity of the police to avoid any charges of police abusing anyone's civil rights also helps people like us.*

After the Kincaids were settled in their motel room, Frank took Jack with him to pick up Chinese takeout from a place near the motel. Both Christina and Alice were sound asleep when they came back. Frank let them sleep. Tomorrow would be a hard day. He wanted to hit the Chicago bank as early as he could, rush to Cleveland, and then take off for Pittsburgh and Washington, D.C. Frank was certain the KGB would have some alerting system when he went into a safety deposit box. In the last five months he had opened all the boxes but took nothing more than a few hundred dollars. If the KGB had an alerting system and had checked the boxes back then, they would have found he had taken nothing.

If the KGB safety deposit box monitoring system worked, they would note that he went to the bank in Minneapolis and then went on to Chicago. A red flag would go up and they would guess that Cleveland was next. In a few more days they may also know his house in St. Cloud was empty with no forwarding address left behind. That would be enough to cause alarm bells. *The next nearest bank was Cleveland,* Frank thought, going through all this in his head. *Someone might be waiting for me there after I hit the Chicago bank.* The Cleveland bank held the smallest amount of greenbacks, gold, and diamonds. He quickly devised a plan to try and throw off the KGB once he hit the Chicago bank. He would call the assistant manager at the Cleveland bank tomorrow, whom he had taken to lunch during his last visit, and tell her he would be coming in tomorrow or the next day and ask if they could have lunch together.

Then, instead he would go straight to Pittsburgh where the largest amount of dollars, gold, and diamonds were stored. He knew emptying the Washington, D.C., bank box would be too dangerous. There were enough KGB agents in D.C. to be waiting for him during banking hours. If he could get the valuables from Pittsburgh, he could pass on Cleveland and D.C. and would still have an estimated four million dollars in currency and an unknown value of diamonds and gold. With this new plan, Frank managed to get some sleep.

The next morning, Frank picked up breakfast from a nearby fast food restaurant and, after telling Alice the plans for the day, he left to be at the bank when the door opened. Again he parked a block from the bank and watched the area from the car for 20 minutes. He saw nothing unusual on the street. Taking his briefcase from the backseat, Frank walked up to the bank, all senses alert for the slightest anomaly in a normal street scene. Inside the bank, the tellers were taking their first customers. Frank knew the name of the young woman who dealt with customers who wanted to get access to a safety deposit box. He approached her and said, "Susan,

I see I beat the crowd. Can you get my box for me? Here is my key and I.D."

"Sure. Follow me. They changed the forecast last night, did you hear? It looks like a storm is going to hit us this afternoon. Are you traveling anywhere?"

"Yes. Unfortunately I have to drive to Cleveland for a day or so. I'll still be in the heavy snowfall area. I hope I can beat the storm."

"You better get started. It's a good five hours to Cleveland in good weather."

Using both keys, Susan pulled the large box part way out and said, "You take it from here. That is a heavy box. Must be full of gold."

"Don't I wish? Legal documents and ledgers weigh a ton. But if we lost our business records, this off-site storage could save our business."

Susan nodded, then left Frank with his box. When the door closed, he transferred the bundles of currency, bars of gold, and diamonds to his briefcase. He also took the identity documents and the .22 silenced High Standard automatic and extra magazines. Frank inserted a loaded magazine into the handgun and slipped it under his belt in the small of his back. He transferred the two bricks from his briefcase into the box and called Susan. When she came in he slid the now lighter box into its slot and said, "Thank you. Now I have to get on the road to Cleveland."

"Good luck," she said with a smile. "See you next time."

Frank left the bank and walked a pre-planned route to check for any surveillance. When he was sure no one was following him, he slipped into a street phone booth and called the bank in Cleveland. When he was put through to the assistant manager in charge of customer services, he identified himself by the name on the safety box and inquired about bank hours and the weather. "I'm trying to get there before the bank closes. I'm in Chicago now."

Harry Barnes, the assistant manager said, "We plan to close at five unless the weather is terrible, and then we may close earlier so employees can get home safely. Oh, by the way your partner called to see if you had checked your box today or yesterday. He said he put some documents in the box you should see. He also said he would be in sometime today. Maybe you two could meet here at the bank. I can make a conference room available."

"No, I probably won't get there until mid-day tomorrow because of this weather. I'll try to get him on the phone. Thank you for the offer," Frank said. He hung up.

I guess I was right about the KGB checking on the boxes when I've opened them. I hope they will believe I'm coming to Cleveland and will set up to deal with me there. By tomorrow afternoon, they will be getting nervous about my no show. Bad weather may lead them to wait one day longer. By that time I'll have emptied the box in the Mellon Bank in Pittsburgh. I'll never get to the Cleveland or Washington, D.C. boxes, and they will no longer stop at trying to capture me. The effort will be to stop me permanently. A sniper set up in Pittsburgh is probably their best shot. At least I now have a better understanding of how this game is unfolding. They cannot use the bank authorities or the police but they can empty the box. I need the contents of the Pittsburgh safety deposit box. I'll have to move faster than they can. The coming storm may help me. They won't drive and if the airlines are delayed or cancelled for several hours, I can beat them. It will be close. It is worth the risk. I'll need the money to escape and hide. In another two weeks, they will have at least one team hunting me full time.

Alice checked the Kincaids out of the motel while Frank loaded the car. They were on the road by 11:00 AM. Fresh coffee from the motel and lunch from McDonald's would hold them for several hours. The wagon's large gas tank was full. Frank figured they were getting 17 mpg on the highway. Once on the super highway, it was a straight shot to Pittsburgh. The radio carried frequent weather updates due to impending storm conditions. They passed several plows and salt trucks in position along the throughway to keep traffic flowing. The storm was coming from the southwest at 40 mph. The leading edge of the broad storm front was behind them but the easternmost part of the front would catch them before they passed Cleveland. From there on, the travel would be hazardous.

The east and south bound turnpikes would bring them to Pittsburgh. An eight-or nine-hour drive in good weather. Frank thought, *America is a huge country. Not as large as the USSR but the roads here are magnificent. Even better, the windshield wipers on the front and back, along with the heater and defroster, keep the windows clear of ice and snow.*

Alice had a good mind and Frank told her about his plan and asked her for her thoughts. "You know you're risking all our lives for the money in the Pittsburgh bank."

"Yes, that's true," Frank admitted. "It is a short-term risk for our long-term safety."

"If we're all dead in the short term, your long term is not so attractive. Tell me the risks you see in taking the contents of the safety deposit box in the Mellon Bank."

"The KGB could have a few people waiting for us in Pittsburgh and Washington, D.C. Not many. We could probably win a short, quick gunfight, but then the police, as well as the KGB would be after us. The box could be empty but still a surveillance team could be waiting for us. Big no-win for us. No more money and hot pursuit. Not a good thing. Best case, I'm counting on my Cleveland ploy to buy us time and force them to scramble to get enough people in Cleveland during a winter storm to capture us. The KGB has limitations in operating here. Personnel from their big bases in D.C. and New York just can't pick up and go to Cleveland.

"They need U.S. government approval and would be followed by the FBI. They have few people like us they can use in this kind of a situation. They also may believe the CIA is helping us now or soon will be. Their greatest fear is that we'll defect to the CIA. That means that they will try to avoid any open violence. Any Russian caught in an act of violence in America will be declared *persona non-gratis*. For a KGB officer who has trained for years to work in America, it is not a good career move to be sent back to the USSR or cause someone to be sent back. You see the odds are not all on their side."

"How much money is in the Mellon Bank safety deposit box?" Alice asked.

"The last time I counted the currency, there was two million mostly in large bills. Hundred dollar bills were the smallest. I can't estimate the value of the gold and diamonds. But the whole thing is larger than both boxes I've emptied so far."

"Can we do this?"

"Remember a few months ago when you signed a few bank cards in that strange name?"

"Yes."

"Well that gave you access to the deposit box in the Mellon Bank in Pittsburgh and the Riggs Bank in Washington, D.C. The plan I like the best is for you to go in the Mellon Bank carrying Christina and ask the person at the desk controlling access to the safety deposit boxes to please get the box for you. When she or he does, simply empty everything in the box into the briefcase you will carry in. There are two bricks wrapped in a towel in the briefcase, put them into the box and have the attendant put it back. The attendant will return your key and you walk out of the bank and out to the car.

"I'll go inside the bank before you with Jack. If you see me use my handkerchief to wipe my face, it is clear for you to go empty the box. If you do not get the go-ahead signal, go up to one of the tellers and cash a hundred dollar bill and go back to the car. In either case, I'll be close. Do not hesitate. Walk without hurrying to the car. It should be snowing hard enough to give us some cover. If anyone wants us, they will have to get close and I'll be ready. Don't worry, we have plenty of time to go over the plan in detail. You will know the inside of the bank exactly. I have a sketch for you. Okay?"

"Yes. Of course I can handle that. I would feel better if I were armed. The KGB will never take me or the children alive. You know, I'm quite good with a handgun. Give me the Browning 9mm."

"It's yours. I'll use the silenced Hi Standard .22. A perfect weapon for close work.

"It's 460 miles from Chicago to Pittsburgh. Should take us eight to ten hours depending on traffic and the weather. Our entire route is on what are called turnpikes here, most are toll roads. I'll need you to drive if I get too sleepy. Just don't speed. Move with traffic. Five miles over the speed limit seems safe. Ten miles over can attract the attention of the highway patrol. Our identities might not hold up if the police do a thorough check. I don't want to kill or injure a cop for any reason. Having the KGB searching for us is enough."

Alice turned from looking out the window to the southwest and remarked, "Have you noticed how dark the clouds are behind us to the south?"

"Yes, I've been watching them constantly. Once we pass the exits to Cleveland and turn south to Pittsburgh we will be driving right into the storm. I'll stop for gasoline soon after we pass Cleveland. You'll have time to take care of the children. I'll help as soon as the car is ready to go. We can get food to go, and you can try to get some sleep. The journey will get much harder when we run into the storm front. They're predicting upwards of a foot of snow, drifted areas would be much deeper. The farther we get from the Great Lakes region, the better. Snowfall is always heaviest near the big lakes."

Christina soon fell asleep in her mother's arms and Frank could see that Alice was dropping off. Jack was sitting in his car seat, looking out the window and chewing on a big pretzel.

Frank had been in worse storms in the USSR but not in heavy, fast-moving traffic. Four-wheel drive doesn't help you stop. He kept moving with traffic but focused on keeping 50 yards between the wagon and the trailer truck in front of him. Some cars were flying by even though the snowfall and winds were picking up, and traffic news was full of warnings not to drive unless absolutely necessary. The farther south they went the worse the storm became. He could feel the gusting winds rocking the wagon's body. The wipers front and back were keeping up, but he had switched both defrosters on to prevent a buildup of ice.

They passed several accidents. Some of them with the emergency vehicles were blocking a lane of traffic. The frantic lane changes of some drivers and the increasing fury of the storm convinced Frank to pull off at the next exit and wait until the worst of the storm passed even though they were still 100 miles from Pittsburgh. *The banks would be closed by now anyway and might be slow in opening tomorrow*, he thought. *We will need to be well rested for tomorrow.*

The storm kept getting worse. Frank saw cars pulling

off the turnpike onto the shoulder. He reached across the front seat and gently shook Alice's shoulder. She was immediately alert and looking around. Frank said, "Just need your help. I'm looking for an exit off the turnpike. It's too dangerous to continue driving in this storm. The traffic is getting heavier and the storm is getting worse. Here's where we are on the map. Look for an exit that looks like it may lead to a cluster of motels and fast food restaurants. We'll check in, get a good night's sleep, and be ready to get back on the turnpike in the morning if the storm has passed."

Alice studied the map. "Five miles ahead there is an exit that leads to a string of small towns, Beaver Falls, Elwood City, and a town with an Indian name spelled A-L-I–Q-U-I–P-P-A."

Frank laughed. "Your Polish tongue isn't up to Indian names. That's pronounced ALI-QUIP-PAH. Help me find the exit. It's hard to read through all the falling and blowing snow." Ten minutes later Alice said, "Slow down. Signs ahead. This should be our exit."

"Okay. Hang on in case we slide a bit. I'm following the guardrails. Can't make out anything else."

Up ahead, Frank saw a cluster of neon lights and, using them as a guide, pulled into a small strip mall with a motel at either end. He picked the one that looked the best and pulled into the parking lot half-full of snow and ice-encrusted cars.

Frank walked through calf-high snow to get to the office. He took a two-bedroom unit and paid cash in advance. Alice was glad to get inside with the children. "Traveling in style. Imagine rooms with a bath. I'm going to get the kids bathed and in bed as soon as they have been fed. That means you'll have to go out and bring in something. You know Jack loves cheeseburgers, and I need something to get some energy. I'm really tired. A bottle of beer would be good also. Check on a place to have breakfast tomorrow. If we're going to get an early start on our bank robbing career, I'll need breakfast and coffee to go. You're the provider. Go do your thing."

"On my way. I hope you didn't overlook the purpose of the second bedroom."

"Don't worry. I always have energy for loving a good law-abiding provider."

"If you're a good girl, you can select a diamond from my diamond supply."

"A handful would be better."

"Typical Polish girl. You can have a handful after we do the Mellon Bank."

****

The next morning it was still snowing but not nearly as heavily as the night before. By ten o'clock they were moving with light traffic past the Mellon Bank. Frank saw a few people dressed for stormy weather going into the bank. He went over the plan again with Alice and gave her chance to ask questions. By the time he found a parking place on the street around the corner and a block from the bank, Alice was ready.

"Give me five minutes then start out for the bank," Frank said. "We'll only be gone about 15 minutes. Jack will be fine in the car. He's all bundled up and half asleep."

By the time Frank got to the bank, his topcoat and hat were covered with snow. He saw a car a half a block from the bank with the engine idling. *A sure indicator someone was in the car waiting for someone in the bank to come out. Something to consider but not enough to abort when we are this close and maybe already under surveillance.* As he got closer to the bank, he could see that the car was covered with snow and ice. Only the passenger door on the side he could see had been opened.

When he entered the bank lobby, he was looking for someone acting busy and watching the door. Frank opened his coat, took off his hat, brushed some snow from the brim, and started working on a bank form at a standup desk. From his position he could see the door and spotted a suspected surveillant. When Alice carrying Christina and a briefcase pushed through the revolving door, Frank's suspect noted her arrival and watched Alice ask the woman at the desk nearest the safety deposit box vault. When Alice was escorted into the vault area, he continued to watch the area with a growing intensity. A few minutes later, the female attendant came out, looked at the man watching, and nodded her head slightly. The man immediately put on his hat and moved quickly toward the exit.

Frank was convinced the man was KGB and followed him closely out the door. Outside, he quickened his pace and caught the man by the left arm, jamming the .22 Hi Standard into his right side, saying in Russian, "Do what

I say or you will die here. Don't look at me or make any signals. I know where your companion is waiting for you. We are going to walk over to your car now."

The snow squalls picked up, reducing visibility. Frank pushed the barrel of his gun hard into his ribcage and said, "Open the door and get inside. I'll put a bullet in one of your tires and nobody needs to die. Do exactly as I say or you're the first to die."

His captive opened the door and Frank pushed him hard inside into the driver. He shot each man twice in the head and then turned to the two men in the back and shot them both before they could bring their weapons up. He reached over, turned off the engine, and locked the doors. With any luck, it would be hours before anyone found them.

Frank crossed the street to a point where he could see the bank door and their car. Ten minutes later, Alice came out of the bank and began walking to the car, carrying Christina and the heavy briefcase. Frank moved to meet her and relieved her of the heavy bag. Alice took his arm. "It went just like you planned it. Everything is in the bag. The attendant seemed a little nervous. I didn't see her after she put the box back and returned my key. Did you get cold just standing around while I did all the work?"

"No," Frank said. "I managed to keep busy." Back at the car, they found Jack still asleep. "We're going to take a different route to Washington, D.C. One of the oldest roads and most important roads in the Colonial era of America is Route 30 that runs over the Allegheny Mountains through a number of small agriculture and manufacturing towns. We may stay overnight in one of those towns. By tomorrow all the main roads should be cleared of snow. Our bank robbing days are now over." He let out a sigh.

After an hour on Route 30 East, just past the town of Jeannette, Frank had finally settled down enough to tell Alice what had happened outside the bank. "The KGB was waiting for us. The woman attendant you said was nervous was working with them. She signaled a man, who was trying to look busy, that you had asked for the right numbered box. He put on his hat and hurried outside. Before I went in the bank, I saw a car with the engine idling. That made me suspicious and when the man in the bank hurried outside after getting the attendant's signal, I went out after him, grabbed his arm, put my gun in his ribs, and spoke to him in Russian. He understood perfectly. I walked him up to the car with the idling engine and when he opened the door, pushed him inside. I had to shoot him and the three other armed men in the car."

"My God, Frank! And I thought I did all the work! Are you okay? What does that mean? Are we in more trouble?"

"The KGB will now be hunting to kill us. I think we were already on the kill list, but now for sure. The men in the backseat were armed with a submachine gun and what looked like a sniper's rifle. At the slightest resistance they would have been shooting to kill. The KGB will keep some effort going to find us for several years. We must not give them any clues.

"We left some things for them to find, assuming the

84

KGB finds the car with the dead men inside. They will cover their tracks, get rid of the bodies, car, and maybe the safety deposit vault attendant. The only thing the KGB will have are the brass casings of the .22 I used. I couldn't take the time to find them all. A first-class police forensic lab may be able to pull partial prints from the casings. I loaded the magazine without using gloves. I always try to avoid handling anything but the bullet part of the cartridge but never can be sure. By the time the KGB even gets around to looking at the brass, if ever, they won't find anything. Hollow points don't give the ballistic people much to work with.

"A police or FBI lab is very different. If they tie the dead men to the bank or the bank attendant, they will do a first-class forensic job. If they get the attendant before the KGB they will get a description of you and Christina from her and the bank cameras. They'll dust the vault for fingerprints but won't find any because you were wearing gloves. The cameras will also pick me up and will link me to the KGB watcher inside the bank, because I was watching him and left immediately after him. I think that is the worst case, and it is not too bad. So, all in all, I don't believe we are in any more danger. But we'll have to watch the evening news for a few days."

Driving east on Route 30 through western Pennsylvania, Frank and Alice talked over their plan for the next month. "Frank, have you ever killed anyone before?"

"No. I didn't have time to think. These men were hunting us and intended to kill us, at the bank or somewhere later. There was no ethical problem for me. It was them or us. An easy choice. There was no thrill or remorse. Those men were hardened killers. Without the snowstorm, we would all be dead. I couldn't take four trained men without the cover of the falling snow and iced-over windows. They had little choice. They couldn't wait out on the street or in the bank. We would have seen them and so would've the bank guard. I'm sure they hated waiting in the car where they were not able to see outside. They didn't count on such an aggressive move on my part. They didn't know about my father and grandfather who killed men many times. Maybe it's in my blood."

"What do we do now?"

"We need to change cars and identities. We also need to buy more clothing so we can fit into a more affluent society. We won't have credit cards for a while so we pay cash for everything. We must look like we are used to wealth and just don't need credit cards."

"Shopping sounds good. My clothes certainly don't fit into a richer environment. My wealthy attitude is natural. I grew up in a privileged class in Poland. Just get me the clothes. I can play the role. Besides, you owe me a handful of diamonds."

"A small handful. Wealth is also a problem for us. We must have 30 to 40 pounds of currency, gold, and diamonds with us now. We can't keep carrying it around and I'm a bit reluctant to put it all in a number of safety deposit boxes around the country. The use of alias identification gets very complex. My idea is to buy a place and hide most of the money on our own property.

The ideal thing would be a remote mountain cabin in good condition. We can hide out there for a while and think about our options. Our trail will get colder over time and the KGB will eventually pull back some of the teams now hunting us."

"Now that we're wealthy can we get something to eat, and a place to rest and get cleaned up?"

"Take a look at the map. I believe there is a small town called Greensburg a few miles ahead just before we enter the foothills of the Allegheny Mountains."

"Yes. It's about four miles straight ahead."

"Good. Now look for a motel. I like being able to park the car right outside the door of our unit. I'm going to pull over when I can find a place to stop for ten minutes so we can change identities again. This will be our last name change for a while I hope."

"I was just getting used to Alice Kincaid."

"Say good-bye to Alice because you will soon be Sally Ann Webb. Your maiden name was Smythe, pronounced Smith. Your family is from Philadelphia, Pennsylvania. You were married July 24, 1971. You have no brothers or sisters and both parents were killed in a car accident ten years ago. You were educated abroad and speak French. You majored in the history of Eastern Europe and Russia. You met your husband, Jacob Allen Webb, at a wedding of one of your friends. You moved to Chicago where our children were born.

"Your husband made enough money in investments and wanted to try a new lifestyle and raise a family away from big urban areas. You didn't like Chicago and were glad to move east. Your credentials are in the brown envelope in my overloaded briefcase. Better wait until we stop and I'll dig them out for you. Call me Jake. You can be Sally or Sally Ann."

"I'll be Sally Ann. I like the flare. Now give me my diamonds and buy me some proper clothes."

"In due time, Sally Ann."

****

Jake left Sally Ann and the children in the rather nice motel just outside downtown Latrobe, while he went to trade the wagon in for another car in the Webb alias. He signed and backdated the title to show a sale from Frank Kincaid to Jake Webb. He had to use his next to last social security number. He was saving the last one for the change to the name of his heritage, Peter Brandon.

At the motel he had studied the local paper and saw that there was a Cadillac dealership a mile down Route 30 from their motel. Jake drove into the lot and was met by a salesman before he got to the show room.

"I want to look at the models in the show room. I'm interested in trading my wagon in on a new or late model Cadillac."

"Good, come with me. I'm sure we can find something you will want. My name is Bill Shipton."

"Glad to meet you Bill. I'm Jake Webb."

In less than an hour Jake drove off the lot behind the wheel of a Cadillac Eldorado hardtop with only 20 thousand miles.

It was a good buy and he felt he had been treated fairly. There was some surprise when he paid in cash. Bill told him that in his five years of selling Cadillacs only one other customer had bought one for cash.

Sally Ann loved the new car. "I never thought I would ride in a Cadillac. Now I own one."

"I paid for it with your handful of diamonds," Jake winked.

"That means I own it for real."

"Yes, it is yours. I'll buy a pickup truck in a few days."

When the children woke up and Christina was fed, the Webbs went shopping at a nearby mall. Jake found a few off-the-rack suits that with minor alterations fit him. After three pairs of chinos, Levis, a leather jacket, some insulated leather boots, a watch hat, warm socks, and underwear, he was ready to go.

He also bought some new luggage. Sally Ann shopped for the children first and when Jake found her, she turned over the children to him and went shopping. The shops weren't like Minneapolis or Chicago but she found three outfits she really liked, a stylish coat, a jacket, and other warm clothes, including Levis and boots. A few colorful scarves, sweaters, and pumps with four-inch heels, and she was ready for her new Sally-Ann-Webb-from-Philadelphia role.

It was growing late in the afternoon but Jake called and made an appointment to meet with a realtor in fifteen minutes. Sally told him she would rather go back to the motel. He could then take her car and go see the realtor.

The realtor, Nancy Elwood, turned out to be a woman in her mid-forties who was born and raised in the area. Jake introduced himself then said, "I might buy later but now I'm looking for a short-term furnished rental with some privacy. An old farm would suit us. If we liked the farm and the area, we could end up buying."

Jake could see he had her attention.

"I have a place like that for sale," she said. "An empty farm house, barn, fenced pasture, and 30 acres of wooded hills. They are asking $175,000 – could you go that high?"

"Yes, I can manage that much if I want the place after living in it."

"The place has been on the market for months. Not much moves here in the winter."

"For immediate occupancy I'll offer $1,000 a month on a month-by-month lease or agreement. Cash up front and a reasonable security deposit."

"The owner no longer lives there. The farm is empty now. I'd want to have our clean-up crew go over it before any one moves in. If your offer is accepted, you could move in day after tomorrow. The owner may want to know if you can afford the sale price. She will also want to keep the place on the market."

"No problem. I'm an investor/builder and have just made a fair amount of money that is in cash."

"I see your Cadillac is not just a front, then."

Laughing, Jake said, "No, I can afford it. If you find something a good bit larger while we're renting, please let me know. I'll finance any place we buy myself."

Ms. Elwood called Jake at the motel the next morning and said, "The owner approved. If you could stop by with the first month's rent plus a $500 security deposit, you could move in tomorrow. There is some furniture in the house you may use."

"I'll be there in an hour," Jake said.

Nine

Moscow, March 5, 1975

General Vassili was enjoying his first cup of strong black tea at his desk. Nothing that he knew about should make this a difficult day for the KGB's Chief of the First Directorate. Still, he would have to cut back on his drinking. Even the best vodka could leave a pounding headache the next morning. *Maybe I should also give up cigarettes and spend more time getting back into shape. How hard could it be to also lose 20 kilos if I put my mind to it?*

The door opened. He had told his very attractive and sexy office manager to give him 30 minutes of peace and quiet.

He scowled at Maria. "What is it that you didn't understand about giving me a bit of quiet?"

"General, forgive me, but you must see this right away. The Director will be calling in the next few minutes."

Stepping forward, she handed him a brief cable from the KGB Residency in Washington. After reading the cable, he slammed his fist on the desk. "Get my operations staff in here immediately."

As the door closed behind her, he thought, *I could lose my job over this. Four KGB senior officers shot dead in front of a bank they were staking out to catch the defector who is stealing from our safety deposit boxes. The men weren't found until the next day. They were all heavily armed and none of them fired a single shot. The safety deposit box was looted right under our noses. The people who want my job will use this to try and destroy me. My own people are helping them with such stupidity.*

He opened his top drawer and took out the file on the defector. *An officer on the fast track. Great training record, impeccable family. Father and mother were awarded Hero of the Soviet Union Awards for fighting in Stalingrad against the best units of the German Army. This defector is very, very good, or he is being helped by the CIA. We need to find him in a hurry.*

When his team of operational officers were settled in his office, General Vassili stared at them and read the cable from Washington. Then he said, "This defector, Ivan Kalin, must be found and quickly. I want an operational plan on my desk in five hours. Maria, contact our Resident in Iraq. Tell him I'm sending a plane for Yuri Kolenko. No delays are permitted. Yuri must be at the airport when my plane lands. Absolutely no excuses. I don't care what he is doing or what he has planned. He is to come directly to my office as soon as he lands."

Turning again to his staff, the General said, "Kolenko and a four-person team will be flying commercial to Minneapolis within 24 hours. All will be flying with business cover aliases and supporting documentation. Get them all the cash and equipment they ask for. Two of the alias sets of documents must include private detective licenses and permits to carry weapons. Yuri can meet with our man in Minneapolis but no one else. Tell our Resident in Washington to cooperate fully with all requests from Yuri. The code name will be *Revenge*. Yuri will have the authority to cooperate with U.S. authorities only with my case-by-case permission.

"Along with the operational plan that you will finish in five hours will be a plan to get American law and order forces searching for a renegade officer turned bank robber and killer. Also prepare a file for Yuri on both Kalin and his Polish wife, whatever her name is. Take all relatives living in the USSR or Eastern Europe into custody. The charge is crime against the State and treason. Now get out of here and go to work."

Ten

S ally Ann loved the farm as soon as they drove up the driveway behind the realtor. The house looked like it had seen better times. It needed painting and some repair of wood rot around some of the windows. The hardwood floors could be brought back with a sanding and refinishing. "Look at this kitchen," Sally Ann said excitedly. "Large, lots of light, and a great view out toward the barn and meadow. I may stand at the sink all day. I like this place."

"Is it large enough?" Jake asked. "Only two bedrooms and one bath. It also has a well system and septic tank in unknown condition."

"Trivial. My husband can fix anything."

"Good. Now make a list of the things we need to live here for a few months at least."

Nancy Elwood said, "I have to go. If you need anything call me."

Sally Ann said, "Thank you. We'll be in touch."

Eleven

Yuri Kolenko and the rest of his four-person KGB team landed in Minneapolis on different flights and times. They were all tourists from Finland, Ireland, Italy, and West Germany. Weapons were delivered to Yuri's room at the hotel. By the next day everyone had checked in and been briefed on what Yuri wanted done.

He was younger than the others but had been on the fast track for years. This mission could make or break his career. They were all given the same briefing. "When you read the file I've given you, read it again," Yuri told his team. "Ivan Kalin is a very intelligent and dangerous man. Without help he killed four of our best with a .22 pistol without anyone getting off a shot. Three of them had weapons in their hands. Before he killed them he emptied the bank safety deposit box of all its currency, gold, and diamonds. He did the same in two other banks, here in Minneapolis and another in Chicago.

"He made us believe he was going to hit the bank in Cleveland next. He set us up with a clever phone call he knew we would get. Then he drove overnight from Chicago to Pittsburgh through the worst storm of the year. His wife is an accomplice. She is intelligent, can handle a handgun, and like most Poles doesn't like Russians. We believe she emptied the Pittsburgh safety deposit box while our man inside watched, and she was carrying a baby in her arms. I tell you this because she is also dangerous and will be difficult to capture. So don't try and don't get caught by the local authorities.

"Control the kill zone. Don't give either one a chance. If the children survive, leave them. Someone will care for them and we cannot take them back. Killing infants is not part of our training or mission.

"Kalin has several problems. Running with two young children is difficult. He has to carry the loot with him. Not only is it heavy, he has to watch over it. Without a fixed address he cannot open a bank account, especially since he cannot give a plausible explanation of where the money came from. Then there is the tax problem. So he will be paying cash for everything.

"Kalin has had the same training we have. He probably used his first alias we gave him to use in St. Cloud, a two-hour drive north from here, until he got to the first big metro center. That is here. From here he needed to change cars and to change cars he needed to change aliases. We don't know what name they are now using. He had to arrange for other aliases without our help once he got to America.

"He has too many problems to last long running and changing cars and names. So he will try to find someplace he can hide and wait us out, while he improves his cover and defenses. He may be in such a place right now. To find him we must find where he changed cars. His need for cars is a big weakness for him.

"What I have told you so far is fact. Now, for some supposition. He would not have gone to a big car dealership. So we leave those for last. He made the purchase maybe weeks before he took off. In that case he had to hold the car somewhere safe. Probably in a pay-for-parking covered garage. Remember, it was bitter cold when he ran. If the car was held outside it would have been covered by snow and ice. With two infants he wasn't going to risk being stranded by a car that wouldn't start or if the doors were frozen. He had to transfer baggage and enough supplies to care for two kids on a long road trip.

"So while half of you cover outlying car agencies, the other two will check indoor parking garages. He will have paid cash in advance for parking. I'm sure nobody was in disguise. He also paid cash for the car. Anticipating bad weather, he would have selected a new or late model with four-wheel drive. With two kids and baggage and with the possibility they might have to sleep in the car, he would not have bought a small sedan, nothing with only two doors. Concentrate on big station wagons or cars. I doubt he would have opted for a van of some type. Few of them are all-wheel drive.

"Okay, you know what to do. Go out and start showing pictures. Show his. Hold hers back for now. Use your P.I. creds. You are looking for a guy who ran out on his wife and young kids. Nothing sensational or spooky and don't act important. Use small bribes if needed. Nothing over 50 dollars. Check back in here tonight."

Twelve

The Webbs had been in their rental farmhouse for almost two weeks. Sally Ann and Jake were in love with the privacy and living close to wildlife. Jack loved to slide down the snow-covered slopes just next to the barn.

Jake bought four backpacks and three sleeping bags at a local hunting supply store and a good .30 Winchester rifle with a 10x scope and 200 rounds of ammunition and a 12-gauge Remington pump-action shotgun with 100 rounds of double-ought shells.

All he needed was the cash and to flash his driver's license. Gun stores were stricter on the sale of handguns but had no requirement to report sales of sporting guns. As soon as Jake got to his small shop in the barn, he unplugged the shotgun so it would hold five shells rather than the limit of three required for hunting small game in Pennsylvania. He also cut thirteen inches off the barrel. It was now an illegal weapon. *But better to be illegal than dead,* he thought. A sawed-off shotgun was the best defensive weapon for close-in targets. If the KGB found him, legal or illegal was not relevant.

He also had a used four-wheel drive white Ford pickup truck and a used Ford station wagon he bought for cash at a small auction in Greensburg. He titled the wagon under the Brandon name using a false address. If they had to flee, he would use the Ford wagon. He had the Ford garage in Somerset check out the station wagon. New tires, belts, wiper blades, fluids, brake check. The wagon passed inspection.

Jake hoped he never would have to use it. He kept it in the barn with the packed backpacks and sleeping bags. Their treasure was hidden under the rear seat. Sally Ann had packed one of the backpacks for each family member and a suitcase full of non-perishable food and water.

Jake was happy. He loved working with his hands and he had a natural skill both with weapons and tools. He was beginning to think they might buy the farm at the end of two months. It was isolated enough that it was hard to approach without being seen. His head was full of plans to improve the house and fix up the barn. Sally Ann wanted some chickens, and maybe a milk cow and a riding horse.

The farm reminded her of her grandmother's farm in Poland. Jake could see that she was really happy for the first time since leaving Poland. The tension and watchfulness was gone. Jake knew the resources of the KGB could find them. He was not ready to use the Brandon name yet. He had made some mistakes, but had had no choice. They had to change cars and names, but in doing so he had left a trail that could be picked up by skillful hunters. Jake knew he was beginning to relax and lose his edge, partly because Sally Ann was so happy and he didn't want to make her fearful again. She carried her 9mm Browning everywhere she went. But it is hard to be eternally vigilant. Jake had high respect for the KGB and had no doubt they would find a clue somewhere and begin to close in.

Thirteen

After 16 days of intensive street work visiting 60 places selling cars and 43 covered parking garages, one of Yuri's team members finally found a lead. After three visits to a large dealership on the south edge of the city, a part-time salesman recognized Kalin's picture and remembered selling him a year-old station wagon. He remembered because it was the first cash sale of a nearly new car he had ever made. It wasn't uncommon but it was his first.

The salesman said, "No, there was no trade-in. Are you cops? Because if you aren't, I'm not telling you any more."

"No, we are not cops but we need to find this man and are willing to pay a $50 fee for any information."

The salesman said, "We are finished here," and walked into the show room.

Yuri's team set up to watch for the salesman leaving after work so they could follow him home, but missed him in the traffic coming and going into the dealership.

At the meeting with Yuri that night, he wasn't pleased they failed to find out where the salesman lived or his name. Yuri split the team to make two teams each with a member who could identify the salesman going or coming from the Ford dealership.

Yuri told them not to come back without the information and to do whatever it took. After three days of watching, a team saw the salesman leaving the car lot. They followed him to a diner and, when he came out alone, grabbed him just as he was getting in his car. The salesman, whose name was Gary Hoyle, recognized one of the team and said, "I told you I wasn't going to give you any more information."

"Look, we're private detectives who are being paid to find a guy who ran out on his pregnant wife and two little kids. Her dad has retained us to find and serve him. We are authorized to pay you $500 for information about the false name he is now using and the VIN and description of the station wagon. Also we will not make trouble for your dealership selling a car for cash to a person using a false name and fictitious address. The court case over that could take months. Please cooperate. No one, including us, needs that kind of aggravation."

"Let me see your licenses."

"Okay," and one of the team handed both licenses to him.

"Looks good to me. But I don't have the file with me. I'll have to get a copy of the sales contract."

"Can you remember the name?"

"Only the last name and that was Kincaid."

"Here's $250. Bring the contract here tomorrow and we'll give you the rest of the money."

"Okay. See you here tomorrow at noon. Can I go

now?"

"Yes and thank you. You have done a good thing."

When they reported to Yuri, he left one team member to meet again with the salesman, while he and the other three went directly to Pittsburgh on separate flights.

Fourteen

Yuri wasted no time in Pittsburgh. After checking into a hotel, he took a taxi to the scene of the four dead KGB officers and the Mellon Bank. The bank was open and he went inside to visualize how it all went down.

A skilled KGB officer like Kalin could have planned and pulled off the looting of the box and the killing of the four officers. In the scenario I believe is true, Kalin had no choice. Once the KGB watcher inside the bank was tipped off by the paid attendant, he would immediately hurry outside to alert the waiting team. Kalin had seen the parked car with the engine running and had to stop them from getting into action. He must have gained control of the watcher as soon as he left the bank and used him as cover approaching the car with the windows iced or steamed up. The men inside had no chance.

Kalin's wife, carrying the baby and the loot from the box, would have been out of the bank by then. Kalin's car, the station wagon, must have been nearby but out of sight from the bank or the parked KGB car. With weather conditions like they were, it would be useless

105

to try to find anyone who had seen the car. I have to put myself inside my old friend's head. Two kids, probably tired and hungry. Four dead men behind him, as yet undiscovered. He had to get out of the area. So far, everyone believes Kalin headed back to an area of the country he knew. They think he probably has a hiding place there ready for the Kalin family.

But they do not know him. Kalin has one of the best operational minds I have ever come across. He would know how his hunters thought and do just the opposite. He would have gone east to lose himself in the vast populated areas of America's east coast. New York, Philadelphia, Boston, Washington, D.C., Richmond, or Miami. He also needed to change cars and aliases again.

There is also another bank with a safety deposit box full of KGB funds in Washington, D.C., but I believe Kalin is done with the banks. He has enough and knows the risk to hit another bank could not be justified. So his main concern now is hiding and breaking whatever chain of clues he believes he left behind. He wouldn't have traveled more than two or three hours after leaving the bank before changing cars and aliases. They would also need a rest. I'm glad he has two very young kids and a wife with him. Without those burdens we would never catch him. The family gives us a chance.

I'm sure he stopped and changed cars and aliases within three hours east of this bank. If he thought it was safe or necessary, he may still be hiding out in the same area. Tomorrow I'll assign my teams to go east 35 miles and start showing the pictures at car sales lots, motels, fast food restaurants right along the highway. I'm gambling that he will avoid the turnpike. Too easy to check traffic and limited exits. He would have chosen Route 30 East. There are thousands of places to leave the highway and travel in any direction. Tomorrow or the next day we will find his trail.

Fifteen

Route 30 East, April 1975

Two days of checking motels, fast food restaurants, and car dealers turned up nothing. It seemed the Kincaids had vanished. Yuri was getting some pressure from Moscow to move on, expand the search area west of Pittsburgh. He stuck to his operational instincts. Yuri had moved his operating base to a motel in Latrobe, Pa., and was actively participating in the search. He needed to make sure the search wasn't so intensive and visible it could attract police attention or media coverage. Maybe if they didn't soon find the trail, he would arrange to get a piece of news into the local papers that might flush Kalin from his rat hole.

On the morning of the third day, Yuri went into the Latrobe Cadillac dealership. When he asked the salesman if he recognized Kalin's picture, the salesman said, "Sure. I sold him a late model Cadillac for cash. I see the car from time to time. He must still be in the area. Why? Can I interest you in a car?"

"Afraid not. Beyond my bank account. But I would like some information on the man in this picture. I'm a private detective working for a Pittsburgh law firm to find this man and get him to testify in a big civil suit against the company he worked for. If you can give me some identifying information, I'm authorized to pay a small fee. It will be at least $50."

"I don't know much about Mr. Webb. I can give you a good description of the car and a copy of the sales contract."

"You just made $150."

"Great. Give me a minute and I'll make a copy of the sales agreement and the trade-in title."

Ten minutes later Yuri was sitting in the back seat reading the contract. He tapped the driver on the shoulder. "Pull into that parking lot and park."

Though handwritten and faint, the name Kincaid was clearly on the copy of the car title.

Turning to the other KGB officer in the passenger seat, Yuri said, "Get on the radio and tell everyone to come back to the motel."

When everyone was present, Yuri started by saying, "Kalin is here is this town. He is using the name Jake Webb.

"They are driving a black, late model Cadillac Eldorado with temporary plates. His wife could be driving, so look for the car. Never mind trying to get a picture. Don't try to take them. Use very discreet surveillance tactics. Kalin is very good at detecting surveillance. Maybe he trained his wife. So be extra careful. Do not get too close. Switch cars often. Your task is only to find out where the Webbs are living. We need that information soon. Do not attract the attention of the local police. The plan is to stake out major crossroads, particularly monitor traffic going and coming on Route 30 west of Latrobe. One car will cruise the town. Break off the stakeouts at midnight and get some sleep. Back on the sites assigned at 7:00 AM. Switch cars and positions every four or five hours. Keep off the radios unless it is important. You have your assignments. Find this traitor."

Sixteen

April 24, 1975

S ally Ann was up feeding and bathing Christina at 6:30 AM. She put Christina back in her crib. She called Jake and said, "Christina and I are going out. You're the babysitter. I need some things from the pharmacy and while I'm out I'll pick up some groceries, anything you want?"

"Yes. Look for the good sausage brand we liked in St. Cloud."

"Okay, I'll try. Make Jack some scrambled eggs and jelly toast."

"Drive carefully."

"No one would dare put a scratch on my new car."

Sally Ann felt at home in Latrobe. *The people are nice. It is much smaller than Ottawa or even St. Cloud, but it has all I need and it is only a few hours to Pittsburgh.* It was good to get out for a little private time and who wanted their husband trailing along in the cosmetic section, anyway? She knew Jake was still worried about their safety but she could feel herself relaxing more each day. Surely they could hide in a country as big as the United States.

111

She found a good parking spot just outside the entrance to the pharmacy she liked, picked up a drowsy Christina, and went through the automatic doors.

Yuri was in the cruising car with the driver. They had just entered the small cluster of shops for a quick drive through and then on to the next shopping area when he saw a black Cadillac Eldorado pull into a parking place practically in front of him. He told the driver to move on and park 20 yards away from the Cadillac. Yuri called the other teams he had and ordered them to join him, but to stay in their cars and be prepared to conduct a three-car surveillance of the Eldorado when it left. "I will direct all movements. Discreet is the word."

Sally Ann came out of the pharmacy and made a quick look around the way Jake had taught her. There was nothing to be seen. She put Christina in her seat and started up the Eldorado for the mile drive to her favorite grocery store. She never noticed the skillful maneuvers of the three cars tracking her. When she left the grocery store pushing a cart with one hand and holding Christina with the other, the three KGB cars began their surveillance ballet. Again she saw nothing. When she turned into the farm driveway, they all kept going past with no pause.

Yuri left one car in position to watch the driveway while the other two cars moved a quarter-mile farther and pulled off on the shoulder. Yuri called the other car to join them and worked out an assault plan.

Sally Ann beeped the car horn to signal Jake they were home and to get some help carrying in the groceries. When she struggled in with Christina and one load, she saw a note on the kitchen counter.

"Took Jack to the Exxon station to fill up the wagon. Back in an hour or so. Lunch date for pizza?
Love, Jake"

How could you stay mad at a husband like that? Sally thought. *Maybe this idea of arranged marriages has some good points. Neither one of us had any choice. I feel fulfilled and very lucky. Getting out from behind the iron curtain is much better than I ever believed. This is what life is about. Without individual freedom, there is no freedom or justice. I'm ashamed of how my parents live a life of privilege while supporting an oppressive regime.*

She was cleaning up in the kitchen when she heard a car coming down the loose gravel driveway. *Good, Jake and Jack are home.* She ran her fingers through her hair while running to the front door. Instead of Jake's wagon she saw three other cars coming quickly toward the house. The last car blocked the entrance to the driveway. She knew immediately they were KGB and ran to get her 9mm Browning and Christina. Snatching Christina from her crib, she raced to the back door.

Bursting out on the back porch, she surprised two men who were coming around the house. She shot twice at the nearest man and knocked him down. The second man couldn't get a clear shot at her and was firing blind. Sally Ann stepped out and emptied her magazine of 11 more rounds at the second man, hitting him several times. Slamming another magazine into the butt of the

9mm, she began to think, *We may get away if I can just get to the wood line 30 yards from the porch.* She took off running hard to the tree line.

Sally Ann had been 200-meter sprinter in college and could still nearly outrun Jake. Another two men came around from the front of the house armed with assault rifles. Both dropped to one knee and began full automatic fire. Sally Ann was almost in the tree line when the first bullets hit her in the back and legs. She went down and rolled over on her stomach to protect Christina and return fire. Her vision was going but not before she hit another pursuer. Everything went black. She never knew Christina was going with her. Neither had escaped the hail of bullets.

Inside, Yuri and two men were searching the house for Kalin and the stolen money. Yuri quickly realized Kalin wasn't here or else he would have been in the firefight. A quick search of the house and barn revealed nothing of interest to him. He took a picture of the white Ford pickup, then checked Sally Ann's and Christina's bodies. He confirmed their deaths and didn't bother to search any further.

He had two dead men and one with a bad stomach wound. Without hesitating, he held the man's hand and shot him twice in the head. They could not take care of any severely wounded and none of his men could be taken alive by the local police. He searched the dead for any identification they might have carried against protocol.

Yuri left the dead where they fell and all his team and cars were out of the driveway on the way back to their motel operations center. They had been on the Kalin property for six minutes. The farm was isolated enough that no one responded to the gunfire. Yuri assumed the local people were used to guns being fired for practice and for hunting.

Maybe we were lucky, Yuri thought. *If Kalin had been there, we all might have been killed. As it was the woman carrying a baby killed three of my team, the last one after she was nearly dead. She died fighting and trying to protect her child. I'm through with trying to trap Kalin. I'll leave one car and one person here to watch the driveway for Kalin. The police may come before he returns. No way we can hang around Latrobe any longer.*

Jake was returning home when he saw the cars pulling out of his driveway. He kept going but as one car turned in his direction, he saw Yuri Kolenko, his old KGB friend from school, sitting in the passenger seat and concentrating on a hand-held radio. Jake saw one of the four cars turn around and pull over to park on the wide shoulder. He hoped Sally Ann and Christina were not home yet.

His first step was to get rid of the KGB officer left behind to watch the driveway. He glanced back at Jack in the backseat. "Jack, want to play a game? See how long you can keep your eyes shut with your hands over your ears. Ready, set, go!"

Jake pulled alongside the watcher's car and motioned to him to roll down the window. With his ball cap and sunglasses the driver wouldn't recognize him until it was too late. As the watcher started to roll the window down and reach for what Jake guessed must be a weapon, Jake shot him in the head three times. He whipped the car around and drove fast up the driveway and slid to a stop. Leaving Jack in the car, he ran through the house, calling for Sally Ann. He saw the bullet holes in the back door and broken windows.

Running outside, he saw the three dead men and Sally Ann's bright red coat near the tree line. Racing up, he saw that she had been hit hard. She still had her 9mm in her hand. Pulling her up and holding her he saw that Christina had also been killed. Screaming and crying, he kissed them both.

"I'm so sorry Marie," he cried. "All I wanted was for a normal life for all of us." He held her close for another minute. "I have to leave you, I have to save Jack. I promise you both, I will save him and take good care of him. Your deaths will be avenged." He kissed them both on the cheek and stood up. The wagon was already packed for an escape so he ran back to the car, kissed Jack with tears still streaming down his face, and sped down the driveway in reverse.

Jake used backcountry roads to get to Route 30 East. The road was open and he had to put miles and miles between him and the KGB in Latrobe. The wagon had a range of more than 300 miles on a single tank. He didn't want to stop until they got to Richmond, Virginia. Jake planned to change cars and names in Richmond. Jake and Jack Webb would become Brandons, Peter and Jack. No more aliases.

Seventeen

Peter and Jack arrived in Richmond very late at night. They checked into a motel and the next day Peter signed a month's lease on a short-term rental in the Fan neighborhood of Richmond. Jack missed his mother terribly and cried saying, "Where mommy and Chrissy?" Peter tried hard to make up the loss by taking Jack with him everywhere he went.

Leaving the wagon in the attached garage, Peter and Jack walked out to a main street and hailed a cruising cab. Peter gave him the address of a Ford dealer. After the cab dropped them and left, Peter picked Jack up, crossed the busy street and went into a Cadillac dealership a block away. A sales man hurried up and asked if he could help them. Peter responded, "Yes. I'm looking for a new or late model Cadillac, probably a sedan."

After looking at the new models with no sale, the salesman said, "We have a late model sedan with very low mileage. It has a few scratches and dents. Would you like to see it?"

"Yes."

"It's the white one sitting over there. Would you like to drive it?"

"No. I assume you have some kind of a warranty?"

"Yes, we do. Just like a new one."

After dickering over the price, Peter said, "Okay. Is it ready to go?"

"Yes, it was just prepped. How will you pay for it?"

"I assume you take cash."

"Yes we do. But it is a bit unusual."

"I'm going through a divorce and do not want to display all my accounts to blood-sucking lawyers."

"Ten thousand will pay the cost of the car. There will be a little more for taxes."

"Draw up the sales agreement. We have a deal."

Back at the rental, Peter transferred all the cargo in the wagon to the Cadillac. Then he and Jack went for a ride into one of the higher crime areas of Richmond. Peter left the keys in the unlocked wagon and he and Jack walked away. Peter had no doubt the wagon would be gone within the hour. He had broken the name chain. There was nothing that could link Brandon to Webb to Kincaid. After resting for a few days, the Brandons left for Florida.

Peter established the first Brandon bank account by depositing $8,000 into a bank that had branches throughout the South. He also rented a safety deposit box and paid three years in advance. He left a sack of diamonds, several ounces of gold, and $100,000 in currency, all in the Brandon name. It felt good. *If only Marie and Christina could be here,* he thought.

Eighteen

The Brandons had been in Florida for two years. Peter had heard of Amelia Island and looked for a house there a few days after they arrived from Richmond. He had found a house on a spit of land on the Amelia River with an acre of land and an in-ground pool. The house design fit the setting. It was expensive, and he had had to find a way to pay for it with cash. Driving a Cadillac and wearing quality clothing helped. No one questioned his cash payment. He now had two more bank accounts and safety deposit boxes. His bank in Richmond confirmed he was a depositor. His aim was to get a large part of his wealth legitimate and taxable.

At the tennis club he met a retired Special Forces colonel named Terry O'Brien who suggested he hire a Vietnamese couple to take care of the house and Jack, as well as cook. Terry said they were great people and fighters who fought with the Provincial Reconnaissance Unit in Quang Ngai Province in Vietnam. Terry worked with them during the war and helped them get to the States. Le Dinh Nguyen and his wife quickly became indispensible to Peter.

They were wonderful with Jack. He was now five years old, and he loved them. Peter felt he could travel without worrying about Jack. Terry also introduced him to a breeder of Bouvier des Flandres. As soon as Jack saw the black, roly poly puppies, Peter knew he had to have one. He selected a male pup and when the puppy was 12 weeks old, he came to live at the Brandon house. From that day on Jack and the Bouvier he named Rip were never apart. Peter was astonished at how the dog watched over Jack. He always stood between Jack and any danger, including dangers only a Bouvier could see. Jack was a strong swimmer, but if Jack was in the pool, so was Rip.

Peter and Terry became good friends. They played tennis together at the Amelia Island club and practiced martial arts together. Peter had been trained in the USSR by North Koreans in their martial arts system called Hapkido, a very deadly fighting style. Terry had some military training in unarmed combat but he was more of a natural street fighter. He was some years older than Peter but could hold his own on the tennis court or in the dojang.

Terry was also an excellent marksman. His specialty was shooting at distances longer than 250 yards. He had been a sniper in Vietnam, often working far in front of Marines in I Corps with only his spotter and a radio. Peter wanted to improve his long-distance shooting skills and Terry volunteered to help him. Over a six-month period, Peter's long-distance shooting skill improved to the point he could almost match Terry's scores. Of course, Peter never told Terry both his father, mother, and grandfather were outstanding marksmen. Peter thought, *Terry would have loved the story of my sniper father and mother at Stalingrad.*

Peter felt he was now ready to pay back the KGB for killing his wife and infant daughter. He wanted revenge but also didn't want to endanger Jack by increasing the resources the KGB was willing to invest to get him. He knew Yuri was beyond his reach, unless he ever got posted to the U.S. for a few years. But he could make a few KGB agents pay. Tomorrow he planned to head north for two or three weeks.

Terry agreed to move in for a few weeks to help the Nguyens and Rip look after Jack. Peter told the Nguyens he had some serious enemies. Their response had been for him to get them two 12-gauge pump-action shotguns and double aught ammunition.

When Peter gave them the shotguns, it only took a few seconds of watching them to know they were trained, experienced warriors. He had no worries leaving Jack with Rip there. Now that Jack had Rip and the swimming pool, he didn't mind his father taking trips.

June 1977

After a 12-hour drive from Amelia, Peter checked into the Washington Hotel near Tysons Corner just outside McLean, Virginia. Driving that distance with his Florida license plates and parking in the hotel lot added complexity, but he didn't want to be without a weapon. It wasn't likely he would run into any KGB agents who knew his face there.

For the past year he had been researching the ranks and assignments of U.S. diplomats to find a CIA officer on the fast track. From his KGB training he knew what to look for. There were several tip offs. One was where the officer lived. Not many CIA officers lived in Washington, D.C., and not many State Department Foreign Service officers lived in McLean or farther west. Daily commuting was a fact of life, and the fewer hours spent in a car going to and coming from work was a strong influence in picking a place to live.

Peter's checklist came up with a number of candidates. He liked one in particular. A Frank Batcher who lived alone near McLean along Old Dominion in an upscale but not affluent subdivision. This candidate was not a graduate of an Ivy League school, had served three years in the military, saw combat in Vietnam, and held a mid-level rank.

Peter wanted no personal contact with any CIA officer. Telephone contact from a pay phone was the limit. No identification and he wanted nothing from the CIA for himself. He only wanted them to help clean up his network of illegal agents posing as Americans. His first attempt at contact had to work.

He prepared a package to put in the Batcher mailbox. He made sure no fingerprints or other forensics could lead back to him. He included in the package one of the two miniature KGB radios he had kept. In the letter, Peter described in general terms information about his network without identifying himself in any way. He made clear he would control all future communications and any effort to identify him would end the relationship.

After ten o'clock at night Peter walked by the Batcher home and put his package in the mailbox. He then drove into Georgetown and called Batcher from a pay phone. Batcher picked up. "Batcher here."

Peter said, "Look in your mailbox. I'll call again in twenty minutes."

In exactly twenty minutes, Peter called from a different payphone. Batcher answered and said, "An impressive package. What do you want?"

"I want nothing but your help in destroying a KGB network of illegal agents posing as Americans. These people are trained and equipped to cause havoc and mass deaths in America, if and when the USSR decides to begin an attack on the United States."

"How do I contact you?"

"You don't. I will contact you."

"I'll need some time to get approval for this activity."

"If you believe that, I've contacted the wrong person and I will have to go somewhere else, maybe to another Agency. In one more minute this call will end."

"If I agree, what is the next step?"

"I call you and tell you everything you will need to pick up a Russian spy. If that works then we will take down another one. I want nothing. No money. No awards. No recognition. If I have anything tangible to give you, I'll tell you where to find it. You do understand dead drops, don't you?"

"Yes."

"Good," Peter said, and hung up.

Peter had told his network to relocate to their assigned areas six months before he broke away from the KGB.

By now they would be in place with the names he had given each agent. Peter was sure these illegal agents now had no way of contacting the KGB unless they had decided not to move when he instructed them. The KGB had a record of their previous addresses, so with an intensive use of resources, it was possible the KGB could find one or more of them. After all, they had found him.

Peter had directed Harry and Mary Jane Hartford to move to the Leesburg area. If they were there, a simple phone book search may be enough. Otherwise he would have to set up an unscheduled meeting. He had to tell himself again that these people he was betraying were killers in waiting. They were all hardcore communists willing to die for their country.

The next morning Peter studied some local maps. Tomorrow he would find the Hartfords, but first he would do his homework and explore the area. He decided to go as far west on Route 7 as Purceville and then double back to the river crossing at White's Ferry, from there go through Poolesville to the beltway and take 495 back to Tysons. It was a pleasant drive and traffic was light after the rush hour.

The ferry barge at White's Ferry was interesting, a bit of private enterprise that would have never been allowed in the Soviet Union. He stopped for lunch in Poolesville and browsed in a local antique store, called Hearthside, recommended by the waitress at the restaurant. He bought some children's books for Jack and returned to his hotel.

Peter was now ready for his first step to destroy the

Soviet network of terrorists under his control. He had a late breakfast in Leesburg the following day. He bought a town map and stopped at a pay phone to look up the Hartfords. They were listed as living on Morven Park Road. Peter drove by the house, a small bungalow on the west side of Morven Park Road, set back from the road, fenced in yard, evidence of a dog in residence, the back of the house not visible from city street, the lot backed onto a wooded area. No good place to set up 24/7 surveillance team. He took several Polaroid shots, dictated some notes, and left the area. No car was visible.

Back in his hotel suite, Peter got out the supplies he had purchased in Leesburg. A ream of paper, sealable envelopes, latex gloves, and a pack of ballpoints. He cleared off the dining table and set up his portable typewriter. His concern was fingerprints. As far as he knew his prints were not in any system and he wanted to keep it that way. When he finished typing in the obvious data such as addresses, physical descriptions, and work skills, Peter added types of weapons in the house according to his own records, the mission assigned, training background, and personality information.

When he finished printing his report, Peter double-enveloped the three sheets of paper. The outer envelope would be removed before putting the information in Frank Batcher's curbside mailbox. After dark he put his report in the mailbox and called Batcher from an Arlington payphone.

When Batcher answered, Peter only said, "Look in your mailbox" and hung up.

He would send Batcher one more report before going back to Amelia Island. The next illegal agent was a bachelor who lived in a rented apartment in Georgetown. Alias Oakley was a dedicated Communist Party member. His mission was terrorism in the Washington area. He liked to kill up close.

Peter wondered how this fanatic got through KGB screening. Oakley's brother had been killed early in the Vietnam War in Hanoi, and he held the Americans personally responsible for his death. He had told Peter he would never be taken alive and hoped he would soon be given the go-ahead to start killing Americans.

Peter felt this was not a case he could trust the Americans to handle. If several of them got killed, Batcher would want Peter brought in. No, he would handle Oakley himself and then put his report in the mailbox.

****

Oakley was good. He was constantly searching for surveillance. He was an intelligence operative who lived only for his mission and the constant effort to improve his craft. Peter had to use all his skill to follow Oakley enough to understand his pattern of movement so he could pick a killing zone and method.

Oakley worked at making his movements as random as possible. Peter knew everyone had a pattern. The effort to avoid leaving a predictable movement pattern was itself a pattern. Oakley parked his car in back of his small apartment building with an outside set of stairs.

Oakley's car, an old Honda, was not hard to find. There were only five or six parking places. Peter had his key to Oakley's pattern and could now establish a kill zone.

He would kill Oakley as he was locking his car at night. There were enough shrubs in full foliage at this time of year. Oakley had come back to his apartment between ten and eleven o'clock the last two nights. Peter bet that he seldom varied his return on the nights he went out. The car lights coming down the driveway would alert him to Oakley's arrival.

Peter was thankful he had found this killer before the KGB had and sent Oakley after him. If he left this trained terrorist up to the American authorities, Oakley would either escape, kill one or more of his would-be captors, or be captured and go to trial where Peter could be exposed and charged with killing KGB officers in Pittsburgh and Latrobe. Not a good ending for the Brandons.

Peter was in place, well-concealed behind some shrubs by 9:30 PM. He was a good waiter. Spies, snipers, and stakeout teams had this in common. Impatience got people killed, missions blown, or both. His was not an occupation for the faint-hearted or advocates of "give everyone a fair chance." Give an adversary like Oakley a fair chance and you could end up dead. No fair chance tonight. Peter chose a hiding place near the most undesirable parking space. Oakley's had been the last car in the previous two nights.

Peter had picked the right place. At 10:30 PM he saw car lights coming slowly down the driveway. He crouched lower, keeping one eye shut to avert momentary blindness. The engine stopped. Lights out. In the darkness of the poorly lit parking area, he saw the door open and Oakley step out and close the door. From ten feet he had a clear shot and took it. He fired twice more as Oakley was falling.

No one could've heard the silenced .22 High Standard. Peter dragged Oakley into the bushes in front of his car, picked up the car and apartment keys from the ground where they had fallen, and climbed the stairs to Oakley's apartment. He wanted to find some incriminating evidence to include with his report to Batcher.

It felt like the entire building was asleep. These were hardworking people. The first door on the left was Oakley's. He slipped inside, locked the door behind him and began to search with his muted, small flashlight. After checking the toilet tank, he stood and let his mind focus on the room. He didn't expect to find anything in the toilet tank, but he had to look.

This man was a dedicated KGB professional who had survived nearly ten years living undercover in America. His hiding place would be in this apartment. It would be easy to open and close. Big enough to hold a handgun, small clandestine radio, encrypting pads, at least one set of alias documentation, and a few simple disguise materials. All incriminating but comforting to have. Peter ruled out the kitchen, bedroom, and sitting room. He focused on a small walk-in closet off the one bedroom.

He studied the small closet for a few minutes and moved to inspect the four-inch baseboard molding. He liked the possibility of the baseboard running from the doorway to the closet wall. Easy access. Good security – Oakley could get in and out of his caching place without have to turn his back on the doorway.

In a few minutes he found the three-foot length of baseboard that was easy to remove. Behind it Oakley had cut and removed three inches of the drywall along the entire three-foot length. Between the 2-by-4 studs, he found what he was looking for. He packed it all into a small valise that he took off one of the closet shelves. Making a quick check, he moved to the door, eased it open a crack, stepped out, and locked the door behind him.

On the way back to the hotel, he went over what he would send to Batcher. *This should make a believer out of him if he hadn't taken down the Hartfords yet.*

After midnight the following night, Peter parked a block from Batcher's house and put his report and the items taken from Oakley's apartment in the mailbox. He called from a phone booth in Georgetown. When Batcher answered, Peter said, "Get your mail. There will be no follow-up call. You should have all you'll need. Remember, no attempts to identify me. There are no second chances. Any media reports will alert other members of the illegal network. They do not know each other but do know how to read and watch television. No mention of equipment or espionage agents. You may want to watch the Hartfords instead of arresting them. There are three more in this network. I won't be using your mailbox again. Goodbye."

Nineteen

Frank Batcher spent the better part of what was left of the night studying what came out of the midnight delivery to his mailbox and what he would tell his boss in the morning. It wasn't every day that a source like this appeared. So far he had managed to hold off all the "do it by the book" people in his chain of command. They all wanted to focus on finding this "potential asset" and bringing him under control and direction. Something in Frank's assessment of this new source was that he was smarter and a better student of the espionage craft than they were, and he would spot any attempt to identify him at the first attempt. Tomorrow morning he and his Division Chief would try to see the Director of Operations.

When Frank and his Division Chief walked into the Director's suite, he was confident they had worked out a good approach. When Frank finished his briefing of last night's event, the Director said, "Frank, what you are telling me is that you want to wait and take no action if and until your new unknown source contacts you again. Is that right?"

"Yes sir."

"You know that will not sit well with all the process

people around here who spend all their time trying to second guess the real case officers who actually run agents. Well, it just so happens I agree with you. It is often better to not make a decision than make one based only on protocol.

"Now you have to listen to me give you my theory about your source. For the last two plus years we have picked up indications that the KGB has been making a big search effort for something. In all my time in the world of clandestine operations, I have never seen anything like it. I'm going to tell you both something that does not leave this room.

"A little more than two years ago the KGB started paying an unusual interest in American banks. We had reports of KGB officers in or near banks in Minneapolis, Chicago, Cleveland, Pittsburgh, and Washington. Four of their experienced case officers were killed in broad daylight in their car parked across the street from a Mellon bank. All the men were armed. Two with AK-47s. None of them fired a shot. I believe a lone man killed them all with a .22 silenced semi-automatic.

"Some weeks later, three cars full of KGB officers attacked a farm house in Latrobe, Pennsylvania. For you golfers, that's Arnold Palmer's hometown. Three of them were found by the local police shot to death. A young woman and her infant daughter were found dead in the back pasture just a few yards from a tree line she was apparently running toward. She had a Browning 9mm and managed to kill three of them, while trying to escape carrying a baby.

"No questions yet. Hold them, please. A woman, two

children and a man were living in that house under the name Webb. A thorough background check turned up nothing. No fingerprints on record. The Webbs arrived in Latrobe the day after the killings in Pittsburgh. They paid cash for everything, including a late model Cadillac from Arnold Palmer's dealership. There is no record of the two-year-old or the man, probably the father. They just vanished. No name and no identified vehicle.

"Two years later, your source shows up. Provides solid proof that he is or was a KGB officer. Does he have a motive for getting even with the KGB? I'll say he does. The radio he gave you is a big deal. We'd never even seen one before. To top that he locates an illegal agent, cases his house, practically tells you how to take him down but suggests watching him might be a better tactic to keep from spooking other Russian agents in the same network.

"He also understands evidence he gave you probably couldn't be used in court without his testimony, which you will never get. The last thing is that he gives you the name and address of a Russian illegal agent trained to conduct terror operations in Washington if war seems probable. He knew this agent's mission, his personality and then to keep you dumb asses from getting killed, he does the job for you. Killing this terrorist, using guess what? A silenced .22. If we find any brass at the scene, I'll bet it matches the brass from the shooting in Pittsburgh.

"Then your source drags the body into the bushes to give him time to take the dead terrorist's keys and search his apartment where in less time than seems possible he finds the guy's cache and the next night puts it all in your mailbox. At least he is human and needs sleep.

"Okay, Frank. I think I saw some bells go off in your head. Right?"

"Yes sir. There is only one way this source could know everything he has told us. This guy is a highly trained KGB officer who was running a network of illegal Russian agents in and around Washington. For some reason he decided to escape from them but recognized it would take a lot of money to hide with a wife and two kids. That money came from KGB operational funds in the banks with all the activity. This guy is smart, tough, and ruthless."

"Yes, Frank. He is my kind of case officer. I want him working for us. I don't care if we ever know his name. No one but the three of us needs to know. No briefing of successors without my direct orders and no support officers, no records. He will get no money. So, no financial records. We need a system to pass him information. Let him come up with one he can control.

"So here is what I want you to do…"

The scheduled 15-minute meeting took longer than an hour. Both Frank and his Division Chief didn't say a word on their way back to their offices.

There is a reason that man is the Director of Operations, Frank thought. *He showed me more in an hour than anyone else has ever taught me.*

An hour after the meeting, Frank was called into his Division Chief's office. The Chief said, "Have a seat, Frank. That was a remarkable meeting. Seldom have I seen the dots connected so clearly. This is going to get complicated. It could turn into a full-time job. I'm bowing out. I want you to report directly to the DDO on this. I've cleared the process with him. He's fine with it. Turn over most of your workload to your deputy. I believe she is up to it. Good luck."

"She is up to it. Thanks for your confidence and support."

"Confidence you have. Support from here is questionable."

Frank pondered that response as he walked back to his office. It wasn't unexpected. His Division Chief had a keen sense of what could hurt his career and wasn't big on taking chances. Frank knew that if this op went south, he was the guy holding the bag, especially if the current Director of the Clandestine Services moved on or out.

The last package from his new source included the identities and general locations of four other Russian illegal agents. For the next several months he had more than enough work. He also needed to hire and train six three-person surveillance teams, with instructions not to make waves. They needed to find and watch the agents pretending to be Americans. No arrests could be made if the court trial seemed problematic. Until proven otherwise, these people had to be treated as citizens with all the ensuing rights. Getting information out of your mailbox after midnight from some unknown person doesn't make Russian spies out of people who look, act, and maybe are bona fide citizens.

Twenty

Peter was enjoying life sitting by the pool with Jack and Rip. The Florida sun was as hot as advertised and a warm breeze came across the marsh from the inland waterway. Peter liked marsh living much more that the noisy, salt-riven lots right on the ocean. He had a Boston Whaler in a boathouse at the end of a pier in the marsh. With its small electric trolling motor, it made the ideal fishing platform for a 115-pound Bouvier, an active, constantly questioning five-year-old who was almost ten. *If only Marie and Christina were here, life would be perfect.*

Terry O'Brien, the only man he'd met he liked well enough to spend time with, had called earlier and asked if he could bring his niece, who was visiting from Ireland, for a swim. Jack and Rip adored Terry. Peter asked the Nguyens to make a picnic lunch.

Rip heard Terry's car come in the driveway and raced around to the front of the house to escort them to the parking area. After receiving his greeting from Terry and meeting his companion, Rip ran back to Peter with his stubby tail wagging and waited for the humans to do their curious meeting ritual. Peter stared at Terry's niece. *This woman is gorgeous. Long black hair, great figure. She is nearly as tall as me. Her Irish accent has a beautiful lilt.* By the time he had recovered, Terry was making introductions. He said, "Peter, this woman, Bernadette O'Brien, is my niece, maybe several times removed. Never mind the lineage. She has always been my niece."

Peter said, "It is always a pleasure to welcome beautiful women to my house. You are the first. Now meet my son, Jack."

Jack took her hand and said, "Now come swim with Rip and me." Bernadette laughed and let Jack lead her away.

As Jack led Bernadette to the pool, Terry said, "She is here on more than a vacation. I'm trying to get her to break with the IRA before it's too late. She is a highly trained IRA assassin, very skilled with knife and gun. I need your help. I don't want her to end up in prison or constantly running for her life. She's not married, has no attachments. I think many Irish lads are frightened being around her. She could take all of them, probably a couple at a time."

"I'll do what I can. Is she in danger now?"

"No. No one from her past knows she is here. According to her, her name is not on any wanted list. The danger will be from her friends if she tries to leave the IRA. I have to go away for a couple of months. Can you look in on her from time to time?"

"Sure. This may sound funny, but I need a governess for Jack. The Nguyens are good, but there is a lot they don't understand about growing up in the western world. I'll pay her a living wage so she will have more options about the future. You know, education, job skill training, or something more general. Whatever she may be looking for."

"Peter, tell you what. Ask her. Whatever she decides is okay with me. She may be young in years but not in experience. She has seen too much and done too much. She's smart and is painfully rethinking her past. I've heard her crying a couple of times. My job as a security consultant requires me to spend chunks of time in bad places. I need the money and I know about violence, security, and physical protection but not much else. Especially not how to comfort my young, troubled niece."

"When Jack brings her back, give me some time and I'll ask her. Okay?"

"You got it."

When Jack came up holding Bernadette's hand, Peter asked him to go help the Nguyens with the picnic lunch and told him he could have one coke. Jack and Rip ran off to the kitchen. Peter said, "Bernadette, please sit down over here. I need some help and Terry told me to ask you."

Bernadette laughed. "Generally, men don't start talking to me about helping them. It's usually more specific but something tells me that if you wanted a woman for sex, you would have no trouble finding one."

"Believe it or not, I haven't even had a date for two years. Sex hasn't been high on my priority list."

Bernadette laughed again. "Now that you've

explained yourself, let's get to the point."

"I need a governess for Jack. Like Terry, I travel a lot and can't take Jack with me. With a governess he would be able to stay here or come with me. I'll pay you well and give you free room and board in my house. It's divided into a couple of guest suites. You can have your pick."

"You mentioned pay."

"How about five thousand a month to start?"

"Dollars!?"

"Yes. But I can do other currencies."

"No. No. I accept," she said and shook Peter's hand.

"When can you start?"

"I already did."

As they were shaking hands, Terry came up and said, "I hope that means you now have a job."

"Yes. A great job and a place to stay. Maybe America is the 'golden mountain' the Chinese talk about. And I'm working right now so don't distract me. Here comes my ward and his dog that weighs almost as much as I do."

After lunch, Terry and Bernadette left to get her two suitcases. They were back in an hour and Bernadette picked her bed, bath, and small sitting room suite and settled in.

Terry left to get ready for his trip and the Nguyens served a light supper with some of the lunch spread and a spicy noodle soup. Bernadette sat with Jack and began correcting his table manners. He bonded quickly with his governess and happily followed her instructions.

After she put Jack to bed, Bernadette joined Peter

by the pool for coffee. She was wearing a short pleated white skirt, with a white halter-top, and open toed platform sandals. She sipped her black coffee. "It may be an illusion, but I'm cold sober and relaxed for the first time in years. I feel safe and that is a happy feeling. I would like to rebuild my life on this start."

"We both have a journey. I still don't feel safe all the time. Mostly it's because of my concern about Jack. I'm going to do something I've never even thought about doing before. I'm going to tell you something about myself that will help you understand my, maybe, over-protective concern about Jack. I don't believe I need to ask you to never reveal what I tell you. Not even to Terry."

Bernadette nodded and sat back in her chair, cradling her cup of coffee in her hand.

"I was married to a woman I loved. We had two children, Jack and his baby sister, Christina. We were making an effort to build our lives when something terrible happened. Jack and I came back to our little farm from a short shopping trip. I found my wife and daughter shot to death. Before she was gunned down, my wife killed three of the attackers with a handgun, while running and carrying a baby. Five more yards and she and Christina might have escaped. I killed one more of them and had killed four others of them a month earlier. I have to operate on the belief they are still searching for me. Now do you still want the job? There may be some danger."

"Thank you for telling me. I sensed there were some hard times in you. You have the look. The one I've seen in top IRA fighters. Yes, I want the job more than ever. On one condition. I want a concealed weapon."

"Granted. Anything else?"

"Yes. I want to sleep with you tonight. You can love me or fuck me but we need to get the male-female tension out of our way. No commitments. We have enough tension without mixing sexual desires into it."

"What if either one of us wants to continue the sleeping arrangement?"

"Easy answer, we do it. I can't believe you're a rapist or the whining type. If I don't want sex at anytime, I'll say so. So can you. Agreed?"

"What's not to agree to?"

"For appearances I'll keep the suite but be with you every night. It'll be fun playing house. You're not my first but I've never lived with anyone before."

Peter took her hand and said, "Let's get started."

"I'm ready. I should tell you it's been over a year since I've had a man, and he was a terrible lover."

The master suite was the most impressive sleeping quarters Bernadette had ever seen. A king-size bed, full bath with open shower, and large garden soaking tub. His and her basins and cabinets. Bernadette looked around then turned to face Peter. "Hurry," she whispered. She was already naked except for her platform sandals. She was not wearing anything under her short skirt. When they were lying together, she slowly opened her legs and eased him into her.

Later in the soaking tub, Bernadette said, "For a guy without any recent encounters, you are very good. I like tenderness but followed by hard, quick sex. Your body is very hard like you have been working out all your life."

"I've worked at martial arts for years, especially Hapkido. Hapkido is a Korean..."

Bernadette interrupted. "I know what Hapkido is and have a brown belt. We'll have to practice together some time."

"What are your other skills?"

"You mean outside the bedroom?"

"Yes. Those skills are impressive."

"Well, my specialty is knife fighting, including throwing. I'm seldom without my throwing knife, except in hot tubs. Don't like to get the handle wet. Throws off the balance."

"What about guns? What do you want to carry?"

"I like the Colt .45 Army issue and four magazines."

"The lady knows her weapons. I'll give you a .45 tomorrow. I've a couple hidden away in the house." They soaked for a while longer in the tub, then Peter took her hand and said "It's time for bed."

Bernadette was soon sleeping, breathing softly in a deep sleep. Peter studied her face and thought *is this the same woman who was such a wanton lover a few minutes ago? I've not had many women but Bernadette is different. She is as composed and confident naked in bed with a new lover as she was fully clothed. She is her own person and I am very glad to have her with me, for my sake as much as Jack's. He is already bonding with her. I must not let him be hurt again. He was young when his mother was killed but he knew something had happened and she was gone. He cried at night for days for his mommy. So Peter, be careful. Bernadette may not be permanent even if I want her to stay with us. She has her own life's trail to follow.*

Twenty-one

Thursday, August 5, 1977

A week later after Bernadette, Jack, and Rip had
formed their own tight group, Peter drove up to
McLean and checked into the Washington Hotel near
Tysons Corner.

The staff knew him now and several nodded or said
hello. People who reserved suites got special treatment.
It was the same worldwide. Money made some things
much easier.

Terry O'Brien had given him the name of an
attorney from South Carolina who was now practicing
in McLean. The attorney, Lee Jensen, had served with
Terry in Vietnam. Peter needed a lawyer he could trust
and one who would not ask too many questions. He had
too much wealth in cash, gold, and diamonds. Somehow
he had to convert most of it into investments and bank
accounts. He had to become a tax-paying citizen with
a social security number and bank credit. Tomorrow
morning at nine o'clock he would meet with Lee Jensen.
Terry had made the appointment a few weeks ago.

Lee's office was in part of a townhouse off Old
Dominion in McLean. It looked as if Lee Jensen was

143

using part of his house as an office. The office had a separate entrance marked with a classic bronze plaque. Peter rang the doorbell and a young attractive woman opened the door and said, "Mr. Brandon, come in please. My name is Amanda. I'm delighted to meet a friend of Terry's. He and my husband have been friends for years. Come with me and I'll take you back to Lee's office. He is expecting you. I just made a pot of black French Roast. I understand you take your coffee black and strong. Do I have that right?"

"Yes, you do," said Peter with a smile, "I see Terry has covered some of the important facts."

"The coffee and that you are a special friend is all we needed to know. Here is Lee's office." Amanda opened the door and said, "Lee, Mr. Brandon is here."

Lee welcomed him with a firm handshake. *He fits Terry's description, slightly taller than I am and a few pounds under my 190. Has a distinct Southern accent and looks like a mild-mannered indoor guy except for the four-inch jagged scar on his right cheek. He or his wife knows antiques. The office is full of 18th century English pieces. Those are Dagestan Orientals on the floor. Also not woven yesterday.*

Lee led Peter to a conference table and poured coffee. After sipping the coffee, Lee said, "Terry didn't tell me much except you are a good friend, needed legal help, and could pay for it."

Peter chuckled. "I wish it was that simple. Yes, I can pay for it. While money is not the problem, using it and growing it is."

"Can you tell me some more? Anything you say

in here is subject to lawyer-client privilege laws and protocols."

"I have been in many countries and made a lot of money. My assets are in the form of gold, diamonds, and cash. I need some of it converted into bank credit, U.S. treasuries, and other securities so I can pay state, local, and federal taxes on future earned income. I want to form an investment company composed of you and me, if you accept me as a client. I don't have the expertise or time to manage the money and do it according to the law."

"How much money is involved?"

"The honest answer is I don't know, but more than ten million and less then fifteen."

"Where is it now?"

"I put it in several safety deposit boxes and small bank accounts where I could deposit eight or nine thousand each month and I have four hundred thousand in my briefcase."

"Well, so far you've done the right thing. What else can you tell me about the origin of the wealth you have?"

"Not enough to satisfy most people. The money was not stolen. It is not income from drug operations or illegal activities and, while some foreign countries would like to cheat me and get their money back, no one legitimate is looking for the money nor is it on any Interpol watch list."

"Who else is aware that you have the money?"

"In this country or its allies, no one but you."

"How do you intend to pay me?"

"I was thinking about a sizable yearly retainer and a

fee for successfully managing my money."

"How large a retainer? I know that sounds crass but I'm struggling to get started here in Yankee land and cannot take on tasks that will not grow my firm."

"I was thinking $250,000 to start and more subject to successful investments."

"That's generous but I have a feeling I'll earn the money. Let's shake on it. No formal contracts or records for now and maybe never. Agree?"

"Agree."

"Okay, let's get started. I'm going ask you some questions. No answer is better than a wrong answer. Tell me if you'd rather not answer."

Lee pulled over a yellow legal pad and started asking questions about addresses, property owned, dependents, heirs. When he asked about father, mother, siblings, Peter shook his head and Lee plodded on. He asked for a social security number. Peter looked at him and said, "Here's where you start earning your retainer. I do not have one."

Lee stopped, capped his Waterman fountain pen and looked at Peter and asked, "Not even an old one when you were a kid?"

"No."

"Birth certificates?"

"Yes." Peter saw no need to tell Lee it was from a grave site in St. Cloud from the family of his grandfather who disappeared in Siberia in the late 1920s. Part of the birth certificate was legitimate, at least the form was, but the rest of it was forged. Jack had a proper birth certificate – only the name and place of birth was forged. Lee might be understanding but no need to push the envelope.

Lee said, "Okay, that gives us something to work with. Do you have any employees?"

"Yes. I have a paid Vietnamese couple that Terry told me once were part of the Quang Ngai Province, PRU."

"Both Terry and I worked with the PRU in I Corps. Very good fighters, men and women. Do they also protect your property?"

"Yes, and my son, Jack."

"The PRU was never slow to shoot. In a dangerous situation they will not hesitate. Anyone else?"

"Yes. I just hired a governess for Jack."

"Wonder how she would feel if she knew the background of your house staff?"

"She's fine with it. She is at least as good with protection responsibilities. She's earned a brown belt in Hapkido in Ireland."

"Jesus Christ, Peter, are you getting ready for a war?"

"No. Just hiring one of Terry's relatives to watch over Jack and teach him some manners beyond eating his meals with chopsticks."

"Is there anything else I need to know?"

"Yes. I may want to buy some property in Pennsylvania's Allegheny Mountains, and I'll need a way to pay for it. Can you set up a company to own my cars and property and also pay expenses?"

"Different from the investment company?"

"Your call."

"You've given me a bit of work. Let me get started. What form is the gold in?"

"Small bars. I haven't weighed them."

"Next time you come, bring them. They'll be easier to convert than diamonds. How do you feel about investments?"

"I need to grow what I have and am willing to take risks with new start ups. I'm also okay with providing seed money to good ideas and committed developers. I expect to be back here in ten days or so. How about buying the property I talked about?"

"Give me some cash and I'll issue the seller a check and arrange for the settlement. Entire process shouldn't take more than a day or two. I'll set up an account you can draw from as you need cash. Later we'll get you a credit line but not yet."

"Great, I feel good about this. I'll give you a hundred thousand as a payment on your retainer and two hundred for you to keep on account for me here. I'll call. Expect me in less than ten days. If I'm successful in buying what I want, I'll be four hours from here for several months."

Lee stood and shook Peter's hand. "Take care, my friend. You've just taken the boredom out of my life."

Peter laughed. "You just taken some stress out of mine. See you soon."

Peter went back to the hotel and spent two hours in the workout facility and then took a nap with his .22 High Standard under his pillow and a chair against the door. Being safe was inconvenient, but so was being dead.

Peter felt refreshed after his nap and drove over to the huge shopping center at Tysons Corner. He bought some clothes at Bloomingdale's, three conservative dark suits, several shirts and ties, dress shoes, and some presents for the Nguyens, Jack, and Bernadette. His clothes needed alterations and would be sent to the hotel in a few days. It was good to live like regular people. After his phone call to Batcher tonight, he suspected the time out would be over.

He filled up his car at an all-night gas station and used the payphone after checking for any outside cameras. Frank answered on the first ring and said, "Batcher."

"Just a call this time. Nothing in your box. Are you acting on the information I gave you?"

"Yes and no. We have the information and have located the people and have them under loose surveillance. As you said, taking them down could have consequences we are not ready to deal with. Your information is very good. So good it is limited to one other person besides me. That person is my Chief's chief. He wants a dialogue of some kind with you. You set the place, time, and rules.

"He is an operational genius and wants you to help us with some problems. He doesn't care who you are or where you came from, he just wants a chance to communicate. He will come alone and you can leave at any time. The man who wants to talk to you doesn't believe we could either pursue you or trap you. He thanks you for saving the lives of his officers by taking down the terrorist/sniper in Georgetown. Are you willing to meet him?"

"Maybe. But I must have total control. I will call you two weeks from today at your office number. When I

149

call he must be ready to go to my meeting site. You may drive him. I will give you less than 30 minutes. It will be nearby. Give me your office number. I will call at noon. Goodbye."

Peter thought, *This might be good or very bad. I have to see. We will need some official help at some point. So far they have played it straight with me. Actually, they told me more than I expected.*

Keeping his suite, Peter drove to Somerset, Pennsylvania, early the next morning. His route out of Tysons Corner was against the morning traffic, and he was in Somerset by noon. He stopped for a cup of coffee in Somerset and picked up the local paper and some free real estate flyers. There were dozens of houses for sale and scores of mountain properties. He saw an ad he liked and noted the real estate office was practically in the center of town.

Peter walked in the office and asked the woman on duty about the ad they had running in the brochure. He showed her the ad. The agent, who wore a pin that said Betty, told him to look on the table next to the door for a Platt map and some pictures, including an aerial photo. Peter liked what he saw. A single building, a large log cabin, sat in the northern corner of a thousand acres of forested mountain land with a small stream running down the valley.

Peter asked if anyone could show him the property. Betty said, "Nancy Squire will be back from lunch in about 45 minutes. If you would like to go out and have coffee or lunch, Nancy will be back when you return. She is free to show the property this afternoon. What is your name?"

"Peter Brandon. Can you tell me how long the property has been for sale?"

Betty replied, "A little more than a year. The coffee shop a few doors to your right is not a bad place for a quick lunch."

After his quick lunch, Peter met Nancy and they started the drive to the cabin. According to the site map, the cabin sat nearly in the center of 1,000 acres on the south slope of the mountain. A chain link fence enclosed ten acres. The driveway was approximately a quarter of a mile from the narrow, hard surfaced road. A locked gate blocked the driveway. As Nancy drove through the opened gate, Peter could see the roof of the cabin nestled against the sharp slope. She pulled into the gravel turn-around space and shut off the engine.

Peter could now hear the subdued murmur of an unseen mountain stream down the steep slope. The sun was high in the sky and the slight breeze swirled in the heavy-leafed branches of towering oak and red maple trees surrounding the small clearing. The back of the cabin was set flush against the steep, heavily wooded slope. Nancy asked Peter if he wanted to see inside. Being a shrewd realtor, she saw that her client was making his own inspection. Peter murmured he would, and she opened the only door into the cabin. The door swung open on well-oiled hinges. The cabin smelled slightly musty. It was empty of all furniture, no wall hangings or drapes. It was larger inside than he thought it would be from his outside view. There was a Pullman kitchen with very old appliances, a sitting room with a slow-burning wood stove, two bedrooms, one larger than the other. Two baths that needed upgrading.

Off the back of the kitchen was a heavy metal door that led to a spacious storage area containing a hot water heater, a pump, and pressure tank for the well. Nancy said, "You probably will want to put in a large generator, in case the long power line in from the State road goes down and it will."

"There is a lot of work that needs to be done to make this place comfortable. I like the setting and the cabin itself is in good condition. I suspect it was built 40 or 50 years ago and has been kept up. I'll offer $250,000 for immediate sale and occupancy."

"Okay. I'll take the offer to the owner this afternoon or tonight, and I'll need to talk to your lawyer about the payment process."

"Good, he will take care of the payment and represent me at settlement."

Two days later, Peter owned a log cabin in the Allegheny Mountains. He asked Nancy, his realtor, to recommend a local contractor who he could trust. When she gave him a name, he said, "I'm not interested in the lowest price. I want good and dependable workmanship. A company that can meet deadlines. Now can your office manage the work and payment schedule?"

Nancy said, "I mostly own this agency. Sales are slow so, yes, I'll manage the work for a 15% fee."

"Agreed. Stay in touch with my attorney. He will be sending the checks out. If you need me, go through him. I travel a lot. Give me a yellow pad and I'll write what I want done."

Twenty-two

An hour later, Peter was on his way back to Amelia Island. He made it as far as South Carolina before pulling into a motel for some sleep. He got a very early start the next morning and was home in time for lunch. Jack and Rip jumped all over him. Bernadette told him later she wanted to do the same thing but uncharacteristically restrained herself. The Nguyens hurried to put on a great lunch in record time. Peter thought, *Life is good. I wish I could keep it this pure and simple.*

That night Bernadette, wearing only her new jade pendant, stretched tightly against him while their breathing returned to normal. She said, "Peter, I have never had a family or even knew what it would be like. This is wonderful. I'm at peace, happy spending time in this place. It is like stepping off the spinning world. I know this can't last but I'm going to bank every day."

"I know the feeling. I'm sorry, but the day after tomorrow I need you to come with me. I must go back up to Washington. I'll need more than your companionship. I need your skills to cover my back while I talk to some dangerous people. There will be time to have fun and I have a surprise for you. Will you help me?"

"Yes, of course, I'd be unhappy if you went into a dangerous situation without me. What will I need?"

"You'll need the .22 Hornet with the 10x scope and the .45 Colt I gave you last week. How comfortable are you in the backup sniper role?"

"Not a lot of experience. But I know how to wait and anything under 150 yards is good. But I'll need to practice with the Hornet."

"Good answer. We'll have time for practice. Do you have any clothes for lying in the woods?"

"No."

"Okay. Tomorrow we'll get you a duck hunting set of camouflage clothes."

"What other outfits will I need?"

"Take your best dress, heels, and bag. Also comfortable shoes, Levis, T-shirts, and rain gear. What you don't have, we'll get. Our hotel is near an upscale mall. Not to worry. The right clothing is part of your job. Look at it as an allowance."

"Why are you being so good to me?"

"I would like to be better to you. I need you and I want to be with you. I feel good with you around and am proud to be seen with you. Besides, Jack and Rip told me you're good."

Bernadette took a mock swing at him and said, "What do they know? They're both too young."

"Go to sleep, you Irish witch, before I want you again."

"Is that a promise?"

****

Thursday, August 12, 1977

The drive up to McLean on Route 95 was much easier with company and two drivers. Peter saw that Bernadette was a natural driver. Her anticipation skills were exceptional. With weapons in the car, they were careful not to get stopped for speeding. Peter said, "It will be good to have a place to keep some weapons and other gear. If we didn't have loaded weapons, we could fly up. I hope to soon have a place to stay. This drive is boring and tiresome. If I never see 95 again, I won't complain."

Walking from the valet parking at the Washington Hotel, Bernadette had to remind herself this was make believe as she entered the hotel on Peter's arm wearing a wedding ring and a two-carat diamond engagement ring. He gave them to her during the drive from Amelia Island. She thought, *It was a good thing I wasn't driving when he gave these to me. A girl doesn't expect to be engaged and married at 70 mph on Route 95.* Peter told her the rings would make the next few days easier. She asked if she had to give them back. He said he wouldn't ask for them.

Bernadette noticed that the staff knew Peter and greeted him. When she entered the suite he usually stayed in, she understood why. Terry told her Peter was well to do but this was ridiculous. She could retire on what he'd spent since she met him.

As soon as the bellhop left and the door closed, Peter said, "Tonight we have a good meal, try out this giant bed, and get ready to work first thing after breakfast.

Tomorrow's dress is Levis, walking shoes, and a dark tee. Also wear this ball cap and your dark shades."

****

Fifteen minutes after getting up from the breakfast table, they were in the car. Bernadette knew not to ask where they were going. He would tell her or not before they got wherever they were going. The road they were on led directly to a park along the Potomac River. The sign at the entrance said Great Falls Park. Peter parked and they got out.

Peter said, "Next Monday about 12:30 PM, a car will pull up over there by that big rock. Our car will be out of sight. One man will get out and walk to the center of this parking lot. Another man, the driver, will remain in the car. There may not be a driver, but one is allowed.

"I will talk with this man for no longer than 30 minutes, probably much less. If I raise my right hand over my head, kill the man with me and shoot at the man in the car. Kill him if you can but do not expose yourself. You will be up on that hillside at least two hours before the meeting time. We will have short-range open radio communications. Keep all messages short, with no names. I know you know all this but I like to cover everything.

"If anything happens to me – killed, hit hard, overpowered by men we missed – hide the rifle and make your escape on foot back to the hotel. There will be a package for you at the desk that will have enough money for you to fly back to Jacksonville and rent a car to go to Amelia Island. Use the car in the garage at my house to take Jack, Rip, and the Nguyens back up here. Use a different hotel.

"The package will have the address of my attorney, a friend of Terry's, give him the note in the package. He will provide what money you need and give you some instructions about moving into the cabin in the Pennsylvania Allegheny Mountains.

"You will see the place tomorrow. You can all wait there, out of sight. Never admit you were in the park. You were shopping when all this happened. You don't know where I went. When we get back we will wander through the mall to help your story. That's it."

"My God, Peter! I've been around men planning operations for the last three years and I've never heard any briefing like that. You have had some serious training somewhere. Let's leave it at that. I'm glad to be on your side. Now show me where I'll be hiding."

****

Back at the hotel they showered and dressed casually to go shopping. First was Bloomingdales. They walked into the women's section. The sales staff paid scant attention to them until one of them saw Bernadette's diamond ring and jade pendant and hurried over."May I help you?"

Peter said, "We don't have much time but this beautiful woman needs some casual and formal wear, head to foot."

Turning to Bernadette, he said, "Darling, why don't

you get comfortable in one of the dressing rooms, and I'm sure the ladies will bring you a number of items. Just tell them which ones you like. I think you need several outfits of dress and casual. Let's see what we can accomplish in one hour."

The sales clerk hurried away and came back with two more sales attendants. To speed things along, Peter moved about the racks pulling off items that he thought would be good on Bernadette and handing them to a confused sales staff. Soon, a steady stream of sales ladies was carrying bundles of outfits back to the largest dressing room.

At the end of an hour Peter called in to Bernadette to see if she had made any selections.

Bernadette giggled and said, "This is really fun. I think I picked about twenty outfits and am now trying to decide the couple to take."

Peter said, "Not to worry. Bring them all." He caught the attention of the nearest sales clerk and said, "Please bring the outfits she likes over to the desk and get the total for me. Don't forget the shoes."

Peter had the packages sent over to the hotel so they could browse the mall without carrying armloads of packages. The entire bill came to $13,291.83. Bernadette had a hard time keeping a straight face. She hadn't spent that much on clothes in her entire life. Peter tipped each of the four sales ladies with a $50 dollar bill.

Back in their suite, Bernadette made Peter sit while she modeled all the outfits. She said, "I know modeling all these outfits for you might seem a bit much, but people like us shouldn't pass up enjoying-the-moment opportunities. Our pure pleasure fun times are limited. So lean back. Enjoy and tell me which outfit turns you on the most."

Peter said, "All of them. You are a beautiful young woman and in these clothes, and without them, you are the kind of woman men dream about. I intend to manage things so that both of us together or separate will have many more opportunities to enjoy the pleasures of life, especially the small ones that just happen. Now leave those four-inch black pumps on, nothing else, and come to bed."

"Good! You do have an erotic side."

Saturday, August 14, 1977

Bernadette was an even earlier riser than Peter. She had room service bring breakfast before Peter finished shaving. He appeared just as Bernadette was going to go get him. She said, "I've been slaving over this breakfast for an hour. Now come and enjoy it before it gets cold."

Peter loved to have a good cup of coffee before he started on the food. The coffee at the hotel was excellent. Peter helped himself to a plate of crispy home fries, eggs over easy, and dry raisin toast. "Today is going to be a super fun day for me, especially as I want to show you what I bought. No. It's not anything in this room. No use in looking around. We have a four-hour drive before we get there. We have to pack up and check out. Please call down and ask them to pack us a picnic lunch for pick up in 30 minutes."

Twenty-three

Peter drove west on Route 7 to Leesburg where he turned north on Route 15. "I could live here," Bernadette said as they passed through Leesburg. "America is such a vast place. A poor Irish girl is lost in this mix of terrain, vegetation, architecture, highways, and ethnic groups. It is much simpler in Ireland, Catholic or Protestant, English, Scottish, or Irish with an occasional Welshman. While Ireland is simpler, its historical angers persist as strong as ever. There weren't enough ingredients for the mixing bowl of differences to produce common goals, hopes, and tolerances for others. I doubt it will ever change."

"Bernadette, I want you to break all ties with the IRA. You are a very intelligent woman. Pick out an area of study you do or could enjoy, and we'll find a university that offers what you want. Paying the bill is part of our unwritten contract. When this current phase of danger in my life lessens, please think about what I said. The IRA is not what it used to be. There is no value in killing innocent civilians, including women and children. How can you justify an organization that uses indiscriminate bombing to further their cause? Where is the honor in that? Where is the justification for killing your own because they chose another path?"

Bernadette thought for a moment. "Yes, I've lost my belief in the IRA. You know, they don't allow members to just walk away. Especially those who know as much as I do. I'm okay for a bit longer. They recognize everyone needs a break and travel to America to further the cause, even with casual contacts, is a good thing. While Terry has nothing to do with the IRA, they respect him and do not want him as an enemy, which he would be if they did anything to me."

"After the killing of my wife and daughter by men who were and are after me, my number one goal is to protect Jack. To give him a chance at life. Even though I love you, if the IRA makes you a target, your presence will endanger my son. Without that problem, I would ask you to marry me right now. The best we can have in the near future is for you to escape the IRA and get an education.

"Depending on what happens, I hope we can see each other. If we're careful, I don't see why not. Even if the time I have to wait to see you seems long, I will wait for you. No other woman will take your place. You are young and can make whatever decisions you choose about life. Compared to you, I'm an old man. Probably 15 years older and many miles behind me.

"What if I get pregnant?"

"I would be proud to have a child with you. If you get pregnant, we will manage to maintain some kind of a family, and the child will have a father and not want for anything. The future is very unpredictable. Maybe none of our enemies will be a problem. Sometime I'll tell you my life story and family history." Peter turned to look out his window.

"Notice we left the rolling hills of Maryland and Virginia and have been climbing into the Allegheny Mountains of Pennsylvania. The wide spot in the road just ahead is Breezewood, a major Pennsylvania Turnpike exit. We'll be taking Route 30 north and west. You will be travelling over one of the oldest and most important roads in the early history of America. I hope you like the outdoors because we will probably be sleeping in a small tent. I have most of the gear we'll need in the trunk, but we'll need to stop in Bedford and get some food and drink for camping. While there we might as well get some lunch. Are you hungry?"

"Thought you forgot about eating. We young Irish girls need to be fed otherwise we get cranky. Hunger kills our sex drive. Nothing I can do about it."

"In that case, I'd better hurry. We'll be at a roadside rest and picnic area in ten minutes. Hope the picnic lunch is good. May be your last good meal for a while."

Sitting in a picnic area alongside the Juniata River, Peter felt a peace he had never experienced before. *The world would be perfect, if I could take this woman and Jack somewhere no enemies could ever find us. Next Monday, the problems will start. No ranking officer of perhaps the most effective intelligence agency in the world would want to see me just to talk. I don't think I personally am in any danger in this meeting. I am just too insignificant for this man to be involved with killing or seizing me. I'm using Bernadette mostly to impress*

*them that I don't trust them and coming after me would
have its downside.*

After their excellent picnic lunch from the hotel
kitchen, Peter asked Bernadette to drive. He wanted
her to be able to find the cabin later and to get a feel
for driving narrow mountain roads. But first they had to
stop in Bedford to pick up groceries for a week.

By the time she drove through Jennerstown,
Bernadette had picked up the skill of mountain driving
with some coaching from Peter to anticipate the curves
and brake, if necessary, before the curve and accelerate
through it. Moving slowly through Ligonier she said,
"This town is even more pleasant than Leesburg. I could
live here."

"Good, but you need to see this place in the winter.
Cold, windy, and heavy snowfalls. The snow sometimes
shuts the town down for a few days. I've never been here
in the winter but the realtor I've been working with told
me winters were hard on newcomers until they learned
to stop fighting it.

"At the bottom of the next steep downgrade there
is a small dam across the Loyalhana Creek." Peter
pointed out the right turn right across the dam and told
Bernadette to follow the road. "But not too fast, you will
soon be turning back to the west and up a steep ridge.

"Okay, there is your turn next on the right. When you
reach the top of the ridge, slow way down. The turn off
is hard to see – there is no mailbox and the opening is
partially grown over with spruce trees. See the slight
break about 75 yards in front on the right? Turn in there.
Don't worry, the branches will brush both sides of the

car. There should have been some trucks in here, but I don't see any signs of them. There is a gate across the driveway. Stop and I'll open it."

"Where is the place? I can barely find it with you telling me every turn. How did you ever get here?"

"A woman brought me here in her car."

"I might've known."

"She was more than twice your age and a sales person."

"Is that your story?"

"The truth is the truth. Okay, the gate is relocked. Drive ahead and park in the small graveled circle."

When Bernadette stopped, she was out of the car before Peter. "My God, Peter this place is like a hidden paradise. How much do you own?"

"As far as you can see from here. Around 1,000 acres. I was hoping work had started but no signs of it outside. Let's go inside. We might not have to use the tent."

Inside on the dining table there was a note from the contractor saying he would be there with a backhoe tomorrow morning to put in the 1,000 gallon diesel tank and generator. Another crew would be there to tear out the bathrooms and install new appliances. They may also be able to get a start on the kitchen. Peter put the note down and said, "I spoke too soon. Looks like the tent will be our home until Sunday. If it rains hard we can hurry back here and share the cabin with the workmen."

"Not my idea of a honeymoon," said Bernadette, flashing her rings.

"Are all Irish ladies so fussy?"

"We're never fussy as long as our man feeds and beds

us often enough. Can we stay here tonight and move out before the workmen get here in the morning?"

"Sure, but in that case come outside with me."

As soon as she stepped out on the small porch, Peter swept her up and carried her across the threshold. "Every woman should get carried across at least one threshold."

"That's a good custom. I can now take that off my 'to do before I die' list," Bernadette said.

****

The weather stayed good. Peter and Bernadette wandered all over his 1,000 acres and much of the adjoining land. Bernadette was intrigued with the way the cabin nestled into the hillside. Peter took her hand and said, "Look at this." He moved some brush aside and exposed the opening to an old family coal mine. Bernadette said, "How deep does it go?"

"I don't know its extent but it goes in at least a couple of hundred feet. I plan to build a hidden room in the shaft that will open into the master bedroom. Enough of this. I want to explore some more of the mountain while the weather is good."

They moved the campsite a few times, but always close to the small stream. Bernadette practiced with the .22 Hornet until they were both satisfied. Both worked on their conditioning. Peter taught her a few deadly Hapkido moves, and she learned quickly.

Bernadette showed Peter her knife-throwing skill. She could hit a five-inch circle from 20 feet nearly every time. As much as he tried, Peter couldn't get the wrist release right and threw a foot right of the target.

Bernadette said, "I hope you are better with gun."

"Why? I'm counting on you to take care of me."

When the contractor packed up for the weekend, he told Peter that the bathrooms and kitchen would be functional by the end of the next week.

Twenty-four

Sunday afternoon they were back in their suite at the hotel. Bernadette said, "Thank you Peter, I really feel that we were on a honeymoon. I'll never forget your mountain hideout."

"I hope we can repeat the adventure several times. Rip and Jack will love romping in the little stream. Late this afternoon I want to go over tomorrow's action. Please question and make suggestions. You have a good feel for the operational flow."

"If these people want you to do something important for them that no one else can, we will still be free after the meeting. If not, we'll be dead for I'm not going to grow old in a British jail."

"Well said, but if you follow my plan you can escape as long as you don't shoot."

"If they come for you, I'll shoot. That's the way I am. Won't even think about it. Thinking too much is not good for taking action. Get in the zone and act. A very good IRA trainer told me that."

"I can't change the way you think, but it would be

easier for me if I knew you were safe and going back to be with Jack."

"Sorry."

Monday, August 23, 1977

Peter hung up the payphone in a McLean gas station and left for the meeting site in Great Falls Park. He had dropped Bernadette off inside the park at 8:30 AM. *I have done all I could. I'll soon know if it was enough.*

He drove west on Route 193 until he came to the park entrance. He made the right turn and parked out of sight of the actual meeting site. Using his small handheld radio, he checked in with Bernadette. She was all set. It was overcast. Rain was promised. No one had come into the park. She had not seen nor heard any movement in the brush- and tree-covered slopes.

At exactly 12:30 PM a black Chevy pulled into the park and parked where he had told Frank. There was a driver in the car. It was probably Frank. He had only caught glimpses of him when he was casing his house and neighborhood. It was beginning to drizzle. A middle-aged man, slightly stout, wearing glasses, and carrying a rolled umbrella in his right hand walked rapidly with the left shoulder leading as if he was favoring an old injury. Five feet from Peter he stopped, looked around, and said, "Is it okay if I put the umbrella up?"

Peter smiled and said, "No. I'm glad you asked for you would be dead now."

The man smiled back and said, "I guess getting wet is a better option."

Peter said, "You have my attention. What do you want with me?"

"No small talk first?"

"We already did that with the umbrella talk."

This time the man laughed. "Maybe you can help me."

"I'm listening."

"First, let me tell you what I think I know about you. I don't expect you to confirm or deny. Just listen. You were a KGB officer who somehow got into this country and ran from the KGB, taking their money with you. In the escape you killed five of them, in Pittsburgh and Latrobe, and your wife killed three more before she and your daughter were killed by AK-47 fire. A remarkable achievement for both of you.

"When you got the chance you contacted one of my officers and gave him KGB equipment and information about a network of KGB illegals, spies, and saboteurs from your own network. I don't know where you are living now and I don't care.

"You have proved to me that we have nothing to fear from you and that you are willing to help. Taking down the sniper illegal agent in Georgetown is all the proof I need of your skills. You can plan and act. Not a usual combination of skills. I need you to help me protect this nation. I suspect that is consistent with your own objectives. Why else would you have come to us when you were already free of the KGB? You also don't seem to want anything from us. Is that right?"

"Your connection of the dots is accurate. No. I do not want anything from you. I'll help the cause of freedom but not at the cost of the rest of my family or a long life here in America. America, by the way, is the home of my ancestors. My grandfather got left behind in Siberia, and we have been hoping to get back to America for generations. The KGB has never connected these dots. Now they cannot. I assume what we say here stays here."

"It stays here. This conversation could hurt me rather badly. I don't want you ever to talk to anyone but Frank or me. Frank reports directly to me. No notes or records. I will not ever expose you to Congress. Some would say I don't have to because there is no money involved. That judgment could change with shifting political agendas."

"What exactly do you want me to do?"

"The short answer is I want you to kill enemies of this nation that I cannot have arrested and tried because of the rules of evidence necessary when foreign spies and saboteurs are given constitutional protection meant only for U.S. citizens. If I apprehend them, it will alert others, because I cannot keep the information away from the media."

"I don't see myself as a government assassin."

"I don't see you like that, either. You will always have the freedom to refuse assignments after being briefed."

"Can you give me an example?"

"Yes. There are three USSR agents in your network who are still free. Some of their missions, if successful, could cause many deaths and damage America's command and control system. Other than your information, I've no basis for arresting or even watching them. I would have trouble getting a warrant, though I probably could. And if I could get enough court-acceptable information to prove they are not U.S. citizens, I might, *might* be able to have some jurisdiction to make an arrest. Then would come the lawyers, the ACLU, and other progressive liberal groups to their rescue. In the end, unless they confessed in front of proper witnesses with legal counsel, they would most probably walk.

"I'm asking you to find them and talk to them about entering some kind of a protection program or voluntary deportation."

"You're asking me to commit suicide. I'm willing to find them and maybe talk to some of them about entering a program that would let them stay here and not be punished, but no deportation. The first thing they would say back in Moscow is that I talked to them representing the U.S. Government. The hunt for me would pick up steam. More resources would be committed. Maybe I made a mistake somewhere. One of them picked up a clue and the search, which I believe has wound down, would get new life.

"I'll find them for you and talk to the one who has the mission of poisoning the water supply of a large city. If he refuses to go into a protection program, he will have to be killed. I cannot take on increased risk for a man who intends to kill thousands of Americans."

"Okay, find them for us, and we'll take it from there."

"Good, I accept."

"There is always one more thing. We have located a possible terrorist training camp. The information came from a long-term illegal agent who came into America through Canada years ago.

"I want you to check out this camp and report back to me what you have found. Are people actually being trained to commit terrorist acts in America, or is it just training so-called survivalists, minutemen, and ardent re-enactors?"

"And, and…?"

"What? Oh, you mean why should you take this risk?"

"That's exactly what I mean."

"It just so happens that I thought of that. May I reach in my coat pocket?"

"Yes, but very slowly."

"Is your shooter that good?"

"Better than you can believe and dedicated. The shooter may have a problem in heavy rain, so I would have to do the job myself. Right now you should be feeling the crosshairs of the shooter's scope just above your left ear."

"I believe you. Here is a letter I drafted. Note it is signed by the Director of Central Intelligence. No file copy. This is the only one. The blank file copy has a torn in half ten-dollar bill stapled to the blank but numbered page. The original I'm giving to you contains the other half of the ten-dollar bill. The bill is your bona fides in case you have to use this letter. The other pages contain what we know of the survival camp."

Peter scanned the letter. It identified him as a loyal American citizen who has taken on dangerous missions assigned to him by the CIA. The bearer should be granted all possible immunity for actions he had to take in performing his mission. He has saved the lives of hundreds of American citizens.

Peter folded the papers and put them in his rain jacket. "This may help. What are you going to tell Batcher about this meeting?"

"As little as possible. Look at him as being my messenger. Now I'm going to go back to my car. Please give my best to your shooter on the slope behind me. I didn't see anything. Just back tracking the line of fire, which you so carefully kept open. Lines work both ways. Thank you. No handshake. I don't want to push my luck."

When the black Chevy disappeared, Peter said, "Come down," into his radio. Bernadette stood up, stretched and loped down the slope. Peter thought, *She moves so well. Wouldn't want her for an enemy. She wouldn't give up.*

She ran up and hugged Peter. He whispered, "Nice work" in her ear. "I felt confident with you having my back."

"I had him all the way. The umbrella worried me. Did you tell him not to open it?"

"Sure did. Told him I just saved his life or something like that. He is a very smart intelligence officer with an understanding of the rough stuff. He's seen his share of action. He asked me to give the shooter on the slope his best."

"What!! He couldn't have seen me. He barely looked in my direction."

"I said he was very good. He noticed the line-of-fire for you that I was keeping open and backtracked."

"He is good. Next time that won't happen."

"A lesson learned. Come on, let's go back to the hotel. Get in the back seat and get out of the camouflage suit. Can't have an Irish Celtic woman warrior march into the hotel in all her splendor."

"Listen, scholar. Celt warriors often went into battle stark naked, including the women."

"As I said, we can't have you marching into the Washington Hotel in all your splendor."

"No. You'll have to wait until I shower. Irish women are quite civilized when they put their weapons down. Now let's get out of here. I can change in the back seat and put this rifle in its hiding place. By the time you get to the hotel, I'll be in the front seat."

"You have plenty of time. My protocol instinct says never go back to base the same way and going to a different base is even better. Let's have a nice lunch in McLean and then go back to the hotel. We have some thinking to do after I brief you on what went down today."

****

After a comfort food lunch in the McLean Deli, Peter drove back to the hotel. After a shower, a nap, and another shower, Bernadette said, "I thought I heard something about a briefing that would tell me what happened today. Right?"

"Yes, come close and I'll do my best briefing."

"Peter! I'm close enough. Your damned briefing, please."

"First, we were right. They want something and for

174

the time being will not threaten our safety. They want me, and people who work with me, to do some dirty work for them. Work they cannot do effectively by following the law. But they encourage us to break the law to protect American citizens. A tactical and moral position that is familiar to all governments."

"They want us to be their assassins?"

"That's close but it is a little more complicated. They have located a camp teaching survival skills and paramilitary training to people holding an anti-American philosophy. There is some evidence that the KGB provided start-up money and a leader to operate the camp. They want me or us to watch the training camp and provide the government with information."

"Sounds like pretty standard government counter-espionage operations."

"Yes. It does. But I wonder why they don't do the job themselves. They have the people, equipment, and charter to handle operations like this. It's possible that they want to do this without exposing a sensitive source. Or they don't want to take the political risk of failure within their own organization, or are fearful of Congressional oversight exposing an operation conducted against American citizens in the U.S."

"You're hurting my Irish sense of morality. I need a world of good guys or bad guys. The people you met must have a very flexible core of values. I neither trust them nor like them. I feel we would be better off if you had raised your arm and given me the take out signal. These people will use you until you become a problem and then make you go away."

"I don't disagree. Right now I need them in ways they don't even know. My plan is to keep them happy until I don't need them any longer. I will need your help."

"You have me. I'm your woman. You couldn't drive me away."

"The danger to you is that I want you too much and will keep you near me long after it is safe for you. I want you to build a new life on my protection and money. A life I can sometimes share. Protecting Jack and you are my top goals in life, and I won't fail either of you. No matter what."

"That's what I love about you, you're so wishy washy."

"Okay, your orders. Tomorrow you fly to Jacksonville. I need you to be with Jack and I need to do some things up here I can do better alone. I will be in Amelia in a week or ten days."

"I'll go but if you get hurt, I'll hurt you much worse for not having me at your back."

Twenty-five

After dropping Bernadette off at Dulles Airport, Peter drove to Falls Church, parked on a side street and opened the phone book he brought from the hotel. Running his finger down the columns of Jones' he found Oscar. How many Oscars could there be with Jones as the last name?

Turning right off Broad Street, Peter drove up Lawton Street until he spotted the Jones house. It was an attractive middle-class neighborhood with good-sized lots that were all well taken care of. Trimmed lawns, shrubs a bit overgrown, and large trees lined the street. A blue hydrangea bush was blooming beside the Jones house. A vintage Subaru was sitting in the driveway. No sign of any kid swings or bikes in the driveway or lawn. Oscar had a long-term live-in he swore didn't know anything about his background. The Subaru was probably hers.

Peter parked where he could watch the house for a few minutes. Fortunately, there were a few 'For Sale' signs in the neighborhood that gave him reason enough to be there. But only for a few minutes.

I don't want to involve the woman. She will have enough trouble with the FBI. No way I can talk to him in his house. The talk thing is not going to work. Oscar is a hardcore card-carrying Communist, totally dedicated to his mission. He won't be taken alive. I'll have to call him. Give him the right keywords to identify myself and get him to go where I can kill him if I have to. The only question is do I take the chance of talking to him first or just kill him. It's hard to have any feelings for a man whose mission is to kill hundreds of people and spread panic. My gut instinct is to just shoot him and get it over with. I'll call him tonight.

Peter hadn't told Frank Batcher everything he knew about Oscar Jones, the KGB agent with the mission to shut down the subway system in the nation's capital by releasing ricin poison during rush hour. Peter last met with Jones three years ago when he gave him instructions to move to Falls Church, Virginia, a suburb in the Washington metropolitan area.

Jones had worked for eight years as a chemist in a chemical plant in Toledo, Ohio. Back then, Peter had had all his agents give him their decoding pads. Without the decoding pads, none of them could receive messages from anyone but Peter. He told them the pads were defective and had to be replaced.

Peter, using the name Mr. Martin, called Oscar from a payphone in McLean at 7:00 PM and, after identifying himself with the right protocol, told Oscar to meet him tonight at 10:00 PM, walking up Great Falls Street toward McLean on the left side of the street past the city tennis courts and to keep walking until they met.

Peter knew Oscar was comfortable with the contact instructions. They were practically right out of the training manual. This procedure gave Peter control of when and where along the walking route he would make contact. If he saw anything indicating his agent was being watched, Peter could abort the meeting and when no contact occurred, the agent would continue his walk for another ten minutes and then return home.

Peter watched Oscar come out of Lawton Street and turn right on Broad toward Great Falls Street. He stayed put in his car until Oscar was out of sight. Noting no surveillance, he drove another route to get near the tennis courts before parking his car and returning on foot to a concealed position in the heavy shrubs near the courts. He would be able to come out of his waiting position the instant Oscar strolled by.

9:50 PM

Peter, peering through a hole in the wall of a large clump of azaleas, could see Oscar approaching right on time. No doubt Oscar was a pro if a bit of a fanatic. Another ten steps and Peter stepped out of the shrubs right beside Oscar, who in spite of his professionalism, jumped and gasped, "Holy God" in Russian. Peter said, "Are you Russian?"

"Martin, you scared the shit out of me. No contact for three years and you jump out of the bushes."

"Okay. My report doesn't have to mention a pro like you cursing in Russian in a very loud voice. You have been left alone for a long time. Let's keep strolling up the street. First question, are you comfortable in your new cover position and new town?"

"Yes. I have a perfect set up. A job that gives me access to the Metro system and I have a small chem lab over my garage that has everything I need to make ricin."

"Do you have enough for your mission?"

"I have enough to do several Metro stations. Just give me the word. I hate these smug Americans and their precious freedom at the cost of their downtrodden class of workers. They need a good taste of Russian-style freedom to work your ass off for the benefit of those who need more than they can earn."

"Is the ricin in a safe place that you can get to in a hurry when we need to strike?"

"Absolutely, it is stored in my lab."

"How about the American woman you live with? Does she know where it is?"

"No. She has no idea. She can visit me in the lab where I work on my research for another degree from a university that works by mail and taped lessons. I have a homemade lock box behind an American flag hanging on the wall. It is not easy to find. Even if anyone looked behind the flag, they would find nothing without finding the secret opening in the wood panel walls. What about my decoding pads? I miss not being able to get broadcast secret messages."

"I agree. It would make my job much easier and safer. But Moscow believes there is a weakness in the system. We have lost a few agents, and Moscow suspects the broadcast system. I can't figure out how that could be.

But I don't tell them what to do.

"One last question. Do you want to go back to the USSR or just retire here when the time comes?"

"I don't want to go back until I get to do my part by killing hundreds of our enemies, and I never would want to retire here. I want to go home whenever the Center decides."

Peter saw that they were approaching the kill zone he had selected to use, if necessary. Oscar was looking straight ahead. Peter dropped back a half step, and in a blur of movement put his left hand around Oscar's head, faking a clockwise twist and then pulling his forehead while Peter's right hand pushed his chin hard in a counter-clockwise move. The twisting motion from both hands and a body pivot to the left snapped Oscar's neck. Peter swung his hip, knocking Oscar into the shrubs and out of sight from the street. He looked around again, saw no one, and continued walking to his parked car a block away on a side street. Twenty minutes later, Peter was back at the hotel. He left again in an hour with a short report for Frank Batcher.

Peter slipped his report into the mailbox and called Frank's home from a pay phone in a McLean gas station. When Frank answered, Peter said, "I lied. I put another package into your mailbox. The agent is dead. His address is in the report I put in your box. You need to get into his house quickly, though you might want to wait until his body is found. He has enough ricin in his lab for several attacks on a metro system during rush hour. His hiding place is described in the report. The woman living in the house knows nothing about who he really was or what he was doing. Goodbye."

The next day, Peter located John Bowers in Poolesville, Maryland. Bowers had been in America for 30 years. He had a wife and grown family who did not know he was a KGB agent. Peter called him and set up a meeting in the small park along the Potomac at Whites Ferry. John, who had met Peter twice as Mr. Walters, was obviously nervous. Peter was waiting for him at a picnic table with a couple of bottles of cold Sam Adams beer. Peter waved Bowers over and shook his hand. As they sat down, Peter said, "It's been more than two years since we last met. How are you doing?"

"I'm living where you told me to go. Kids are doing well. Your extra money helped them finish their educations without a crushing debt. My wife is unhappy, she wants to go back to Wisconsin. My report is in this envelope."

"Keep your report. I have some good news. You have two options. The first is to go back to the USSR next month or to relocate anywhere you want in Wisconsin."

"What?"

"You heard me. Back to the Motherland or back to your wife's family roots. What is so hard to understand about that?"

"This is a test. You know I have to say back to the USSR."

"No test. You've done what we asked. It would be hard and expensive to relocate you and your family to Moscow. I want you to just disappear in the United States. Much more secure and inexpensive for us. We may contact you someday, but I doubt it. Your choice."

"I'm still afraid this is a trap. Our Agency does not operate like that. If I opt to stay here, you will come after me someday."

"Think! I don't care where you go. Don't tell me. How can anyone find you? I never turned in your current name. I have no idea how you got your wife to accept the name change. She must really love you or you're a great convincing liar."

"When can I go?"

"Soon as you can. I have a bit of advice. Do not use any name the KGB knows and do not settle anywhere near any address on record or your wife's family's home. Go at least 25 miles away or they will find you."

"I don't know why you're helping me, but I appreciate it."

"One more thing. Here's an envelope for you. It contains $25,000 to help with the resettlement. This is our last meeting. You will never see me again. Be free but careful. Goodbye."

Peter felt good about his meeting with John Bowers. He had done his time and deserved to be left alone. Peter had done his best. Neither the KGB nor the FBI should be able to find Bowers.

****

Thursday, August 26, 1977

It took Peter most of the morning to find James B. Casey in Frederick, Maryland. Peter had seen Jim Casey on only one occasion but they hit it off well.

Peter had a genuine desire to help the Caseys escape from their espionage past. He thought, *True, they are here illegally. So what? There are millions of illegal immigrants in America. These people are paying taxes. So far they have done nothing to hurt America. From a KGB viewpoint, they have adjusted too well. There are no kids, and both husband and wife are agents. They will have the smarts and experience to keep the identities I gave them and stay right here or go anywhere they want to go. They don't need the hand of American security forces watching them. In five years no one, not even me with my inside knowledge, could find them.*

Peter called Jim Casey and Jim asked him to come to their house for dinner. Peter accepted but wondered why Casey was breaking protocol. A handler of agents like Peter never went to the home of one of his agents. The security risk was too high for the agent in case the handler had made a mistake and had picked up some FBI surveillance. Years of work, risk, and preparation on the part of the illegal agent could vanish with nothing positive to show.

For the next hour Peter debated what he should do. He had too much at stake to walk into a possible trap. He decided to play it safe and called Frank Batcher at his office number. He used the telephone name Frank had given him and was put through immediately. He explained the situation to Frank and recommended that a team show up instead of him at the Caseys' home at 6:45 PM.

Peter parked his car three blocks from the Casey

house and walked to a place he could see the house from a distance.

At exactly 6:45 he noticed two casually dressed couples walking toward the Casey house. He suspected the back of the house would be covered as well. The couples continued on their walk and a single male pulled up, parked his car, and hurried up to the front door and rang the bell. The door opened, and the two couples came up at a hard run and pushed inside. A quick burst of gunfire and it got quiet. There were now two ambulances at the curb. Two stretchers came out with covered bodies. A squad car arrived and the two officers surrounded the house with crime tape. From his vantage point 75 yards away, Peter saw two handcuffed men and a woman led out and put in a black van that had just arrived. He had seen enough. Somehow the KGB had found the Caseys or the Caseys had alerted the KGB. He had to be more careful. No longer could he think the danger was less than it had been. The search was still active and had found a loose thread somewhere. He had almost disregarded his instincts. Never again. This was a close call. He would start back to Amelia Island now, after making sure he wasn't being followed.

Twenty-six

It was a 12-hour plus drive from McLean to Amelia Island. Peter was within three hours of his destination before he gave in to sleep and stopped in a motel near the exit to Hilton Head off Route 95. He was back home before lunch the next day. All was well at home. The Nguyens served a curried chicken and a medley of curried vegetables for lunch. Both Jack and Bernadette sat close to him at lunchtime. Rip had matured slightly in his absence. He was now curled up under the table. It was a strict protocol that Rip was not fed from the table but anything that fell on the deck was his. Somehow, Jack always managed to drop something with an innocent look of "how did that happen?"

After lunch when it was time for Jack's nap, Bernadette led Peter up to the master bedroom and demanded a briefing. Peter said, "How can I brief you when you're sitting on my lap and wiggling?"

"Come lie down and let me get the wiggling urge out of my system, then you can brief me."

Lying beside Peter with one long, shapely leg still lying across his body, Bernadette said, "Okay, I'm almost done wiggling. Now the briefing and don't hold anything back."

"First I missed you very much and missed the comfortable feeling that my back was covered. In two cases some people died. One I killed, and the others tried to trap me but I figured it out and sent the good guys to show up for dinner rather than me. It was a trap and at least two were killed and maybe three others arrested. I watched from some distance but don't have any more details."

"What do I have to do to convince you that you're safer with me than not?"

"Nothing. Jack's safety is more important to me than my own. So I feel safe when I know you're here with Jack. You are probably the deadliest governess anyone ever had for their son. If you weren't so good I'd have you with me all the time."

"Okay. That's a good answer. I have to have more time to think up a response." As she rolled over on Peter, she said, "Your briefing is over. My turn."

****

Down at poolside, just before tea, Bernadette said, "Terry's coming for dinner tonight. I told him we are lovers. He's good with that, just worries about either one of us getting hurt."

"Good. I'm glad you told him. I think he knew this would happen. Anyway, I have an idea I want to talk over with both of you."

After a cookout by the pool with Terry doing most of the cooking and after Jack and the Nguyens had gone to bed, Peter, Bernadette, and Terry sat in a net-covered small pavilion discussing Terry's last trip to the Middle East. Terry's thesis was that sooner or later radical Muslims will declare war on the Christian West. "The two religions are and always will be incompatible and the minority of Jihadists will be the voice of Islam.

"The moderate Muslims will remain quiet, partly out of fear and partly because they, too, are tired of Western wealth and dominance," Terry said. "On the personal side, it looks like I can have work as long as I want to work. A number of people and companies with a presence in the Arab world are paying big bucks for people with my skills."

Peter asked, "With all your big-paying jobs, can you take two months off? I need your help and will cover expenses and extra pennies for your services."

Bernadette broke in and said, "What about me or haven't I shown you enough?"

Peter laughed and said, "I was taking your help for granted."

"Right answer."

"Of course I'll help. I need a break anyway. What will we be doing?" Terry asked.

"Trust the Irish. Right to the point. No foreplay at all. First, I bought a mountain cabin and about 1,000 acres of mountain land. The cabin needs work done. There is a contractor doing some things right now, but there are other things I want done that I don't want anyone except present company to know. That will be the first month's work."

"And what will be the second month?" Terry said.

"More work in the mountains. Hiking, shooting,

spying, and lying. Some people I know that Bernadette has seen through her 10x scope have asked me to do something for them. I really can't refuse. One of those kinds of things. These people can be considered to be the good guys as long as I cooperate. Also they are part of the law. There is a suspected terrorist-training camp they want me to look into. They've told me where the camp is but don't know much about it. They said it's possible the camp is legitimate."

"Oh," Bernadette said, "that makes it okay? I still think I should have shot them."

Terry said, "I don't even want to hear about my innocent niece getting involved with guns and things. What will her IRA friends think of her?"

"While we are cabin building, I want you to improve Bernadette's shooting at targets 200 yards out."

"Tell me more about the second month in the mountains."

"The easterners call them mountains. To the people who have seen real mountains, they are just steep hills covered with forests. The work is straight forward. All we have to do is check out a camp teaching tactics, sniping, and general outdoor skills. Most, if not all, of the students are would-be terrorists holding real or bogus American citizenship. We collect some information and maybe close the camp down. There are some indications that the Soviets are involved. Just a routine assignment."

"I like your friends even less," Bernadette said.

Terry said, "Well, at least we have a month to think about it and work out some possibilities."

"Terry, can you go to the Pennsylvania cabin the day

after tomorrow?"

"Don't see why not."

"Bernadette, will you organize our caravan? The Nguyens, Jack, Rip, you, me, and Terry. Buy anything you need, including vehicles. Be nice to have a pickup truck. Get the Nguyens to buy the food and drink we will need. They can both drive. Maybe let them drive the pickup or Cadillac. It is, at least, a 15-hour trip. Set up stopping places for gas, meals, and sleep. We can't caravan safely the whole way, but we can have organized rendezvous. Three or four short-range radios may be useful. Agree?"

"Yes. I love to buy cars. We'll also need some blankets or sleeping bags. I didn't mind sleeping in the tent. We'll be very short of indoor sleeping accommodations."

"You're in charge. Make it happen."

Twenty-seven

After a tiring two-day trip, the Brandon caravan of a new pickup truck and Peter's Cadillac pulled into the cabin's parking area. The workmen were gone. Even the extensive repairs to the six foot, black chain-link fence enclosing the cabin and ten acres was finished.

Everyone helped unload the vehicles. The Nguyens delayed any food preparation until Mrs. Nguyen got the kitchen scrubbed down. Bernadette tried to help but got chased away. She then took charge of getting the tent set up down by the creek. Terry walked around the cabin, noting where floodlights and sensors should be installed. Rip and Jack went into exploring mode and soon had covered the cabin and fenced grounds. The small creek was the best. Rip and Jack romped and splashed in the creek and made enough noise to scare wildlife miles away. Peter and Bernadette stopped the setting up of the campsite to watch the now full-grown Bouvier and Jack frolic in the brook.

Bernadette said, "Why can't it stay like this? Watching them makes me want to have a baby sister for Jack."

"If we can get through one more year and get you

away from the IRA, who knows. With luck maybe your wish can come true."

****

The Brandon crew had been in the cabin for almost two weeks. It was as if the outside world didn't exist. The contractor finished his work, and the daily coming and going of trucks was over. All were in love with the privacy and views of the forest-covered mountains. Jack loved to run down the grassy slope with Rip and jump in the creek. Peter enjoyed going to town in the new four-wheel drive Ford pickup truck and was putting the skills he had learned as a carpenter's helper in Canada to good use. He was happy. He loved working with his hands and he had a natural skill both with weapons and tools.

With Terry's help, he replaced the outside door with a modern steel-line door and a dead-bolt locking device. They also added an alarm system that covered all the outside windows and door as well as the driveway. Motion-activated sensor lights were put on the cabin's four corners.

As they were standing at the entrance to the mine, Terry said, "I think the first 100 or so feet of this mine is the original cave. At some point, maybe a 100 years ago, a family living on or near this site used this cave as the first part of a coal mine. Notice where it narrows severely. That is where they started digging."

Peter said, "I want to extend the master bedroom into the cave to create a hidden room to store weapons and use as an escape route from the cabin if ever necessary.

My plan is to prepare the entrance to the cave, pour a six-inch concrete slab inside the cave, and then build the extension room inside the cave. Later I'll simply join it to the bedroom by a hidden door."

Terry said, "No problem. With some hard work and a rented backhoe, we could easily build the extension into the mine. When we're finished, it would look as if the cabin's back wall was flush with the hillside. Six months after it's completed, I doubt anyone could tell from looking at the outside."

Peter said, "Are you telling me that you can run a backhoe?"

"Yes and a bulldozer, if necessary. Part of the skills I picked up between jobs and summers, when I was struggling to get through Furman University without owing anybody anything."

"Let's go rent a backhoe and I'll call the contractor and get him to pour a floor in the cave for a storage area."

"If we get a backhoe today, your contractor can come tomorrow to get ready to pour the floor. A couple of hours to do the pouring and a couple of hours to finish off the floor. In three days we should be able to start building your secret room," Terry said.

"I think we could finish by two weeks from today," Peter said. "I'll have the contractor run power to the storage area, too."

****

Two and a half weeks later, the storage area in the mineshaft was nearly completed. Peter, Terry, and Bernadette built a wall-to-wall, floor-to-ceiling bookcase on the back wall of the master bedroom. Behind the space for a TV set, Peter installed a switch hidden behind a power plug to swing open a door-sized section of the bookcase. The switch, operated by turning the power outlet lower plug one-half turn counter-clockwise, caused a section of the bookcase to smoothly rotate on its center support.

The finished hidden room was about 15 by 30 feet. Several black, good-quality metal four-drawer filing cabinets lined one wall. A large gray metal desk with an IBM electric typewriter, a black metal supply cabinet, and three metal chairs completed the furnishing.

The concrete block walls were painted white with a textured paint. The cement floor was painted light beige with three small oriental carpets to relieve the sterile atmosphere. A large white board with an array of markers and a cork wall to hang maps covered a side wall.

The atmosphere in the room did not have the damp musty feeling of an underground storage area. The thermostat controlling the electric baseboard heaters maintained a constant 68 degrees. Two large grated vents in the ceiling provided heat and cooling. A metal conduit containing the power lines ran down both long walls. A metal door was set into a cement block wall at the back of the room. Behind the door was the beginning of a small, well-stocked armory. A glass case of handguns lined one wall. On the opposite wall a series of gun cabinets held an assortment of sporting rifles and shotguns. Terry said, "Later we can add some automatic weapons like, M-16s, the shortened AR-15 version, Uzis, and AK-47s. None of them are hard to buy, but it takes time to find the right sellers."

"I like the escape you built into the back of this hidden room," Bernadette said. "Who would believe that behind the next door was a way out of here?" She raised the locking lever bar and stepped into the darkened space beyond. Peter and Terry followed her into the tunnel. A small point of light identified a light switch that dimly illuminated a long narrow tunnel that seemed to lead deeply into the mountain. Except for a few ventilation shafts and old shoring timbers, the tunnel was bare. After about 30 feet the tunnel turned sharply to the right and angled toward the surface. Another 10 feet and there was an aluminum ladder fastened to shoring timbers. At the top of the ten-foot ladder was a trapdoor.

Bernadette started up the ladder. Peter whispered to Terry, "Do you think she can open the trapdoor?"

"You're damn right I can and stop whispering like a couple of school boys."

She reached the trapdoor and opened the locking bar. She pushed upward. Nothing happened. Bracing herself, Bernadette put her shoulders against the door and pushed steadily upward using her legs. The trap door started to swing up. She gathered her strength and thrust up as hard as she could. The door swung up and crashed open.

"So much for a quiet escape," Bernadette muttered as she was climbing out of the hatchway. She moved to one side to let Peter and Terry climb out. They were all in a small cave that looked out over the valley. The cave was only big enough for three people to sit under the short overhang. The trap door had been concealed with small stones, loose dirt, and leaves. Bernadette said, "Okay, who is the woodsman that weighted the door to camouflage it?"

Terry said, "I guess I over did it a bit. I'm surprised you could open it."

"It's a good thing I went up first. You two wimps would have needed help. What good is an escape route that almost can't be opened and then makes a huge noise in opening?"

Peter said, "How about an excellent Vietnamese lunch?" They all started back through the tunnel to the cabin.

Bernadette said, "It's a good thing I've been working so hard or I'd be fat as a pig by now. The Nguyens are excellent cooks. I've no interest in going out to lunch. With them here, I could live here permanently. I don't know how they do it. One of them is nearly always awake. I took a walk outside the tent before first light a few days ago. Mr. Nguyen was moving quietly on the slope leading to the tent. He saw me. Stopped and raised his shotgun over his head to keep from scaring me even more. I'm glad they're on our side."

"You wouldn't believe the firefights they have been in," Terry said. "Between them, they have more combat experience than most Special Forces troops."

Peter said, "With them watching at night and Rip

never leaving Jack's side, I can almost relax. Jack and Rip have learned how to entertain themselves without constant adult supervision. One of the workmen got too close to Jack, and Rip moved between them and growled. He's full-grown but will add more muscle. He knows his job.

"Given that Bernadette and I have some bad enemies, I want to keep the existence of this place to our small group. Do we want to stage out of here to check out and possibly take down the training camp?"

"I like it here," Bernadette said. "I feel safer here than in the city. IRA types aren't as comfortable in the mountains and forests as they are in any urban location. My vote is stage from here. Thanks to the gun shows we've hit in the last three weeks, there is a better selection of weapons here."

"Don't let this go to your head little niece, but you are very good," Terry said. "I've seldom had such good students. Either one of you can have my back. Peter, you are a natural. It must be in your blood."

While Terry was talking, Peter wondered what Terry would say if he told him both his mother and father were decorated snipers, and that he had been conceived on the Stalingrad battlefield.

"Your set up is a little unorthodox but the results are outstanding. I agree with my beautiful and lethal niece. Let's stage out of here."

"Okay, here it is! Bernadette, we need you on this trip. I wish we didn't. I'd feel better if you were here with Jack. For his sake as well as yours. I feel we are a family, including brother Terry, and I don't want to lose anyone. On this trip it is not the mission first. Our safety is first."

****

Later that night when Peter and Bernadette were sitting around a small campfire by their tent, Peter asked Bernadette about her uncle. Peter said, "I see a six-foot-two heavily muscled man who is immensely strong with hair clipped as short as the clippers could cut. Beyond that and my respect for his integrity and kindness, I only know I like him very much."

"I read some papers he had lying on his desk when he was making an application for foreign security work of some kind. I'll give you what I remember." Bernadette stared at the flickering small flames and started to recite. "Terry left the service as a colonel with multiple tours of special operations combat duty in Vietnam and as a combat advisor in Angola and Central America. Two Silver Stars, three Purple Hearts with the scars to go with them, and numerous campaign ribbons were listed under awards. They didn't mean anything to me and I didn't focus on them. There was practically no weapons course he had missed. Weapons training, operational planning assignments, and intelligence collection and analysis were where he excelled. He is good with languages with a natural ability to learn languages. In addition to Chinese he speaks Spanish, French, and German."

"Bernadette, you have amazing recall."

"I've always been able to recall and see things in my mind, if it was important to me. Focusing is the important part. You want me to tell you about our first night together?"

"No. I'd sooner you show me."

"Okay! I'll lead, you follow. I knew you had some promise."

Twenty-eight

September 12, 1977

Leaving the Nguyens, Jack, and Rip at the cabin with the Cadillac, Peter, Bernadette, and Terry climbed in the big cab of the pickup. A locked box secured into the truck bed contained their weapons, camp gear, extra clothing, ghillie suits, and provisions. Peter drove. "My hope is that we won't have to go into the camp. From the maps and photos we looked over, we should be able to find a place where we can camp a mile or so from the training camp in a good defensive position with multiple escape routes.

"Three days of observation and photographing with our new super duper long-range camera that weighs too much should give us time to collect what we need. It's possible we may have to go in the camp building or buildings, but not until we totally understand the tempo and activity of the camp.

"I'll drive through Charleston on the main drag looking for the turn off to County Route 20. We'll continue for ten miles southwest on Route 20 and look for a place to get this truck off the road and far enough into the tree line, so with our black tarp thrown over it, we can leave it for a few days. My estimate is it will take us a little more than a day's walk to get into position. If for any reason we get separated, we meet at the truck. I know we've been over this, but I like to cover the essentials to refresh our plans and maybe discover some flaws."

"Our radios are in the clear," Terry said. "We must be careful how we use them."

"Yes. Only messages of a few words. I don't think there is an intercept capability any place near here. But Terry's right. Act as if your communication could be intercepted."

Bernadette asked, "What kind of a camp are we going to set up?"

"Minimal. No tent. We'll tie up a tarp if it rains. I don't expect we'll get out of these clothes until the job is done. We won't have to wear the ghillie suits in camp. No sense in scrubbing the green and black skin paint off. A very small, no-smoke fire for hot liquids, coffee, and soup. Meals are all prepackaged. We will have one person awake at all times in a position to watch over the camp. If we need to we should be able to move our camp in minutes. We will try to always be in sight of each other. Any person in an advanced position will always be covered by two rifles.

"I want to avoid any firefights. But if one happens, we take no prisoners. It's better to mess up the mission rather than lose one of us."

Bernadette said, "We've gone ten miles. Our map shows a series of fire roads in the forest. A couple cross Route 20 just ahead. I suggest you take the second one."

201

Peter slowed and shifted into four-wheel drive.

Terry said, "Up there about 50 yards. See that slight break in the tree line?"

Peter checked his mirror, braked, and pulled into the fire road. He said, "Now look for a place to hide our black truck."

Bernadette pointed. "Straight ahead, on the right by that large pine tree."

Peter said, "Looks good," and powered the Ford through the soft pine branches and parked in a grove of 20-foot pines. When they had their gear out of truck and covered it with a black plastic tarp, it was almost invisible. Peter and Bernadette had selected the AR-15 as their shoulder weapons. The automatic rifle was light with a choice of 20-or 40-round magazines. It was not a burden to carry 300 rounds of the light ammunition. Terry stuck with his favorite, the US M40A1 Sniper with the 10x scope.

Terry had the map spread out on the Ford's tarp-covered hood. Bernadette, looking intently at her compass, said, "Okay. What am I to do with this?"

Terry laughed. "Okay, Irish city girl, watch and learn."

With Bernadette watching every move, Terry laid his compass on the map and drew a line from their current location to a destination close to the suspected terrorist training camp. Terry said, "Once we get to this place I've marked on the map, I'll do the same thing again, getting closer to the camp each time. Professionals like me call those lines azimuths. Use your great memory to remember the degrees of each azimuth. To find the truck from our next destination, simply follow the reverse line, or azimuth."

"I hate to say it but that sounds simple. I understand it and never had any of your fancy courses."

"The only other lesson for you is to always trust your compass. In doubt, it is right and you are wrong."

When they reached the high point of 1,000 feet, Terry asked Bernadette to lay out the next line of march, which she did correctly in quick time. Before they started out, Terry said, "Let's check our packs. I think I heard some pack noise from my point position." Terry quickly found the problem in Bernadette's pack and padded the rattling items. He also put the heavier items on the bottom to make the pack less top-heavy.

Terry took a quick look at Peter's pack and said, "You've done this before. Bernadette, note where Peter is carrying his ammo, right where his left hand can quickly get a loaded magazine. At the next stop we do a foot check and another one two hours later. We cannot deal with bad blisters or turned ankles. We have to be able to move very fast without worrying about a sore foot or painful ankle."

Bernadette insisted on carrying an equal load. Peter noted she showed no signs of fatigue even though they had been climbing steadily. He thought, *this Irish girl is incredible. I didn't think after my wife was killed that I could ever love again. I was wrong. I love this woman and must protect her. I wish she was back with Jack. So far this seems too routine. I have to keep my edge. Terry is good at this stuff. This is probably a walk in the park to him. Must remember these people are serious and very dangerous.*

An hour before the light began to fail, Peter said, "Okay, this looks like decent campsite. I judge we're within two miles of the training camp. We should be several hundred feet above the camp of the bad guys. I'd like to keep that advantage.

"Tomorrow morning we'll find the camp and set up our hides. The camp shouldn't be hard to find. There is a jeepable road into the camp from the east. We'll be approaching from the west and should not be in their extended training area. I don't know how their shooting ranges, if any, are oriented. If we stay a few hundred feet higher than their camp we shouldn't have to contend with any danger from their firing range.

"There is another problem. I've no idea what they are teaching in the camp. Logically, they are not teaching standard military skills, such as patrolling, use of mortars, heavy machine guns, or shoulder-fired rockets. I expect they are teaching casing of targets, communications between cells or individuals, recruitment of sources, placement of explosives, maybe bomb making, small arms, and standing up to interrogation techniques. The training subjects make me believe they won't be roaming in the hills around their camp but they may have lookouts posted. Now a treat. I always travel with some scotch but in this case I have some Irish whiskey. Does anyone pass?"

****

The supper of hot soup, trail mix, and instant rice

with hot sauce was over and the small fire was dying down. Since sundown it had been growing colder. Terry volunteered to take the first watch from a promontory a hundred feet above and south of their camp.

Bernadette said, "I don't care if my uncle is sitting up above us. Put these sleeping bags together. I'm cold and want you to love me. I promise I won't scream. With the kind of life you lead, I want to be with you. Not wasting a day. I feel the odds are going to catch up with us before I can give you a house full of Brandons."

"Bernadette, as long as we are facing so many dangers, enjoy each day. I don't want to live my entire life being so careful and protective. I don't see any relief for at least two years. I want to hold you close and not make your life so difficult, you may decide to leave."

"No chance. You couldn't drive me away. I'm here and here to stay. My uncle has already told me living with you would be dangerous. My life has always been dangerous. You have given me something to live for. Before I met you, all I had was a belief to die for. This is better. Now it is bed time."

September 13, 1977

They were up at first light. Terry had a small fire going and cooked a great breakfast of bacon, fried eggs, pan toasted wheat bread, and coffee despite Peter's instructions of prepackaged meals only. No one complained. After breakfast, Peter packed up the food and used a light nylon line and pulley system to put the food far enough up a tree to keep bears from raiding the camp while they were gone. Food scraps were tossed in the latrine ditch and covered over. Packs shouldered, weapons checked, and an azimuth was shot toward the location of the training camp. It took another 30 minutes before Terry was satisfied with their ghillie suits and face paint.

They moved out in a no-talk routine at a careful pace with Terry in the point position and Peter bringing up rear. After an hour of a slow, careful pace, Terry held up his hand and motioned Peter and Bernadette to come forward. "We're close. I smell wood smoke and believe I heard a faint motor noise, probably a gasoline generator."

Peter moved up beside him and listened. He already smelled the wood smoke. Peter opened all his senses and stood very still.

The day in mid-September in West Virginia could have been clear and bright, but it wasn't. This was more like September in Moscow. The cold, damp overcast sky settled down over the forest. When he was a young KGB trainee, he and a few others used to wander the forests on the Western edge of Moscow. If it rained or was just too cold and windy, they would go into one of the many cement pill boxes built to stop the German advance, the same way his parents fought at Stalingrad to stop the Germans. He hadn't thought of those earlier times in Russia for years. Now here he was carrying a rifle in the mountain forest of West Virginia to stop a Russian-backed training camp for terrorists. Like his parents and those forgotten Russian soldiers who fought from those crumbling fortifications, he would not fail.

He felt the blood of his wilderness warrior grandfather coursing through him. For the first time in his life, he felt like a warrior.

"Peter! Peter!" said Terry. "Where are you?"

"I'm here. Just thinking. Wait here, I'm going ahead to find an observation hide where we can spend some hours getting the pattern of the camp down cold."

He was back in 30 minutes. Peter motioned for Terry and Bernadette to come in close. "We're a lot closer than I thought. There is a steep drop-off just 50 yards ahead. The drop-off forms the western wall to a small valley maybe a mile by half a mile. At the bottom of the western wall is a cluster of six small recreational vehicles and two large tents. A larger cement block, flat-roofed building is approximately 75 yards north of the RV cluster.

"I saw a dozen people walking around, all armed. Before I came back here they all went into one of the large tents. Near as I could tell, one tent is for classes of some kind and the other is the mess tent.

"The leader, or at least the man who looks like the leader, is huge. Over six four and must weigh at least 250. He also carries a whistle and uses it to get people to move. No shoulder weapon but wears a large revolver on his right hip.

"Get our camera set up. Who is the best at taking pictures from cover?"

Bernadette said, "I'm good. Learned from my father before the British shot him. I've done a lot of casing for the IRA."

"Okay, you're it. Get set up. Terry, watch our back.

I'll watch and take notes while our photographer works. Terry, I know this is old stuff for you. When Bernadette comes back, come up and do some sketching and distance marking in case we have to go in at night."

All day they manned their observation hide and collected information. Peter asked Bernadette and Terry to go back to the camp at dusk.

When Bernadette objected he said, "I want to watch to see their activity at night. I've carried my night vision gear. It is now time to use it."

"I just don't like you being here alone. Can you find your way back in the dark?"

"Yes, I have my compass, there will be decent moonlight tonight, and I have night vision gear. Just have some hot soup ready for me. I'll only stay here a few hours longer. Now go with Terry. Okay?"

"Okay, but I still don't like it."

Two hours later, Peter finished his recon of the cliff's edge, moved back to the observation hide, and was preparing to pack up and start back to the camp when he noticed a growing source of light across the valley where the jeep trail came through a small pass. He thought, *That has to be a vehicle. This might be interesting.* He switched off his night vision gear and picked up his spotting scope. As the vehicle drew closer, he could see that it was a gray Ford pickup with several passengers. The pickup parked practically right below him. He could hear the doors close and some bits and pieces of conversation. Two of the men were speaking Russian. He focused his scope on the two men who had walked off a few yards to have a private conversation.

The man facing him lit a cigarette. In the glare of the match flame he saw his old KGB friend, Yuri Kolenko, the man who led the team that killed his wife and daughter. *If Yuri is here, something big is going on. I'm betting he will not stay the night. I've got to go down there.* Peter used his radio to call Bernadette and Terry. On the second try he got Bernadette and said, "Come back here with Terry. Some big game has just arrived."

September 14, 1977

In less than an hour he heard Bernadette and Terry coming through the scrub pines. He slowly worked his way back out of the clump of mountain laurel covering their observation post and went back to meet them.

"Something big is going on down there. I just saw a Russian expert on terrorism, whose picture I've seen, get out of a car right below our observation post. His face was lit up by match lighting his cigarette as I was focused on him. There is no doubt the man is Yuri Kolenko. He would only be here if something big was going down. We may have to stay here for a while. I found a small spring just 20 yards down the western slope.

"Two things have to be done. The first is get into that cement block building and the second is to block the road out of here. We don't have the tools or manpower to build a blockade they couldn't remove in a few hours. So we ambush the first vehicle leaving the valley. "Anyone have any ideas?"

"Will we have to shoot our way into the building?"

Bernadette asked.

"No. They won't be expecting any opposition. I can pick the lock and take a look inside. I expect the building is a bomb-making location, and no one will be on the inside unless they are working on a bomb.

"We have to be careful moving around. I saw three two-person teams go out on patrol. I suspect one team will remain in the valley and the other two will patrol the ridgeline around the valley. Most likely 20 or 30 feet from the edge of the ridge. It will be a while before they get here. Bernadette, you and I have to get out of our ghillie suits. They won't help us once we are in the camp.

"Questions, scenarios, comments?"

Terry said, "It seems to me that if there is a bomb, it's the priority item. We should do our best to avoid the patrols. We don't know if they have radios with them, but they should. If we have to deal with them it has to be fast and quiet."

"Bernadette, any comments?"

"Yes, I'm thinking that the sooner we get in the valley the better. There is some natural movement by the people left at the site. We may be able to mimic their movement pattern. We've seen both males and females in the camp. Peter and I should take on the building recon, while Terry covers us with his rifle from a point where he can see the building's entrance with the night vision stuff."

"Makes sense to me," Peter said. "Let's do it. Remember who these people are. Don't hesitate to shoot. No prisoners. No extra risks. Terry, let's go over your sketch of the camp and plan our route to the block building and return."

Terry spread out his sketch and with a dimmed flashlight planned a route to get to the target building. Terry's sketch with distances was clear. Peter asked, "How accurate are these distances?"

"Maybe an error margin of five yards every hundred."

"Bernadette, can you put this map into your wonderful recall memory and count steps as we go?"

"Sure, let me focus on it for a few minutes."

Peter walked over to his pack and took out 175 feet of nylon line and a set of gloves. He asked Bernadette, "Do you know how to repel down a cliff face?"

"Yes, but I have only had limited experience and mostly down buildings."

"That'll work. Get your gloves out."

Terry broke in. "I've plotted a route for you. It's better if you don't take the sketch with you. Give Bernadette one more look, pick your time, and go. I figure a patrol could be by here in 15 minutes."

"The nylon line is dark," Peter said. "We can leave it in place. If anyone is looking that close, they'll find our boot marks coming down the mostly bare clay slope. Okay. Bernadette, let's go. People down there are carrying rifles so we can carry ours."

At the cliff's edge, Peter said, "I'll go first. As soon as I tug on the line, start down. Do not hesitate to shoot because they are civilians and we're in West Virginia. These are very bad and dangerous people. The man I saw from Russia is not to be underestimated. He can shoot, think fast, and will have a plan to counter us as soon as he sees what is happening. Use the radio if you have to. We'll keep the volume very low. After leaving the building, we'll disable some vehicles and then hurry to the other end of the valley and set up a roadblock and ambush. Terry, get there when you can. I don't want the Russian to escape. If you get a clear shot, take it. At least stop the vehicle."

Standing on the valley floor waiting for Bernadette, Peter judged the cliff to be 90 or 100 feet. For them both to go back up the rope would take too much time if they were being pursued.

Bernadette slid to a stop at his side and said, "I like your kind of repelling. Buildings are harder and steeper."

"Okay. Check your weapons quietly. Walk on my left side. Fire at targets only on your half of the circle. If it gets chaotic, shoot anywhere you have a target. It's a good 100 yards to the cement block building. Let's get started. If anyone questions your accent, just growl IRA and tell them to back off.

"Over here the IRA has a tougher image than they've earned in the last several years. Bombing civilian targets indiscriminately is not a thing to be proud of, no matter what the enemy has done. Killing non-combatants on purpose to deliver some kind of a message is pure terrorism. Later we can talk, but I want you to make a complete break. The cause is lost. Prior to the bombing of civilians, the IRA had a proud reputation. Now they are terrorists and thugs. Am I getting through to you?"

"Yes, but it's more complicated than you seem to realize."

"Let's drop the subject, but keep chatting, makes us

212

look more normal."

"The building has no windows. How are we going to get in?"

"The lock is probably a good-quality dead bolt. I should be able to pick it."

"Well, if you get into trouble, call me. I've some skill in the fine art of opening things."

"Noted. We must fit in. At least five people have seen us reasonably close in the light provided by the pole lights on the perimeter."

"Yes, I hear the generator loud and clear. When we get to the door, I'm going to unscrew the light over the door. Stand behind me. When I pick the door open, I'll hood my flashlight and look around inside the door area. If I see nothing I'm going in. Back in behind me, close the door, and lock it."

When Peter opened the door and stepped inside, Bernadette, following, softly closed and locked the door. There was no ambient light. Peter's hooded flashlight created a small puddle of moving light. When they stopped moving, there was no sound. Peter whispered to Bernadette, "I think we are alone."

"I'm not sure. It feels to me someone is in here besides us."

Suddenly a loud voice said, "Who are you? You know no guns are allowed in this building. Don't move. I'm turning on my flashlight. But first I want to hear you put your rifles on the floor. Do it!"

Bernadette put her rifle down loudly on the floor and said in a soft voice, "Put it down. Trust me."

Peter's rifle clanked on the cement floor. He noticed

Bernadette had moved to his right a few paces. When the flashlight beam switched on and swung toward them, Peter saw that the man had a handgun pointed in their direction. The light and handgun centered on Peter. Just as he was going to say something, he heard a whirring noise and the flashlight clattered to the floor. Its owner was clutching his throat as he fell hard. A knife handle was protruding from the center of his throat. Peter switched on his light and said, "Where did that knife come from?"

"I told you I was good with a knife."

As Peter watched, Bernadette walked over to her victim, pushed him on his back with her foot, pulled out her knife, and wiped it on the dead man's jacket.

"You're better than good. You're phenomenal. Where do you keep the knife?"

"Up my sleeve or down my back just below my neckline. In this case I eased it out of my behind-the-neck sheath as soon as this would-be guard opened his mouth. I could have taken him in the dark but I wouldn't have been so accurate. The difference between a target just over six feet and one or several inches under six makes a difference. In the dark I couldn't be sure."

"How could you know you wouldn't miss a quick-kill area?"

"Simple, I don't miss."

"You're one scary lady. Remind me to never make you mad. Now, let's see what is here. Stay with me. I don't want to split up. This is a big building to search without good lighting. Did you hear what the dead guard said about no guns in here? Why would he say that?"

"You know why. They make bombs in here. This building has little or no ventilation. Probably afraid a gunshot would ignite the fumes that build up when making a bomb in an enclosed area."

"What do you know about making bombs?"

"Never made one. Never been a part of a bombing operation, but I have heard stories."

"What have you heard?"

"Getting ready-made explosives is very hard. So terrorists turn to making their own bombs. Fertilizer and diesel fuel are the principal ingredients. The hard parts are the detonator and timer."

Back against the north wall they found more than a truckload of bagged fertilizer and a large above-ground tank of diesel fuel. Some distance away across the open-floored building they discovered a well-equipped electronic workbench with a number of remote devices. A further search turned up a gasoline-driven generator large enough to run the lights and power tools and a small ventilator fan high in the wall.

"Any ideas how to destroy this building and not us?" Peter asked.

"Fire. Spread some of the diesel around the fertilizer and use the gasoline to set it off as we get out of here. The fire and possible explosion will alert everyone minutes after we are out the door."

Peter said, "Okay. Let's do it. There are at least six five-gallon cans of gasoline near the generator. We'll dump two on the fertilizer, one on the diesel tank. Without power for the tank's pump, I don't see how we can get the diesel fuel to flood the floor."

"Not to worry. The gas is enough. The heat will ignite the diesel when the fire gets going."

Ten minutes later they were through with setting the stage for a powerful fire. Peter was backing toward the door leaving a trail of gasoline as he went. Bernadette slipped out the door to provide covering fire for Peter, in case anyone was lurking in the area or saw Peter run out leaving the door wide open.

Bernadette saw the flash of light from the gasoline fire just as Peter ran out the door in her direction. When he joined her, Bernadette said, "Let's get out of here."

"Right. Run hard for the wood line on the edge of the valley. Once under cover of the forest, slow down to a steady run and move to the end of the valley where the road comes in. We had no time to disable vehicles. So there will be a lot of action at the ambush we're going to set up. I hope Terry is already there."

They heard a loud whoosh, followed by a flash of light. Both turned to look back from a high point and saw the building engulfed in flames. Flames were rising above the roof. Bernadette said, "Chalk up one wiped-out bomb-making plant."

Peter said, "Pick up the pace. There is movement around the vehicles in parking area. Ease out of the wood line. We need to make time. Get to level ground where the footing is better and we can run harder. We're only a 100 yards from the road entrance. Check your rifle. It looks as if we'll have to begin shooting as soon as we arrive at the pass out of this wretched little valley. I haven't been able to contact Terry."

Bernadette, showing her youth and athletic ability,

pulled slightly away from Peter in their race to get to the road entering the valley. She reached the road first and ran up to where the roadway narrowed on a rutted uphill stretch and settled in behind a tree. Seconds later Peter took up a position opposite Bernadette. Looking back toward the burning building, he could see vehicle lights starting down the valley.

Peter called out to Bernadette, "Here they come. Concentrate on the Ford pickup when we get the road blocked with vehicles. Let the first one get close before we fire."

Looking down from his position, Peter saw they were in an ideal position to stop the flow of recreational vehicles streaming down the valley. The road into the valley was slightly wider than a one-lane country road. The Ford pickup was third in line as the scurrying vehicles entered the uphill climb.

As Peter was picking his first target, he heard gunfire in the distance. *It sounds like Terry is in action with one of the patrols he saw earlier.*

****

Terry was getting ready to move fast toward the road at the far end of the valley when he heard voices and the noise of people moving through brush. He knew the patrol was between him and the planned ambush site. It would be suicide to try to move through or around the patrol. *Probably two people armed with automatic rifles.* He had the advantage of concealment, fire cover and surprise. *When you have the advantage, don't give it up for no gain.*

The two people will probably walk between me and the steep drop-off into the valley. When they get there, I'll take them. At a time like this I would like to redo my choice of a shoulder weapon. This rifle has a five-round magazine. Fine for the slow, steady fire of a sniper, but not ideal for close in fire fights. Too late now. I'm not even carrying a handgun. In my ghillie suit, I'll be hard to see until I shoot.

The noise of clothing rubbing against brush and scrub pines was growing steadily louder. He smelled cigarette smoke. Now, using his night-vision optics, he could see two green shapes moving along within 15 feet of the drop-off. One looked like a woman. *Damn, I've never killed a woman. Maybe I can shoot the male and capture her. Time for thinking is over.*

Terry shot the male, who went down hard. He called out, "Drop your weapon! You're surrounded by police! You have no chance!"

The woman yelled, "Fuck you," and emptied her magazine in a sweeping 180-degree arc. Terry fired one round that caught the woman in the chest. Two of the bullets from her weapon hit Terry in the groin and high on his right side. He fumbled with his radio and raised Peter who answered while firing to take out the leading vehicle. Terry heard the firing and said, "I'm hit hard! Near our cliff top hide. Killed two on patrol. One was a woman. I gave her too much slack. Take care of Bernadette. Kill the bastards!"

Both Peter and Bernadette were firing on full automatic. All the windshields were blown out and some of the tires on all the vehicles were flattened. Some of the terrorists had managed to get out of the RVs and were using them as cover to return fire. They hadn't pinpointed the location of the attackers and their fire was ineffective. From their crossfire positions, Peter and Bernadette were steadily cutting down their opposition.

The lead RV was burning. The Ford pickup was partially hidden in the blowing smoke. Peter was sure the pickup was disabled. He knew Yuri and his huge companion were not going to stay around in a firefight. At the first chance they would disappear. Knowing when to break off a firefight is a useful art. Peter knew it was time to leave this one. He took advantage in a lull in the shooting and raced across the road to Bernadette's position. "We'll each fire one more magazine and then withdraw east to the valley wall and head back to our original position."

After midnight, Tuesday, September 1977

"Why not stay here and make sure the Russian is finished?"

"Terry's been hit and needs our help. He's more important than our Russian."

"My God! Let's go! What can you tell me?"

"Not now, we have to focus to get out of here. There are still shooters out there just waiting for us to make a mistake. Fire your magazine and follow me close."

The smoke from two more burning RVs helped cover their withdrawal. It was a quick climb out of the valley. The surrounding cliff was not as steep on the eastern end of the valley. Once on top they made good time and in 15 minutes found Terry.

Bernadette cut off the clothing surrounding the two bullet wounds. A glance at the groin wound and she knew it was the most serious. "Peter, stop the chest wound from bleeding. I don't think that wound is critical. Stand by to help me with the gunshot in the lower right abdomen. That one is the problem."

Bernadette had learned years ago that if you don't have what you need in a crisis, it is too late to get it. Her first aid kit was lightweight but extensive, including forceps and two pints of plasma. A syringe of morphine helped Terry to stop thrashing around. A plasma drip was next. With Peter holding the light, she probed for and found the bullet in the abdomen and was able to clamp off two of the major bleeders. Next she extracted the bullet in the high chest wound. She left a cut off plastic tube in the lower wound, and then she stitched up both wounds and gave Terry a big dose of antibiotics.

"My God! Bernadette, that was wonderful. Where did you learn all that?"

"Some because I had to, but I did have some real training from an IRA doctor with a lot of battlefield experience. If you can keep focused and cool, have the right stuff, a lot of luck, and a strong patient, they sometimes recover from worse wounds than Terry has."

"What about moving him?"

"No way tomorrow. Maybe a short distance the next day. He has to be kept warm, dry, and hydrated. I know people will be swarming all over this valley before he is ready to move."

"That's what worries me. I'm sure some bad guys are still alive down there. I'm going to push the two Terry killed over the cliff. Better they are found on the valley floor than up here. It's very likely that the fire, small explosion, and our firefight will have been heard and reported by someone. If so, the authorities will be here tomorrow.

"The light from our flashlights and fire to keep Terry warm can be seen from the valley or the surrounding ridges. We'll have to be alert tonight. I'll take the first watch. You try and get some sleep. Tomorrow will be a hard day."

During his watch Peter thought about tomorrow. *We can try to save Terry by bringing our truck into the valley. A time-consuming operation. I don't know where the track that comes into the valley begins. The only way to find out is to follow the track out of the valley. Most likely on foot. It would save a lot of time if I could get one of the shot-up vehicles to run. Probably some terrorists still alive down there. Have to deal with them before trying to get a vehicle running. I'm sure Yuri and the big thug are still alive. They would have stayed out of the firefight and right now are thinking how to get themselves out. They will check all the vehicles first and if none can be used, will plan to walk out, probably down the track they came in on. Also he will know the people who set up the ambush are gone, and they will have seen the light up here on the ridge.*

Yuri will be thinking about coming up here. By now he knows the U.S. Government personnel were not the attackers, and the attackers were not strong enough to

221

conduct a clean-up operation. Yuri and the huge guy with the whistle will be up here tonight. I'm lucky if the night optics batteries last another hour. Bernadette and I should get into our ghillie suits now.

Peter moved over to where Bernadette was sleeping and gently awakened her. When she sat up, Peter whispered, "Put on your ghillie suit and check your weapon. I think we're going to have visitors, the Russian and the huge guy with the whistle. They know we are a weak force, otherwise we would have stayed in the valley cleaning up."

"What do you want me to do?"

"Put out the fire and get in a concealed position where you can protect Terry and watch for movement along the way we came back here. I'm going to the spot where we repelled down the cliff and retrieve the rope. I'll set up right there. Except for that small sector, you can fire anywhere."

"Terry is holding on. His color is better and the bleeding is stopped but he is still very critical. He will need more expert help than I can give him, especially out here. I think his best chance is to move our truck into the valley."

"Yeah. I had the same thought. The biggest problem is that there are still some shooters alive and the worst of them is Yuri and his sidekick. We have to secure the valley before we can even try moving Terry back to the valley. If the Russian and his partner do not show up here tonight, I'll have to go down and look for them."

"Not without me."

"You need to stay with Terry."

"No! Terry may not live, and he will have no chance if anything happens to you. I can't deal with two wounded men and I can't move him by myself. So I have to watch your back. Discussion over."

"No time for more talk! Okay. I'll come back shortly after first light. I won't go down into the valley without you."

Peter pulled on his ghillie suit and moved back to the clump of mountain laurel and retrieved the 175 feet of nylon rope. With the green face paint and camouflaged suit he was nearly invisible as he settled in to watch the trail.

By the dying flames of vehicles and the block building, he could see some movement through the scope on Terry's rifle. Most of the movement was at the ambush site. He couldn't see any purposeful activity, like clearing the blocked road or working on an RV. *Either they have left the valley or are hunting for us. They still outnumber us. I'm sure a few of them survived the firefight.*

The stillness of the night settled in. He could hear the chorus of crickets breaking the silence. An occasional popping sound came from the valley floor as the dying flames suddenly ignited a small pocket of trapped vapor. Voices from the tent below him brought him to alert. There were three separate voices from snatches of conversations he could hear in his hide.

Peter knew he had to kill anyone hunting for them. People with the courage and know-how to hunt an unknown enemy at night in a forest were too dangerous to leave alive. He doubted Yuri would not be part of any group hunting the attackers. Yuri would know it was time to save himself. He would not expose himself to more risks. He wasn't trained that way. By now he was already on his way out of the forest. Somewhere he had a rendezvous point and a waiting vehicle. His work at this camp was over. His huge companion who ran the camp would be left here to destroy anything or anyone who could provide evidence the Soviets were involved.

Peter stopped his musing and focused. The forest was quiet. The chirping crickets had stopped their endless chorus. His night vision gear was marginal with the dying batteries and he slipped out of the cumbersome gear. He needed all his senses at full alert. Minutes passed, and he heard a faint footfall, followed by more. He could now hear the faint sound of fabric brushing through the scrub pine trees. The sounds were coming from his right. Focusing on the faint game trail, Peter could make out the slowly moving form of a man, stepping and pausing. He let the first man pass. When the second man passed and he was sure there were only two, he shot the second man in the back of the head. He went face down on the trail.

As he swung his rifle to take the other searcher, he saw the man had spun and launched himself toward his hide. Before he could get a shot off, the man landed on his rifle, knocking the weapon out of his hands. Without a pause the man grabbed handfuls of Peter's ghillie suit and pulled him face down in the tangle of the clump of mountain laurel.

Peter sensed his attacker was a professional and would soon have a knife in him. He feinted a roll to his right and when he felt his opponent resist, he rolled with all his speed and strength downslope to his left. The quick movement put the attacker under him. He knew by the power and size of the man that it was Yuri's huge partner. The man's arms closed around Peter's chest and began to tighten. The pressure was incredible. Peter slammed his palms against the attacker's ears. The man winced but kept tightening his hold.

Peter repeatedly struck the giant's temples with vicious middle finger knuckle strikes. He felt the crushing grip loosen and then tighten more as the giant thrust his head under Peter's chin, forcing his head back and arching his back. Peter felt his focus slipping and a darkness enveloping him. He tried to fight more but nothing would respond.

Suddenly, the terrible pressure lessened, and he heard the giant thrashing and sputtering. The weight on his chest was gone and a warmness spread over his neck and chest. As his full consciousness returned, he realized he was being gently cradled in Bernadette's arms, who was wiping blood from his face.

She said, "Don't try to talk yet. Have a drink of water. The fucking giant is dead. I rolled him over the edge."

Peter sat up, taking another long drink from his canteen. He said, "That was too close. I've never been overpowered like that. What did you do?"

"I heard your shot and moved fast toward the sound. I nearly fell over the one you killed. You and your friend were making a lot of noise. He was so intent on breaking your back, he never heard me. I used my knives to cut both of his carotid arteries at the same time and pulled him off you. He had a knife in his belt, but I guess he wanted to kill you with his bare hands. If he had used his knife, you would be dead."

"How is Terry?"

"Better than I expected. He's very weak and lost a lot of blood. If he doesn't get an infection he should live if we can get him proper care in the next 24 hours. I'm out of antibiotics. I've been saving a little morphine to use when we move him."

"How big is the other man?"

"I only stumbled over him. I didn't measure him. Why?"

"If I can wear his clothes, carry his weapon, and know his name, I can make a quick trip into the valley before the sun comes up and they find the giant's body at the bottom of the cliff."

"I still say why."

"I want to find Yuri and kill him, and I want to see if any of the vehicles down there can be made to run. Getting Terry proper care means getting one of those RVs running or trekking back to our truck and bringing it into the valley. The only other way is to hope the authorities of some kind get here tomorrow, and we turn Terry over to them. I really don't like that plan. Getting him back may be very hard with all the bodies lying around."

"What do you want me to do?"

"Like always, keep saving me. Stay up here with your radio. Protect Terry, but don't give your life away. Terry is a warrior, he would understand. I'm going to repel to the valley from here and probably come back to this place. If I find a vehicle that can run, I'll alert you to get Terry ready. We'll lower him down right here, put him in whatever I got running, and get out of here. The Russian is probably gone by now. I may have to shoot any terrorists down there who can put up any resistance. Try to follow me using Terry's rifle. The night vision gear is finished. Commercial stuff just isn't up to military specs. I love you and you need to be very careful. Do not expose yourself. Move like you know someone is trying to find you. Give me three of your magazines."

Peter squeezed Bernadette's hand and disappeared over the edge. She heard a few sounds from his descent and then quiet. Peter stayed in the shadows from the flickering dying light from the still burning building and a few RVs. He carried his rifle openly. Everyone still conscious would be wary of anyone moving. They probably believe a force of at least ten people attacked them. They had been professional enough to send out patrols, probably of the most fit. No way to know how many are still patrolling.

He saw one RV parked near the undamaged tent area. Checking it, he found it had the keys in it. He took the keys, checked the tires and moved toward the ambush site. He keyed his radio. When Bernadette responded, he said, "I've found a vehicle at the tent area that looks okay. I'm not going to try and start it until I get back from the ambush site."

"Good! We need to get Terry better care than I can give him."

Peter crossed the small valley just outside the light

cast from the smoldering building. He wanted to retrace the route they used to get to the vehicle track entering the valley after setting the fire. He moved slowly, conserving energy and being careful to pause and listen every 40 or 50 feet. It had been more than 36 hours since he had any sleep. Munching on candy bars and staying hydrated with water kept him moving.

Creeping through the mountain laurel and scrub pine, Peter heard voices and froze his position. The next time he heard the voices he was able to get a direction and began to move slowly toward the voices. He was now close enough to distinguish three voices, all male. Carefully, he crept closer.

Now he could make out words.

"Never mind looking around. I say let's get out of here now."

A more modulated voice said, "There may be wounded here and back in the valley. We need to find them. If we can't help them, we kill them. If any of them are captured, it will be the end of us. Our Soviet friend has already left. Horace is out patrolling somewhere. Did you ever see such a big man move so quietly?"

The third voice said, "No and I hope I never see him again. I think if he comes back he'll kill all of us. He's very close to that big-shot Soviet. We've all seen the Soviet guy and know the target.

"Funny, he had just briefed us a few hours before the whole place went to hell. Must have been 20 or 30 people in the assault group. Maybe they left because they think we're all dead."

"Bullshit! Those people were professionals. They

left because they were done. They weren't the cops. No attempt to arrest anyone. Just destroy the bomb factory and pour heavy automatic weapons fire on us as we tried to get out of this rotten valley. They won't be back but the State Police will get here and lock us all up. That's why I say let's go now."

The first voice said, "If we leave now, where will we meet?"

"Meet? Are you crazy?" the third voice said. "I never want to see any of you again. Period."

"We have to meet again. We've got all the casing of the target done. All we have to do is build another bomb and we're back on track."

The modulated voice said, "I'm certain we are the only ones alive. No more patrols are out. The Soviet big shot is gone, and Horace is still out there roaming around. If we're still here when he comes back and we tell him we're through, what do you think he will do? I'll tell you. He won't hesitate one damn second. He'll kill all of us. We know all about driving the RV bomb close to the Old Executive Building in Washington and that the KGB and IRA are working together. No one who knows what we know can walk away. It's run and hide now or go on with the plan. Me, I vote for making tracks right now. Who's coming with me?"

Peter heard the other two agree and the noise of getting up and checking weapons. Holding his flashlight along the short barrel of the AR-15, he switched it on and swept the group with automatic fire. It was all over in five seconds. All the would-be terrorists were down. They wouldn't be building any more bombs.

He remembered there were four RVs and one Ford pickup at the ambush site. He quickly checked to see if any of them could be used. All had fire damage and shot up tires. There was only one good inflated tire in all the vehicles. He found spots of blood in the pickup. No bodies nearby. The blood was on the passenger seat.

Peter thought, *Yuri wouldn't have been driving. It was not his style. Yuri and Horace must have been the only ones in the pickup. Horace sure as hell wasn't wounded. Not the way he nearly killed me. It must be Yuri who got hit. No vehicles left the valley once our attack started. Yuri must have left on his own. Able to walk but bleeding. Probably not too bad. Felt he could send Horace to have a look around while he waited somewhere along this unused fire or logging road. I may still have a chance to get him. But getting Terry out is first.*

Peter slapped a fresh magazine into the AR-15 and started running at a ten-minute mile pace up the valley. The three men he had just killed thought everyone else was dead, but he took nothing for granted and didn't use his flashlight. He ran straight to the RV near the tents that wasn't part of the rush to exit the valley. A quick check showed no damage, no bullet holes and no flat tires. He switched on the ignition, leaving all lights off. The interior lights were already covered with duct tape. The fuel gauge showed three quarters of a tank. Using his belt knife, Peter cut out two of the seat belts and put them around his neck. *All looking good. Now to get Terry down the cliff.*

Peter used the in-place repelling rope to walk up the

cliff face. Bernadette was waiting for him. She hugged him when he stepped on the top of the drop off. "God. The gunfire scared me. I was debating coming down when I heard noise around the RV below us. Figured that had to be you. What's all that stuff hanging around your neck?"

"That, my lady, is the going to be the harness we use to lower Terry down this little cliff. Is he ready to go?"

"Yes. Do we just walk away from both of the campsites?"

"Not much choice. I'll clean up this one a bit and cover over our fire site. It's possible no one will find this camp and our observation hide. The other campsite is a problem. I don't think the police can track any of the things left there to us. But we left a bunch of fingerprints there. Especially on the tarp, cooking pot handles, and packaging of food items. If we don't get it cleaned up now, it will be too dangerous to go back there later. If it's found, some smart person will stake it out for a few days. For now let's concentrate on getting Terry in the RV. Has he been awake much?"

"Not as much as I would like. He'll wake up when we start to move him."

"Help me get this improvised harness of seat belts on him. I don't think it will put any pressure on his chest wound. But I'm worried about pressure on his groin wound."

"Do your best and I'll pad it well," Bernadette said. "How are we going to get him to the edge of the cliff?"

"Fortunately, it's not far. We'll put my jacket under him and use the seat belt harness to drag him. He's too heavy to carry without a risk of opening his wounds. We can move slowly to the cliff's edge. Once there I'll come back to the camp site and do some clean up and backtracking."

Thirty minutes later Terry was at the cliff's edge. He was awake and lucid. Peter said, "The trip down is going to hurt. I believe everyone down there is either dead or gone. Bite on this stick instead of yelling in case I'm wrong."

Bernadette repelled down first. Peter attached the repelling line to Terry's harness and took a turn around a nearby sapling and eased Terry over the edge and slowly lowered him to the valley floor.

Bernadette waved to Peter to come on down.

Peter used the repelling line doubled so he could pull it down from the bottom of the cliff face. The RV was old and sparsely equipped but there was a pullout bed for Terry. He was awake and said, "You guys are good. I thought I might have to shoot both of you for torturing a senior citizen."

"We aren't out of here yet. Somehow this old RV is going to serve as a tow truck to open a lane in the jumble of wrecked vehicles for us to get through.

"Okay, now the real test," Peter said as he hit the starter. The engine cranked and coughed once before quitting. The battery sounded weak. On the second try the engine caught and kept running. "It's probably been here for a while and it was left here because no one wanted to trust it in an emergency.

"Bernadette, when we get to the ambush site, you drive. I'll take our trusty repelling line and use it if we need to pull a vehicle out of the way. Also I found blood on the passenger seat of the Ford pickup. I think the blood belongs to the Russian. I believe he sent the giant thug up on the ridge to see what he could find to explain this disaster to his betters. When the giant, who I heard called Horace, didn't come back on time, the Russian headed out on foot. Probably to some previously agreed upon rendezvous. He will be watching for a vehicle coming from the valley and will probably believe his friend Horace is driving this RV."

"How can you think all that out in the midst of everything that has gone down this night?"

"I really don't know. It just comes naturally to me, like a clear image. This is close enough. I'm getting out to find a path through this mess. Keep your weapon ready. No lights and keep the engine running."

The moon was now up and the cloud cover was breaking up. Peter could make out the damaged vehicles and the one-lane track. His night vision was sharpening. Clearly the RV in front of the Ford pickup ended up sideways on the track blocking the Ford pickup. Peter put the pickup in neutral. The hand brake was not engaged. He turned the steering wheel hard right and walked back to talk to Bernadette.

He leaned in the window and said, "Pull up behind the pickup and when you see me wave my arm push straight ahead. Start out slow and accelerate until the vehicle starts to move. Push until it's off the road. Keep your RV on the road."

Peter stood beside the pickup with the door open and one hand on the steering wheel, keeping it locked in a tight right turn. He waved Bernadette up. When the bumpers mated, she increased power and the pickup, on its flat tires, rolled off the road into a shallow low spot.

Moving the other RV from its cross-road blocking position was more complicated.

Peter had to use their repelling rope to drag the rear of the stranded RV downhill toward Bernadette's RV. Peter stayed in the towed RV until it reluctantly rolled off the road and rocked to a stop against a tree. The road was now open. Bernadette wasted no time in moving out.

Peter opened the sunroof and stood on the seat with his chest and arms resting on the roof, his rifle scanning for any stragglers or the only man he badly wanted to kill. Bernadette had her bright lights on and kept the speed down. The road was deeply rutted and Terry couldn't take too much rolling around. They were coming to a sharp rise and a narrowing of the track between two boulder-strewn steep hillsides.

Peter came back to the passenger seat and said, "Lights out. Keep the engine running. If you hear gunfire go fast through the small pass. Don't stop for another half mile. That road feature is exactly the kind of place the Soviet would have remembered. If his guy, Horace, was to pick him up, this is where it would be. He can also easily kill anyone coming through. From behind those boulders he could almost put his rifle barrel against the driver's window. Keep a close watch for anyone sneaking up while I'm gone. I'm going to the west and then cut back east to come on the choke point from his blind side. Wait here for 30 minutes, then go fast. Watch for a blinking light, three short blinks. A pause, then two more. Pull up into the pass and wait, weapon ready at all times. Okay?"

"Got it. Please be careful. This is as bad as the IRA ever was. Give me a good luck kiss."

Peter eased the RV's door open and slipped out, moving into the roadside tree line. Just to be sure he took a compass reading and then when his night vision peaked, moved quickly due west for ten minutes. Peter thought, *Yuri was not hit hard. The amount of blood in the pickup didn't look like anyone had a bad wound. Also he wouldn't have left on his own if he was really hurting. So he must be alert. He saw our lights. Saw them stop. His plan must have been for Horace to drive right into the chokepoint. Therefore he sensed danger and moved to a better defensive position where he can see the narrow road and the planned pick-up point. He's thinking he can't be sure the vehicle is not being driven by Horace or someone sent by Horace.*

He will be on high ground close to the road. He'll not be making a sound and I have to move in quickly. I'm bound to make some noise. If we didn't need to get Terry medical care, I wouldn't be doing this. I'd get in a good position, and Bernadette and I would bracket the high ground and search for him in daylight from cover. Much better odds than now. He has the advantage. It depends on how badly he is hurt.

****

Yuri was settled in a good defensive position on high

235

ground. Come daylight he would be able to command the area. He knew someone was out there in the dark near this little pass. He couldn't understand why the vehicle stopped and turned its lights off. Horace wouldn't have done that. Yuri had struggled to get this far. A bullet had carved a deep furrow high in the outside of his left thigh. He had gotten the bleeding stopped but it started again when he moved positions.

Yuri knew the attack wasn't by government forces. They would have completed the attack and taken prisoners and collected evidence. No, the camp was attacked by a few highly skilled professional fighters. What did they want? Were they looking for him? Horace must be dead or captured. Otherwise he would have been here hours ago.

He had a half canteen of water, some candy bars, and an extra 13-round magazine for his 9mm Browning automatic. If Horace didn't come, he would have to walk out through the forest tomorrow. This place will be swarming with security forces shortly after sun up. He ate two of the candy bars, drank deeply from his canteen, and came to a decision. He had to leave now. His ride wasn't going to happen. The longer he stayed, the worse the odds of his escaping became. With that thought, he was on his feet and moving into the forest close to the road. Even with his slow pace he would be back where he could get help by nightfall tomorrow.

Peter entered the small pass area from the west, as Yuri left eastward. If Yuri had waited another five minutes, he and his old friend, Kalin, would have met in the darkness.

Twenty-nine

Before dawn, September 16, 1977

Peter signaled Bernadette to drive up into the small pass. He jumped in when she stopped. He reached over and squeezed her hand.

"Good to see you again."

"It seemed you were gone for hours."

"I found signs of his being there. Bloody bandage made from a torn shirt, candy bar wrappers, and cigarette butts. Higher up in the rocks when I chanced using my flashlight, I found a few spots of fresh blood. He's not hurt badly. I think he saw the RV stop and go lights out. He had no good option. Stay and fight an unknown number of opponents or move on, probably down the road we're on. He will hear us coming and hide until we pass. I'll bet he is only 40 or 50 feet off the right side of the road in the tree line.

"When we get in the Charlestown outskirts, find a payphone. I need to make a call about medical care for Terry."

The narrow-rutted road dead-ended on County Route 20. Peter said, "Turn left, it is only a short distance to our truck. Less than ten minutes out of our way."

Peter found the pickup just as they left it. He told Bernadette to follow him. Thirty minutes later he was talking to Frank Batcher from a pay phone.

"Frank, I know this is an open line. If I'm giving you too much detail, tell me. I need some emergency help. The terrorist camp is destroyed. Everyone there is dead except for a Soviet KGB Officer, Yuri Kolenko. He was in charge and escaped. The terrorists were planning on driving an RV packed with explosives near the Old Executive Office Building. Where and what that is I don't know. There was a large 50- by 70-foot concrete block building that was the bomb-making plant. It was destroyed.

"One of my people was hit hard. He's had good battlefield care but is still critical. I don't want to take him to a local hospital with two bullet wounds. The police will tie him to the shootout at the terrorist camp. Not a good thing. Can you help?"

"Yes. Take him to General Hospital in Charleston. It's on the 800 block of Riverside. Park next to the helio pad. One will be there in an hour. Pilot's name is Bill Wilson. Your friend will be taken to one of our care facilities. No questions and no costs. When he's able to travel, he can leave. I assume you will make arrangements to have him picked up. He will have to sign a no-talk about agreement. It's no big deal. I don't think his kind would talk too much anyway."

"My other friend will be with him in a brown RV that belongs to the terrorist camp. There were five RVs in all.

238

The Soviet was in a Ford pickup. All those vehicles are still in the valley. There is some blood on the passenger seat where the Soviet was sitting. Later I found a bloody bandage when I trailed him. I had to break off to get my friend to a hospital."

"Leave the RV. We'll take care of it."

"The cab inside is covered with our prints and a lot of the AR-15 brass at the camp site will have our fingerprints."

"No problem. I'll take care of the forensics and thank you for such an outstanding mission. We'll have a recon team in the valley in two hours. Call me any time for an update on your friend. By the way, how many people in the attack team?"

"Me, my friend, and a woman."

"What! You did all the damage with three people?"

"Yes. It wasn't that hard. We only committed two members. I kept one in reserve. He was shot by a random security patrol. Take good care of the patient. I'll be in touch."

Peter walked over to the parked RV. "Bernadette, drive to this address, it's a General Hospital with a helio pad. There will be a chopper there in about 45 minutes. It will take Terry to an excellent trauma facility. No questions asked. We can't go with him or visit, but we can get telephone updates on his progress and as soon as he is fit to travel, we will pick him up. We can't visit because I don't want our names known.

"Is Terry awake?"

"Yes. He has a slight fever but is lucid. I'm a bit

worried by the looks of an infection around the groin wound."

"You can brief the medic on the helicopter when they pick him up. I'll park near the entrance and be watching. Leave the RV and walk out to the street. I'll be there. It's probably useless but wipe off your and my prints as much as possible. I don't think there is anything we missed transferring to the truck when we picked it up. Right?"

"I'll look around. But believe we are good to go. See you at the hospital. Where are we going from there?"

"Back to the cabin and Jack. We'll hold there until Terry is with us and recovered most of his strength. Okay, I need to talk to Terry."

Peter climbed in the RV and knelt beside Terry. He looked pale but was sipping water from a canteen. He looked at Peter and said, "Some walk in the mountains. How did we do?"

"We're the only ones left standing. The Soviet got away but bleeding a bit. He's got a long hike ahead of him. How you feeling?"

"Not worth a damn. What's going down?"

"My friends will be picking you up in a helicopter in about 30 minutes. And you can ride inside, not strapped on an outside stretcher. You don't need to answer any questions from anyone about who you are or what happened, except for medical questions. Bernadette will brief the medic on the treatment you've had. We can talk to you on the phone when we call. You can't call us or anyone else. You're going to a first-class facility with high security standards. When you're fit to go, we'll pick you up. Relax and don't fight the process. It will be okay. Anyway, the top guys think you're a hero, and I couldn't change their minds. Never mind any questions. We have to go now. See you soon."

Thirty

After Terry was picked up and taken to a trauma treatment facility, Peter and Bernadette stopped for breakfast. "I'm almost too tired to eat," Bernadette said. "I badly need a bath and a good 10-hour sleep. But I'd sooner drive back to the cabin. If you can drive long enough for me to get a two-hour nap, I'll take over and let you sleep."

"Sounds like a plan. We've pushed our bodies hard. I don't have much more. Adrenalin can only last so long. We're almost past that. With a huge coffee to sip on, I can drive for a couple of hours. How good is it to get a decent breakfast? People in West Virginia know how to serve up a great one."

"Give me a chance to go to the ladies room and I'm ready to go. Hope Terry is okay."

"He's in good hands. I trust these people to take good care of him."

"By the way, although I asked no questions, I'm very impressed how a payphone call delivered a medically equipped helicopter with first-class medical people on board. Obviously there is a dark government hand in

242

this somewhere."

"Knowing when not to ask questions is just one of the things I love about you. During my short call I gave a quick summary of the valley action. I was asked how many people were in our team. I said three, two men and one woman, but only two of us were in the attack force. The other man was on watch and in a standby mode. There was astonished silence on the other end of the line. They will have a recon team there in a few hours."

"You know we are good, but we can't keep up action at that level. I may have to go back to Ireland and the IRA."

"Listen to me, woman warrior, you are done with the IRA! Stick around. I guarantee the level of violence of the last two months will stop. But we will always be in a defensive watchful mode."

"Good. I'll join you in the truck in five minutes."

By the time Peter and Bernadette finished their breakfast and were back on the road, Terry was in the operating room of a small but first-class trauma facility. Frank went up to see the Director of Operations to brief him. Just as he finished briefing the Director of Operations, the phone buzzed. The Director frowned and picked up the secure phone. He told Frank to pick up the extension. Fifteen minutes later the report from the Recon team in the valley of the terrorists' ended. The Director shook his head and said, "I knew this guy was good, but I was thinking your report was embellished a bit. Now from what was reported by the Recon team, it was understated.

"This strange man is the best operative I have ever

heard about. The Recon team leader thinks for security reasons I'm not telling him what unit hit the valley. It was a major bomb factory run by the Soviets deep in the West Virginia mountains. Their bomb plot against the Old Executive Office Building might have worked.

"The Recon team spotted a small camp from a helicopter search, probably where our guy staged from. With a badly wounded man, he couldn't go back and clean it up. We need to get it cleaned up before the cops or FBI people find it.

"The Recon leader said they monitored the local police network for their own protection and heard about a carjacking very near the first hard surfaced road near the entrance to the old fire or logging track into the valley. Both the driver and a woman passenger were killed. One shot to the head. That must have been the Russian. Use your contacts to raise the priority of the search. Bring the FBI in. Tell them we don't know what happened in the valley. We were just checking out a low-level lead from Moscow that there was a training camp for spies and terrorists in the area. No mention of our guy and his team. Our Recon team was in fact a search team attracted by the smoke.

"Frank, handling this asset is a full-time job. I want him protected at all costs. Mostly from our process people. No written reports of any kind. Clear all your instructions to him with me and no one else. Also, no effort to find or identify him without my express personal order. If he wants us, he will find us. He will notice any attempt of ours to find him. His reaction would probably be to kill you and maybe me and disappear. When we need him, we run the ad he gave us in the Wall Street Journal one week every month until he contacts you.

"Remember, this guy is not a defector. He wants nothing from us. He is an all-pro from our toughest opponent who shares our interests. Doesn't happen very often. Until now I would have said never."

Thirty-one

Peter let Bernadette sleep. By the time he pulled the Ford pickup into the small circle of gravel that passed for a parking area at the cabin, he was done. Before he and Bernadette could get out, Rip had his muddy front paws on the door window and Jack was running as hard as he could up the slope from the creek bed. Mr. and Mrs. Nguyen joined the welcoming group. Bernadette was touched. She nudged Peter and said, "Your warrior house staff know we've been in battle. They know the after-battle look. I'm wiped out. Help me up the steps."

Mrs. Nguyen ran up to help Peter get an exhausted Bernadette in the cabin and started running a bath. Mr. Nguyen opened the locked chest in the truck bed and took out the weapons. He shook his head and mumbled to himself about the condition of the weapons. He carried them up on the porch and got his cleaning kit and started on the weapons. Peter saw him, after he left Bernadette half asleep in the tub, and said, "Thank you, I didn't have time to clean them. Too much fighting. We've not gotten any sleep for two and half days."

246

Mr. Nguyen frowned and said, "Can't fight with dirty weapons. Not work for you when dirty."

Peter smiled. "You are right. You've been in more fights than I have. I accept your advice."

****

Everyone, including Jack, worked hard at getting the cabin ready to stand unoccupied during the winter. Peter concentrated on finishing the room built into the mineshaft.

He had time to work with Rip who was very smart and almost as stubborn. Rip was beginning to assert himself as the alpha male in the cabin. After several "talks" Rip understood he had to wait awhile before becoming head of the cabin pack. Bernadette watched this process with great amusement. Here was the most competent, fearless man she had ever seen competing with a dog barely out of puppyhood, even if a very big, strong one.

She was amazed once when out for a walk with Jack and Rip, Jack ran back to the cabin to get a sweater and she told Rip to stay with her. Seeing he might not listen, she took a firm grip on his collar and found herself being dragged on her stomach down the trail. After letting Rip go, she understood Peter had some strong competition. She learned never to get between Rip and his duty to watch over Jack.

Nine days after returning to the cabin, Peter was told that he could come and pick Terry up. Terry could continue his recuperation at home. Peter and Bernadette drove the Cadillac to Leesburg, Virginia. The pickup place was a popular restaurant in the historical district.

They found Terry having coffee and a piece of pumpkin pie while reading the local paper. Bernadette slid in beside him and hugged him. Terry said, "No too hard, you Amazon. Your uncle still has some sore spots."

"Oh Terry, I'm sorry. I was so worried about you."

Peter sat on the other side of the booth and reached across to shake his hand. "You know your uncle, he just likes sympathy."

"Where were you treated?" Bernadette asked.

"The truth is I don't know. I had great care, the doctor and staff were very good, even kind. But no one would tell me where I was and I still don't know."

"Couldn't you look out the car window?"

"No, my Irish Princess. They used the old black hood technique. It was taken off right out there when they pulled into the curb. They made sure I could make it to the door and said goodbye after putting this thick file under my arm. They said this is for the battlefield surgeon that saved my life and you would tell me about my treatment and be in charge of my recovery. If any problems come up, you can call them."

"Did they give you any prescriptions?"

"Yeah, there's a bag of pills and stuff in the folder."

"Aside from all the medical stuff," Peter asked, "how do you feel?"

"I'm tired and get tired very easily. Pain is not bad. I've a lot of work to do to get back. A week or so at the cabin will help. Thinking about that place kept me going."

It was dark when Peter parked the Cadillac at the cabin and helped Terry into the master bedroom. Peter and Bernadette moved back into their tent camping site. Jack was back on the couch with Rip. The next morning Bernadette took Terry for a walk. A couple of hundred yards from the cabin and Terry said, "How about I sit down for a while?"

"Good sign. You're in touch with your body. I was afraid you would play macho male and overdo this rehab thing. You cannot hurry or force your recovery. It will be six months to a year before you feel you're back."

October 15, 1977

Three weeks later, Terry was looking much better. His appetite was back and he was sleeping well. His wounds were healed and the pain was nearly gone. He was even running a bit.

Peter had finished the hidden room in the mine tunnel, and to his satisfaction, the cabin was now complete and could stand empty during the Pennsylvania winter.

Bernadette and Peter had put themselves through a grinding physical fitness program. Peter was now in the best shape he had ever been. He and Bernadette often went on 15-mile runs through the surrounding mountains. They practiced frequently with an assortment of handguns. Peter liked the Browning 9mm because of the 13-round magazine. Bernadette stuck to the .45 U.S. Army 1911A Colt because it fit her hand better even though its magazine held half that of the Browning.

She made great progress in Hapkido. Peter told her that she was good and she had incorporated her knowledge of Aikido into her own fighting technique.

At dinner Peter asked, "Is everyone ready to go back to Florida?"

There were all yes votes. Jack wanted to go swimming again. Mrs. Nguyen said, "Yes, it's getting cold here." Peter said, "Okay that's it. Tomorrow we go."

"Good," Terry said. "Let's get out of here before it snows. I thought it was going to snow this morning."

The Brandon caravan was on the road by eight o'clock the next morning. Peter, Bernadette, and Jack rode in the Ford truck and Terry took up the back seat of the Cadillac. One overnight stop in South Carolina and they arrived in Amelia Island in time for an early afternoon swim. Peter felt the tension leaving his body. He felt safer at this house than anywhere he had lived. Terry soaked up some Florida rays and let Jack see his Purple Heart scars.

Thirty-two

Bernadette drove her uncle home the next day and helped him unpack. There was a note in the mailbox for Bernadette O'Brien. She found it and one more when sorting Terry's mail. There were no stamps on either envelope. She thought, *This is not good.* Opening the first envelope she read a note of cut and pasted newspaper words.

"This is our second attempt and last nice attempt to get in touch. Call the number below by October 22 or we will call on you."

There was no doubt in Bernadette's mind who the note was from. She had been expecting some form of contact. She thought, *They must want me to do something either here or in the UK. They won't ever accept that I want out. I know too much and they know too much about me to let me go. If I do one more job for them, there will be another and another. I might as well face up to the problem now. I'll have to tell Peter but I must not allow the danger to spread to Jack. Terry is still too weak to*

251

be of much help. He doesn't need any more bullet holes. There are just too many of them willing to die for the cause. For the time being, I'll handle this myself. First I need to set up a meeting place they don't control.

Bernadette called the number in the note and when someone answered she said, "I'll meet you tomorrow on the city beach at 10 AM. If I don't know you by sight, you'll need to convince me you're in some leadership position."

"Good to hear you again. Tomorrow is good at ten on the Fernandina City Beach. I'll be wearing a blue windbreaker. I think you already know me but no names. Come alone. I don't want to see your uncle. Cheerio."

Bernadette left a note for Terry and, with a plan forming in her head, drove the few miles to the Brandon house carefully checking for a tail as she approached the gated community. She loved the setting of the Brandon house on a spur of land jutting out through the marshland into the Amelia River and the Inland Waterway. The view was spectacular.

As soon as she stopped the truck, Rip and Jack came charging up, competing for attention. She dropped to one knee and hugged them both. It was hard to tell which one was wriggling the most. Maybe the one that was licking her face. Peter came out a few minutes later carrying two cold bottles of Bass Ale. He said, "I didn't expect you back quite so soon."

"I didn't expect to be. I got a note in the mail we need to talk about." Bernadette reached in her shoulder bag and handed the note to Peter. When he finished reading the note, she told him about the phone call and meeting arrangements.

"Before we talk about this problem, I want you to know I'm aware of bringing more danger to you and Jack. I was very careful to check for anyone following me on my way here."

Peter said, "I wasn't thinking about that. I am wondering if we can get rid of these people."

"There are too many of them and they don't care who they kill. Terry's in danger, and he's not well enough yet."

"What do you think they want?"

"Something illegal, very illegal. Like killing someone or casing targets. They will never let me alone. All I want is to be able to live a normal life with you and Jack."

"We both have enemies with resources and motivation."

"Right now I can't think long-term. What can I do tomorrow? My plan begins with following my contact after the meeting back to wherever they are hiding. If I find them, I'll kill the lot of them, and Terry and I will disappear."

"First, I'm part of this plan. Meet them and find out what they want. I'll be there to back you up and follow them after the meeting with you. It's possible we can get the lot of them arrested. In any event we have to make plans to move you and Terry."

For the next two hours Bernadette and Peter worked out a plan for the meeting tomorrow. Bernadette left in the pickup to bring Terry back to the Brandon house. She only told Terry Peter needed him. Once again

Bernadette checked for any tails.

"What's up? Why are you checking traffic so closely?"

"Something's come up with the IRA. Once we get to Peter's house, you'll get the full story."

Sitting around the pool in the warm Florida sun and drinking Bass Ale, Bernadette told Terry about the note and phone call.

"God damn those people! Can't they understand you're done with them?"

"Terry, these people are terrorists. You cannot reason with them. You either cooperate or you get punished. In my case, punishment will be death."

"Terry, here is the beginning of a plan. Short term we must find these people and get them arrested and jailed or deported. Failing that, we kill them. They will not understand a warning or threats, and Bernadette doesn't believe they can be bought off.

"Long-term, you two have to disappear. New location and new name."

"Hell, I don't like that. I've been Terry O'Brien a long time. I'm proud of my name and record. I can't or won't give up my veteran rights and pension, and don't say you will make it up for it isn't the money. But we don't have time now for that debate. I'm in for the short-term plan. Lay it out."

Peter said, "First of all, you must keep out of sight. They will be looking for you. And when real professionals look they want eyes on the target. That's you. If you're not under observation, they won't go through with the meeting. The next meeting site would be Bernadette's choice and they might send a painful message.

"They will come to the beach in a car or motorcycle. They don't know me. I'll set up where I can see the parking lot. I'll take a few pictures and follow the person or persons that show up to wherever they go. All Bernadette has to do is listen, act normal, and not give them a definite 'no.' Leave open another meeting in the same place if possible. If not, pick a shopping mall that has activity during the time of the meeting.

"Bernadette, wear one of your bikinis with a beach wrap to cover your knife. It's okay to bring your .45 but leave the gun in your beach bag with all the stuff ladies take to the beach. They might try to follow you after the meeting to see what you do. Run some errands, go shopping, go back to Terry's and take a nap, anything that seems natural. Don't come to my place until late afternoon. If there's trouble, call and come immediately.

"My intent is that your IRA friends never figure out what happened or who is to blame. How's the plan sound to you?"

Terry said, "Plan sounds good and I won't ask how you got so good at it. You must have been to a good school."

"I think it just comes natural to him," Bernadette said, "Like some people can sing or paint or write poetry or shoot. I haven't had much coaching in knife throwing but I'm pretty good at it. No school teaches knife throwing 101. What school would teach operational planning?"

"I'm glad you like the plan. Now let's get into the details."

Thirty-three

October 19, 1977

Peter, driving the black Ford pickup, pulled into the parking lot at the beach and parked where he could see the entrance. It was now 8:30 AM. He doubted the IRA advance person would arrive before 9:15 AM. Maybe they would use an advance person to recon and monitor the meeting site. It was also possible this wasn't a meeting but an opportunity to grab or kill Bernadette. He had convinced Bernadette to keep a small commercial transmitter in her beach bag. If she yelled for help, he would hear her.

The tide was coming in and a storm at sea was causing bigger than normal breakers. Some East Coast surfers were trying without much success to catch a decent wave. Peter walked over to the beach restaurant and got a large takeout coffee. He was certain the coffee would be poor but drinkable, especially as a cover prop. He wandered down to look at the beach and strolled back to the truck. With his Levis and light rain jacket, he fit right in with the growing beach population.

Camera ready, he settled in the truck, sipping coffee and waiting for the main characters to arrive. It was now

9:00 AM. If the IRA was going to cover this meeting, the person or persons should be arriving soon. The lot was now half filled. There were several more pickup trucks. Fortunately, none of them blocked his line of sight lanes.

At 9:30 a motor scooter arrived with two people and parked near the bike rack. They looked out of place. The man was big but not overweight, the woman was wearing a very revealing tiny bikini and was white as snow. She was carrying a beach bag that looked heavy the way she was carrying it. The man reached over and took the bag. It was very obvious they were not at home on the beach.

Peter shot a couple of pictures with his 35mm Minolta with a distance lens. If they weren't IRA reconning the meeting site, they should be. Perfect casting for comic relief. Thirty minutes in the Florida sun and they would be in misery in a few hours.

Bernadette arrived on schedule at 9:55. She parked Terry's Toyota and walked down the short stairway to the beach as if she hadn't a care in the world. She spread her beach towel near the high tide line. In another hour her spot would be covered. From the seat of the truck Peter could see Bernadette with her short robe covering her knife and not much else. The motor scooter couple picked up their towels and moved to within ten yards of Bernadette. *The stage is set*, Peter thought. *Just waiting for the main actors.*

Focused now on the entrance, Peter saw an old model VW camper with a passenger and a driver in the front seat. The driver stayed with the VW. The passenger moved directly to the beach. Peter hurried to get the photos he wanted. The VW was parked 20 yards closer to the beach entrance by the restaurant. The driver was watching the main actor as he moved toward the meeting site.

Peter thought, *This has all the earmarks of a snatch.* His instincts told him this meeting was not going to be nonviolent. He switched plans, got out of the truck, and moved toward the VW. The driver was still watching the meeting site. Peter approached on his blind side, reached through the open driver's side window with his right arm, hand cupping the chin, and broke the driver's neck in one quick move.

Climbing inside the camper, he found a Luger fitted with a sound suppressor on the seat next to the dead driver. He put the Luger under his belt and took the driver's cap and wrap-around sunglasses and pushed the body over the bench seat on to the empty bed of the camper and covered him with a ratty blanket conveniently spread out on the floor. There was no doubt in Peter's mind that the blanket was meant for Bernadette.

They were going to torture her before telling her what they wanted from her. Both to teach her a lesson and to find out what she had been doing in the last couple of months. If they didn't like the answer, they would kill her. There will be some torturing here, but not of Bernadette.

Peter moved quickly to the motor scooter and let the air out of the front tire. They would believe a flat tire but not a knife cut in the tire. While near the sea wall, Peter checked the meeting site. He was surprised to see the man in the blue windbreaker walking closely beside

Bernadette. The scooter couple was still on the beach obviously playing the rear guard role.

Peter ran back to the VW, opened the sliding side door, and stepped inside. When the IRA thug with Bernadette approached he said, "Harry, get behind the fucking wheel. I got her." The blue windbreaker pushed Bernadette inside and got in behind her. He didn't see Peter and yelled, "Harry, get moving." Blue windbreaker pushed the sliding door closed.

Peter hit him behind the head with the Luger's butt. He sank to the floor. Bernadette was in his arms. She said, "I knew you would save me. But I was getting worried."

"You are not completely saved yet. They're two more out on the beach. They'll be along any minute. We've got to get going. Mr. IRA thug is a practical sort. There's a roll of duct tape back here. Very convenient. I'll get this thug wrapped up. You take my truck keys and Browning and follow the scooter people. No chances. Just see where they go. They'll be bewildered. The VW camper will be gone.

"Their scooter has a flat front tire. I let the air out. Get the truck someplace where you can see them coming out. They'll be going fast. Just stay close enough to keep them in sight. Probably brought at least one handgun, and now they have your .45. Their job was to do clean up."

As Bernadette was getting out of the VW she said, "His name is Sam Conners. And he is a bad one. He's killed several people, including IRA members who he thought were out of line. He told me he was going to rape me and then beat me so badly, I would never have to worry about any other man wanting me."

"He will never bother you again. After you find out where the scooter people go, come home. I'm going to put Conners and the VW in the detached garage and boat house in the marsh behind the house."

"Okay. Take care, Peter Brandon. These are mean, treacherous people. Conners will have had a gun and a knife."

"I got the snub nose .38 Smith and Wesson. It dropped out of his hand when I hit him. Remember no chances. Just get home safe."

Bernadette hurried back to the pickup truck. Looking up she saw the VW with Peter at the wheel wearing the driver's cap and sunglasses. She moved the Ford out of the beach lot to a street position where she could see the exit of the public beach lot and be able to move to follow the scooter no matter which way they turned coming out of the lot. She knew it would be at least 15 minutes before the scooter couple could get their front tire checked and inflated.

Peter headed straight for his house. He had the remote from his truck that controlled the resident's gate in his pocket so he didn't have to risk the guard at the main gate wanting to check the run-down VW camper before allowing him through. It wasn't every day that a guard could find a dead man and another one taped up under a blanket on the floor of a vehicle driven by a resident.

Turning into his driveway he punched in the access code and when the gate swung open he drove around to the back of the house, past the pool, and down a narrow, unpaved track to a detached garage and boat house some 100 feet from the house.

Peter closed the garage door and made sure Conners could not move or make any noise. He then called Terry from the boathouse phone. When Terry answered after several rings, Peter said, "So far okay. It was a snatch operation, only we snatched the leader instead. Bernadette is okay and should be here soon. But I need you now. Be careful coming over. These people are serious. They sent four armed people to get Bernadette.

"Come straight back to the boat house when you come. I'll be inside waiting for you."

"I'm on my way," Terry said.

Peter walked to the main house and checked in with the Nguyens to tell them to keep the shotguns handy and Jack under watch. And to prepare a picnic lunch for six out by the pool.

Peter heard Terry's car coming down to the boathouse and went out to meet him. Terry got out and said, "What's going on?"

"Come up to the pool with me and I'll bring you up to date."

Seated in a cabana, Peter told him what went down at the beach. Terry grew visibly angry as he heard the story. "As soon as Bernadette checks in, let's go kill the bunch of them."

"That's what will probably happen, but we have to question Conners and get both of them ready to go in the river tonight. I don't think Conners will talk at first. He thinks he's tough. He told Bernadette first he was going to rape her and then beat her so badly no man would ever want her again."

Terry clenched and unclenched his huge fists. "Please let me talk to him," he said.

Peter replied, "Okay. But don't kill him until he's answered our questions. And let's give Bernadette some more time to check in here. She may have information that will help our questions' focus. We don't know yet what they wanted her to do. Maybe Connors never told her. Maybe this rogue faction of the IRA just wanted to clean up a loose end. While we're waiting for Bernadette and lunch, let's go and check on our prisoner."

Before opening the door into the garage, Peter said, "Don't make any noise. I want him to stay bewildered over what happened. When we rip off the duct tape from his mouth and eyes, he may be ready to talk. I don't care what he sees and hears then. After dark he will be shark bait."

Looking in through the VW windshield, they could see Connors trying to move. He could make slight noises but nothing that would be heard outside the garage.

Back at the cabana Terry and Peter talked over dumping Connors and Harry out in the Nassau Sound. Peter said, "I've not had the Boston Whaler out much. It came with the house."

"Don't worry. I'll get it running. I used to cruise and fish these waters in the same type boat."

Peter jumped up when he heard Bernadette driving down the driveway. He laughed because Jack and Rip beat him to greeting Bernadette. She hugged them both and let them escort her to the pool, where she dropped her beach robe and did a flat dive into the pool, followed by Jack and Rip. Both were now strong swimmers. Peter yelled "lunch is served" and Bernadette swam over to the cabana and offered a hand to Peter who pulled her out. She said, "I needed that and I need some serious lunch."

Peter handed her a cold Pabst Blue Ribbon and an Italian sub made by Vietnamese standards. Bernadette said, "You know I'm getting to like nouc mam. I think Mrs. Nguyen uses it to brush her teeth. Okay, I've settled myself after this morning's horror show and am ready for some serious talk. Have you briefed Terry?"

"Yes. He knows as much as I do. Your turn to brief."

"Okay. I followed the scooter couple to A1A North toward St. Mary's. They pulled into a cluster of what you call in America, doublewides. It was a trailer park. Laid out in lanes. In the back of the site there were two doublewides almost touching each other. I saw the scooter people go into the double wide on the right as you face them. Before they went in, they stood around outside as if waiting for something.

"Probably the VW camper with Connors, Harry, and me. I should have walked up and asked them if they were waiting for me and then shot them. I'm sure they didn't see me or notice the truck. They were speeding as much as one can on a scooter. I was never closer than 100 yards. It's easy to follow the only scooter on the highway. Okay, that's my report."

"Did Conners ever tell you what he wanted you to do?"

"No and I asked him before things turned bad. He said the higher ups wanted me but he didn't. He planned to make up a story of what he found out and kill or almost kill me for his made-up accusations. There's no question he knows the plan or at least the target. My mission for the IRA almost always involved casing hard targets. I have a good memory and can sketch rather well. Occasionally the mission involved direct violence but my reputation was centered on my casing ability."

"How do you suggest we interrogate Conners?"

"He's tough. But he is very afraid of water. He can't swim and is known for his fear of drowning."

Terry said, "That is a big help. I'll use a Special Forces procedure that gets good results and doesn't injure the prisoner or mark him up. All I need is a couple of towels and a bucket of water. The process works on mental fear of suffocation not pain. It is unpleasant. I know. It was used on me in a training exercise."

"Did it work on you?"

"Yes, after a number of sessions. I figured I'd held out as long as I could."

"Okay, you're on. Bernadette, can you write up a number of questions for your friend, Conners?"

"Give me ten minutes."

Peter went in the house to talk to the Nguyens. He said, "I have some bad men in the boat house that tried to capture and hurt Bernadette. They wanted her to do something she didn't want to, and they were going to rape and torture her. I captured them and now it's time to question the leader."

Mrs. Nguyen said, "I have many times questioned prisoners. If he won't answer your questions, call me. He will answer for me."

"Thank you. If he refuses to answer, I'll ask you to help."

Before the interrogation started, Terry said, "I want to see the Whaler before we start."

"Go ahead. The door is unlocked."

Terry came back 15 minutes later and said, "I got it started. Did you hear it?"

"Yes and I'll bet Conners also heard it. If your towel trick doesn't work, we can take him out in the boat. That may be more humane than turning him over to Mrs. Nguyen. Not that I care."

"It's time to introduce ourselves to Mr. Conners."

Peter opened the garage side door and turned on the lights. "There is more room in the boathouse. The door in the back of the garage leads downstairs to the boathouse. He isn't a big man. Let's take him there."

Terry said, "Bring the tape. We'll put him on the empty workbench."

Peter opened the sliding door in the VW and reached in to pull Conners out. Peter took his upper body and Bernadette pushed Terry out of the way and said, "Sorry big guy, but no lifting for you. Remember, I'm in charge of your recovery."

Starting down the set of ten stairs, Peter said, "Just drop his legs, I'll drag him down from here."

Once Conners was taped down on the workbench, Peter stripped off the duct tape over his mouth and eyes. Conners' eyes roamed around the boathouse and stopped when he saw Bernadette. He said, "You bitch, you're a dead traitor."

Peter leaned over him and slapped him hard across

the mouth and nose, which immediately caused him to bleed. Peter said, "We'll do the talking here. You talk only when we ask you a question."

Conners tried to spit in his face and Peter slapped him again harder in the same place. "Maybe you didn't understand. Do you understand now?"

Conners said, "Fuck you, whoever you are. You will also die. You don't know who you're fucking with."

"You mean the IRA? Guess what, unless you do what we tell you, your days with IRA are over."

Terry said, "Enough of his phony tough talk," and put a towel over Conners' face and began pouring salt water over the towel. After 30 seconds, Conners started to struggle. Terry poured more water on the towel. When the struggling slowed, Terry pulled off the towel. Conners gasped for air, sputtering water.

Terry said, "How about some more?" and started to put the wet towel back on.

Conners screamed, "No, no more! You people are crazy. You'll drown me!"

"Does it look like we care?" Bernadette whispered in his ear.

Peter said, "First question. Answer truthfully or the towel goes back on. Where is the rest of your group?"

"They're in a motel South on A1A toward Jacksonville."

Bernadette shook her head. Terry put the towel back on and poured more water on it. Conner began to sputter and struggle. This time Terry waited until the struggling stopped and pulled the towel off.

Conners' face was blue and for a moment Peter

thought Terry pushed it too far. Then Connors gasped, coughed, and spit up water.

Peter said, "Shall we take you closer to drowning this time? Same question, please answer."

Bernadette said, "Listen Sam. I've been with these people for several months now. They are killers. Your only chance of not being drowned is to tell them what they want. They don't care. I've seen them do this to someone a lot tougher than you who in the end told them everything they wanted. This man is now living under a different identity in South America. Do you want to drown or cooperate?"

"My people are in a trailer park on the east side of A1A going north toward St. Mary's. It's the Sunset Park. We have two big ones on the south end of the park."

Peter described the scooter couple and asked, "Are those the people?"

"Yes."

"Who else is with you?"

"No one."

Peter stepped back and nodded to Terry who stepped forward with the wet towel.

"No, no! There are two more."

"Who are they?"

"They're shooters. Bernadette knows them, Casey and O'Malley."

"When you and Harry didn't show up with Bernadette, what will your people think?"

"They'll think we took her some place to fuck her before showing up at the trailer. Where is Harry?"

"I ask the questions. Do you want the towel again?"

When Conners shook his head, Peter said, "Harry was in the back of the VW with you. Didn't you two talk?"

"I thought there was someone back there with me."

"Harry was there but he is dead now and will soon be with the sharks. You may be with him, only you won't be dead. We'll see how far you can swim with a 20-pound anchor. Not far I guess. Are you a good swimmer?"

"Christ! Don't do that to me. I'll help you."

"You had better start now. The boat is ready. Harry is waiting for you. He doesn't want to see the sharks alone. So tell me, who gives you your orders?"

"I can't do that. The lads will kill me."

Bernadette moved in close and said, "I told you he won't help. Let's put him in the boat and go finish the rest of them in the trailers."

"Okay, I guess you're right. I'll tape him up. Connors do you want to go swimming with your eyes open or taped closed?"

Conners started thrashing on the workbench, yelling "No, no please! The guy in Boston gives me orders. I check in at O'Keefe's, an Irish hangout. O'Hara is the IRA fund-raiser. He uses O'Keefe's as his headquarters."

"What does he look like?" Peter asked.

"He's a little man but mean as a snake. Has a beard and walks with a cane. Also wears glasses with no rims. He's in a back room at O'Keefe's after ten most nights."

"Maybe you *can* help," Peter said. "Now tell me exactly what orders O'Hara gave you."

"I was ordered to find Bernadette and get her to come to Boston. O'Hara said he had a job for her. If she refused to come, I was told to kill her."

"But you decided to kill me and lie about my willingness to help, right?"

"I've never trusted you. You thought you were too good for me. I was going to teach you a good lesson."

Peter said, "Never mind. What else did he tell you?"

Conners hesitated and Terry moved to put the towel over his face. Connors looked at the three of them and said, "You have to help me. If I tell you more, there is no place in the world I can live. They will find me if it takes them years. That's the way they are and always have been."

"Well, you are in a tough place, because if you don't tell me in the next minute your worries will be over." Peter then turned to Terry and said, "Will that one anchor hold them both down long enough for the sharks to eat them?"

"I think so but I'll add a heavy chain just to make sure."

Terry left to find the chain. Peter nodded at Bernadette who said, "Don't kill him before throwing him in the shark channel. I want to cut him just before we throw him overboard. The flowing blood will attract the sharks."

"NO! NO!" Conners screamed. "A bomb! bomb! I was told they would have a bomb for me to pick up and guard. The bomb was coming from a bomb factory hidden in the mountains. The Russians are involved in some way. There's a big-shot Russian, O'Hara calls him Mr. Harris, who's running the whole show. I know the RV bomb is going to be used in Washington but I don't know where."

Peter wondered if Terry or Bernadette noticed his reaction when Conners said the name Harris. His sworn enemy, Yuri Kolenko, used that alias every time he could. Yuri had to be the one involved with the bomb plot. The Harris name, Yuri's presence at the bomb factory in the West Virginia mountains, and the fact his expertise was planning and using terrorism was proof enough.

"You'd better do better than that," Peter said.

"I only know Bernadette was needed to case a building near the White House and some woman was going to drive the mobile trailer, called an RV. O'Hara brags he gets information from someone in the American Parliament and will know if they're on to us. Nothing more, I swear!"

"Okay. You won't go in the channel with Harry, but you'd better keep cooperating," Peter said.

He taped Conners' mouth and eyes and went to find Terry in the garage. Peter said, "Let's go up to the house for tea and a planning session. After that we'll take down the trailers."

Mrs. Nguyen brought out a tray of tea, biscotti, and chocolate chip cookies. Peter said, "I have an idea for the trailer people. I've checked the local maps of the general area. It doesn't lend itself to a sneak attack or a surprise attack. My main concern is that we don't get hurt or worse. Remember the Trojan horse gambit at Troy to get through the defensive barriers? Conners is our Trojan horse."

When all the details and options of Peter's plan had been gone over and everyone knew their part, Peter said,

"We have several hours before we go after the trailers. I'd like to get rid of Harry but he'll have to wait. I don't want to dump him in Nassau Sound in daylight. Too many boats on the water and too many people looking at the Inland Waterway with telescopes and binoculars. We can take care of Harry when we come back from the trailer park."

****

Just after dark, Terry parked the Ford pickup along 1A1 in a closed-up plant nursery, 100 yards south of the trailer park. Thirty minutes later he was settled in some palmettos fifty yards from the entrances of the two doublewides. Porch lights were on and he had nearly perfect line of sight with his 10x power scope on his sniper rifle, the USM40A1. *Okay*, he thought, *I'm ready. The show can start anytime.*

Terry had been in place for twenty minutes when he saw he VW camper pull into the trailer park and come to a stop near the two isolated doublewides. He heard the horn beep twice then saw the doors of both doublewides open and two people come out of each trailer and wait near the steps.

The light was going fast but with the porch lights on he was good to go. He saw Peter, wearing Harry's clothes, and supporting Bernadette who was barefooted and wearing her bikini with the top ripped in half. She hung limply between Peter and Conners. Bernadette's hands were behind her back, holding a Browning 9mm. Peter held the sound-suppressed Luger in his right hand behind Bernadette's back, and rammed against Conners' ribs.

The four people came down the steps from the small porches. The man who rode the scooter yelled, "Sam where in God's name have you been?"

Peter whispered in Bernadette's ear, "Show time. I'll take the two on the left. You have the two shooters on the right. No one is carrying a weapon. Go!"

Peter took the scooter team down in four shots, Terry hit one of the shooters, and Bernadette hit the other shooter. Bernadette, Peter, and Conners walked up to the bodies. "See, I told you I could be useful," Conners smirked.

Peter said, "Thank you," and shot him twice in the head. Bernadette dashed inside to check for any documents, maps, or sketches. Peter put the Luger in the hand of one of the shooters. He then rushed back to the VW and wiped the steering wheel, door handle, and other things he touched while driving. The VW was wiped clean back at the boathouse. Terry moved in close to guide Peter and Bernadette, wearing Peter's shirt and sandals back through the palmettos to the truck. In a quiet voice he said, "Four minutes, time to go now."

Bernadette put the Browning 9mm in the hand of the scooter driver and joined Peter and Terry moving through the brush. She had found her .45 Colt automatic on a table in the doublewide.

They were in the truck going east on the highway leading back to Amelia Island. Peter said, "I think we left a confusing crime scene for the local detectives."

"More than you think," Bernadette said. "There were

drugs inside, loose large bills in one of the bedrooms, and several weapons. A very interesting crime scene. I suspect the VW was stolen."

Peter said, "One more task. Burial at sea for Harry. I don't want Jack or Rip to find him in the boathouse. Terry, how are you holding up?"

"Tired and bit sore, but not so much I can't be your guide at night to the Nassau Channel."

Thirty-four

After resting and spending time with Jack, Rip, and Bernadette and getting a good sleep, Peter eased out of bed at 6:00AM Monday. He used the bath down the hall to keep from waking Bernadette. *God, what a woman and warrior.* He'd sooner have her at his back than any man he had ever known. Terry was good, but she was better.

Peter grabbed a cup of coffee and some homemade coffee cake and slipped out the door. He needed to talk to Frank at the CIA. The information he had couldn't wait. Not having a secure line handicapped communications but he could get the most important information to him. Peter headed east on A1A, the back way to Jacksonville. He didn't want the CIA to know he spent time on Amelia Island. No one should ever completely trust an intelligence officer or the organization. They have their own set of priorities and ethics that do not always apply to their agents, which is what he was. A damn good one, he knew, but still expendable.

Peter stopped at a shopping mall in Jacksonville and called Frank. Frank's secretary answered, and when he gave her the name Frank had given him, he was put through immediately.

Frank said, "You're up early."

"Yes. I've been a bit busy and have some very timely information."

"Okay. I'm ready. I'm going to record this if you agree."

"And if I don't you will anyway."

"In most cases that would be true but I'm under the strictest orders to do what you want and never to make any effort to locate you. Your performance has earned that respect."

"Okay. On Tuesday morning a team of IRA killers tried to kidnap, torture, and kill one of my people. Those killers are now all dead. During an interrogation of the head man, whose real name is Sam Conners, we learned he took his orders from an IRA fund-raiser with the name O'Hara who used a back room at O'Keefe's in Boston for his headquarters and that his mission was to kidnap and bring my person to D.C. to case some federal building near the White House. When he got back in Washington he was to pick up and guard an RV full of explosives from a bomb-building site in the mountains of West Virginia. The bomb-building site and this operation had KGB support. A Russian using the name Harris is in charge, according to Sam Conners.

"When Conners expressed some concern over the high-risk of a bombing in Washington, D.C., O'Hara said, 'Not to worry, I have a source in the American Parliament who will alert me if anyone is on to us.'

"Conners was frightened. The interrogation was

quite skillful. I have no doubt he was telling the truth. Which brings me to the question, did information about my last operation in West Virginia go to anyone in the Congress?"

"The honest answer is I don't see how. But I will check as soon as I hang up. Call me back in twenty minutes."

"If you want us involved further, please tell me then."

****

Frank called back right on time. He said, "No information had gone anywhere yet about West Virginia. My boss, whom you met, wants you and anyone with you who understands the IRA to please come to Washington. This is a very serious plot, and we have no one who is as up to date as you and your people."

"We could save time and fly up but you would have to provide us with equipment, including weapons. Can you do that?"

"Yes. What will you need?"

"Three Browning 9mm with sound suppressors. Each with four magazines. One AR-15 and one sniper rifle, preferably a US M40A1. A couple of car-tracking beacons, five short-range push-to-talk radios. Three protective vests, two large, one medium. A half-dozen concussion grenades. One night vision unit. Two sets of cop flash credentials with a blank place for thumbnail photos. One small motorized 35 mm camera. That's it."

"Good list. We can do it. Where do you want it?"

"I'll tell you later. We'll be there tomorrow. I'll

check in. In the meantime you have in your legislature a Congressional Committee called the HPSCI that oversees the government's intelligence activities. You might check the Committee roster for Irish names and any recent, last five years, travel to Ireland. Also anyone supporting Irish causes."

"Okay. I'll do that myself."

"That's all I have. Goodbye."

Thirty-five

The United Airlines flight from Jacksonville to Dulles International Airport touched down smoothly on the long runway and the shuttle bus moved them to main terminal. Peter went to pick up the Ford wagon rental, leaving Bernadette and Terry with the luggage.

Traffic was surprisingly light and they made good time to the Washington Hotel near Tysons Corner. Bernadette was elated to be back in the same suite. Terry said, "This is good. I like your style. If you two young and uninjured people don't mind, the old man is going to rest a bit. Something tells me the next few days are going to be long and hard. So carry on. Wake me if you need me."

"I understand old men need their rest. Bernadette and I will be doing some shopping in the mall. We may wake you for dinner."

Walking through Bloomingdale's, Peter took Bernadette's arm and said, "You are beautiful and deserve to have some matching clothes for Boston. It will be cold and damp. And we will be moving in some so-called elegant circles and you should have clothes to

278

fit the occasion. Pick some that change your appearance, so if we run into any IRA veterans they won't recognize you. I noticed that I have to listen hard to hear your accent. Your cover story is that you are studying political and cultural history of the Sub-Continent and are planning a field trip to Mohenjo-Daro and Harappa. That will make most people's eyes blink."

"Lover, you have impressed me again. I had no idea you even knew anything about ancient civilizations in India and Pakistan."

"So let's dress you up as a snooty intellectual with an artsy flair."

"I like that. I'm ready to get all tarted up."

Two hours later, Bernadette finished shopping and met Peter at the store's main entrance. His call to Frank hadn't taken long, and the equipment he wanted was in a self-storage facility in Vienna, just a few miles west of McLean. The storage facility was locked with a combination lock, making two-way exchanges easy. Also the site had few cameras, none aimed at entrance to unit 273. Frank also put some information he dug up in with the weapons and other equipment.

Peter decided there wasn't much to move from the storage unit into the Ford wagon. *Bernadette and I can handle it and let Terry rest. He is not back to his fighting level of strength and energy. Those two bullet wounds took a lot out of him.* Peter also suspected that Terry was deeply concerned about his tentative handling of the woman who shot him.

The situation in Boston may be very violent. O'Hara, the IRA fund-raiser, will have a couple of hardcore shooters handy, and my KGB nemesis Yuri Kolenko, using the name Harris, must be the Russian in touch with O'Hara. I want to have another chance at Yuri.

Bernadette and Peter picked up the supplies and weapons from the storage site and headed back to the hotel. Not only had Frank delivered everything they asked for, he had it all wrapped in various sizes of cardboard boxes. Peter pulled a tarp over the cargo and had no worries about parking the wagon in the hotel parking building.

Back in their suite, Peter studied the file Frank included with the weapons while Bernadette went to check on Terry.

The attached unsigned memo read like it was written with the carefree but intense style of Frank's boss. He must be one of those people who write like they speak. The memo said the mission in Boston was to find evidence linking the IRA fund-raiser and terrorist to anyone in Congress. The Russian, Harris, was also a high priority. No violence was required but no one would miss O'Hara or any of his people if things got rough. Peter was asked to call in any leads they uncovered to anyone in Congress that was or is in contact with O'Hara in any way. The attached brown envelope contained photos of O'Hara, regular patrons, and O'Keefe's Pub, where O'Hara had set up his headquarters. Photos of the building were from the street and inside, including shots of both sides of the street for a block. There was also a blueprint of the entire three-story building and a detailed street map of the area around O'Keefe's. An internal envelope contained two sets of cop credentials that identified the carriers as Federal Investigators.

Just as Peter finished going through file, Bernadette and Terry came in. He handed her the file. She spread it out on the dining table so Terry could see it. A quick examination and she said, "You have some powerful and competent friends. This is an excellent casing file. I couldn't do any better myself. Will there be any on-the-ground support?"

"No. As far as I know, we are it. They do stress that the mission is collection, but if it turns violent we defend and withdraw. They don't want any of us to get hurt."

"Everybody get a good night's sleep. Tomorrow just after a 0800 breakfast, we start off for Boston. We'll stay in a downtown hotel with good security and look at O'Keefe's tomorrow night. To get the evidence we need, I see no alternative to breaking into O'Hara's office very early in the morning. So we'll be checking out door locks, alarm systems, cameras and guards, including dogs."

October 22, 1977

The eight-hour trip passed quickly. Terry slept in the back. Peter and Bernadette took turns behind the wheel. They stopped once for gas and a pit stop. The hotel had provided Peter with one of their excellent travel lunches. By 6 PM, they were checked into an old but classy hotel in the historical section and ready to do a shopping walk-by on State Street and check out O'Keefe's.

Some time before 9 PM, Bernadette would go inside and get a table and tell the waiter that she was expecting two more for dinner. Fifteen minutes later, Peter and Terry would join her and order dinner. Peter had a motorized Olympia camera that he could conceal in his palm and shoot pictures with a high-speed black and white film.

Their first pass of O'Keefe's was made from across State Street. Bernadette said, "It looks like a bit of Ireland was just dropped into Boston. Even the specials displayed in the windows look authentic."

After an hour of casual shopping, Bernadette walked out of a shop alone and made her way into O'Keefe's. It was already getting crowded and a band had just started to play. Bernadette thought, *This place is out of my recent past except I never had these upscale clothes and the cash to bribe the maître d's to give a single woman a booth when the restaurant was nearly filled. I can even hear people speaking my mother tongue. If this is an IRA hangout, I haven't recognized anyone yet. This booth is perfect for casing this place.*

She settled into the booth. *I'm a bit worried about Terry. He seems to be a long way from the way he was before he was shot. Some of the older IRA cadre talked about losing their edge as the years passed. One of them said, as long as you recognize you've not got the same quick reactions, you can make do. If you don't see what's happening with age, you'll get someone or yourself killed. In truth, I no longer trust Terry to have my back or Peter's.*

Just then, she saw Terry and Peter come in. She waved and they started over. *Peter looks so handsome in his tweed jacket. Terry's bomber jacket sort of hangs on him. He has lost some muscle mass.*

"Well, how are you, pretty lady? Bernadette, you really brighten up this corner." Peter slid in the booth beside her and Terry took the other side of the booth facing the bar. The waitress hurried over and took their order for Guinness drafts. While waiting for the drafts, Terry announced he was going for the Shepherd's pie, Peter said, "Sounds good to me." Bernadette said, "The corned beef special for me."

"Bernadette, how does this place fit the real Irish scene?" Peter asked.

"It is right on and I mean right on. No wonder it's an IRA watering hole."

"Do you see any one you recognize?"

"Only one, I think I've seen the big man at the bar who's nearly bald somewhere before."

Bernadette quickly turned her head to face Peter and said, "I spoke too soon. I know the three coming in the door now, two men and a woman. The woman is Mary Callahan. If she sees me, she will recognize me and come over. Terry, you are my uncle and Peter's a new boyfriend. She will believe me and want to talk to me later. She has an uncanny eye for sensing money. My clothes, jewelry, and Peter's outfit and Rolex watch will be noticed and immediately filed in her gold-digging head. She is a known IRA groupie and has slept with more men than most girls for hire."

"As long as my body is screening you, I don't think she will see you. When she moves away, I'm going back to the men's room to take a look at the entrance door to O'Hara's office," Peter said.

The waitress came up to take their dinner order, providing additional screen for Bernadette. By the time they finished ordering, Mary and her two escorts had moved farther into the pub. Peter got up and went in search of the men's room. He found it halfway down a hallway in the very back of the club. There was a door at the end of the hall that looked to Peter like it was a door to the outside. *O'Hara must have a key to the outside door and the only other door, halfway down the hall, must be the door to his headquarters.*

He could see no cameras or sensor systems. The lock seemed similar to the outside door lock, which was a deadbolt type lock. *When O'Hara's in residence, there would probably be a guard in the hallway, watching both doors. A real problem,* he thought. *If we go in while he is in the office, there is bound to be a gunfight. We would win but the consequences may be bad. Cops would be here quickly and take everyone who might have been involved into custody.*

He had seen all he needed and made his way through the crowd to their booth. He saw Mary and her group at a table near to the hallway corner he had just cased. *If Bernadette comes this way, Mary will see her for sure.*

Back at the table, Peter said, "Okay. Here's the way it is going down." He explained the layout he had seen and compared it to the blueprint Frank gave him. It all checked out. The end door was an outside door and the other door led to a two-room suite. When Terry and Bernadette were familiar with the layout, Peter said, "I'll call the waitress over and pay the bill, leaving a big enough tip to let Terry keep the booth and order a dessert. Bernadette and I will go out and down the alley to the outside door.

"Bernadette will cover me while I open the lock. We'll go inside and I'll open the door to O'Hara's office. Terry gives us five minutes and then goes back to the men's room. By that time, Bernadette and I should be in O'Hara's office. If anyone comes in and heads for the office door, follow them and push in behind them. We will hear the door bang against a chair I put there and come to the door with guns out. Kill anyone who looks like they are going to be a problem. We'll use our cop credentials if we have to. Anyone who surrenders, we can tie up and leave. But we can't leave anyone alive who's recognized Bernadette.

"Your friend Mary and her crowd would see you for sure if you walked to the back of the bar. Okay, here comes our waitress. The clock is ticking."

Peter and Bernadette were out the door before Terry's dessert arrived. They were outside the alley door to O'Keefe's forty-five seconds later. Bernadette stood with her back to the wall beside the door, partially screening a crouching Peter from anyone looking down the alley from State Street. He said, "A few more seconds."

"You don't have any more time. Here comes trouble. Three young men think we're an easy mugging. They'll be here in five seconds. Pin me against the wall like you're fucking me. I'll pull up my skirt. The sight will put them off guard. When they get up close, I'll moan as the signal for you to show them they had a bad idea."

The leader of the three stopped and said, "Will you look at the legs on that bitch? Bet her tits are world class. Let's have a closer look."

As they moved in close, Bernadette moaned and Peter spun and drove the heel of his right hand into to the chest of the nearest attacker but not hard enough to kill him. Bernadette took advantage of her legs free of her skirt to hit the second attacker in the side of his head with a sweeping inside crescent kick. Peter put the last one down with a neck lock that shut off the flow of blood to the brain. He would wake up in a few minutes with a sore neck and headache.

Bernadette helped Peter drag the three unconscious muggers behind a dumpster. He ripped their pants and shoes off and threw them in the dumpster and said, "By the time they get moving, we will be inside. Our five minutes is almost up."

When Peter eased the door open, he could see Terry standing near the ladies' room like he was waiting for his woman to come out. It took Peter less than 30 seconds to open the office door. Inside he relocked the door, put a chair up against the doorknob, and joined Bernadette in searching the office. There were no windows so they felt comfortable switching on one light at a time. Bernadette quickly found a wall safe but both knew there wasn't enough time to even try to open it. Instead they concentrated on the two four-drawer file cabinets whose locks were simple.

Peter found two empty cardboard boxes and began dumping any documents that looked important into the boxes. He wanted to be in and out in no more than five minutes. They were pushing the time. Without getting into the safe, they had done all they could. Peter called to Bernadette it was time to break off and leave.

They each picked up a box and headed for the door when they heard the door being unlocked. Peter moved the chair he had placed under the doorknob. The door swung open and several men started to enter. Peter and Bernadette flanked the door. There was a sudden commotion at the door as Terry charged, pushing everyone inside. The group was surrounded by three people pointing guns at them. Peter spoke, "No talking. Anyone even looking like they are reaching for a weapon will die. Everyone on the floor face down. We're just looking for a chance to kill you. Don't give it to us."

Bernadette pointed out O'Hara. Peter walked over to where he was lying uncomfortable on the floor and showed his I.D. that he was a federal agent. He then grabbed O'Hara by the front of his suit coat and pulled him to his feet. When he had O'Hara away from the others, he said, "I'm going to give you two minutes to open your safe. If you don't, I'll put the first slug in your knee and go on from there until it is open. You won't be alive if the safe doesn't get open in two minutes."

"You don't scare me. The FBI does not operate like that."

Peter chuckled, "We are nothing like the FBI. I don't intend to arrest you if you cooperate. That's the good news. The bad news is if you don't cooperate you will die or almost die, depending on how I feel. Now open the safe."

O'Hara hesitated and Peter shoved the sound suppressor on his 9mm hard into O'Hara's throat, just under his chin. He looked hard at O'Hara and said,

"Last chance."

O'Hara moved to open the safe, and it was open in less than 30 seconds. Peter put O'Hara back on the floor and not very gently. After dumping the contents of the wall safe in one of the boxes, Terry and Peter collected wallets from all the men. Bernadette was out in the hall. O'Hara hadn't gotten a good look at her.

Bernadette and Terry, carrying the boxes, went out the back door to the Ford wagon. Peter stayed behind to give them more time for the getaway. He pulled the phone out of the wall and took all the car keys. The door to the office required a key to open from either side. Seeing two of the guns had left the room, one very big man started to get up. Peter hit him behind the neck with an axe kick that drove him back on the floor. No one else moved. Peter took a picture of each man, then left, locking the door from the outside with O'Hara's key.

The wagon was standing by to pick him up as he left the alley. As Peter got in the car, he was smiling. Bernadette knew what he was smiling about. She, too, had seen the three muggers dumpster diving for their shoes and pants. They wouldn't forget attacking the romantic couple in the alleyway.

Thirty-six

October 23, 1977

The return trip to Tysons Corners in Virginia was even easier than trip up to Boston. The stress was gone. The operation had gone smoothly. Their adjustment to unforeseen events was nearly flawless. No one got hurt, not even the muggers. They will never know that they had flirted with death and escaped. During the entire fight, both Peter and Bernadette had weapons ready to fire in their hands.

Peter and Bernadette had quickly scanned the boxes of documents. They found nothing about a terrorist attack on the Old Executive Office building next to the White House and under White House Secret Service protection. Nor did they find anything about Soviet involvement. But Terry noted one of the wallets taken from the men on the floor contained an I.D. badge to the House of Representatives.

Peter talked to Frank at the CIA and told him the borrowed equipment and their take from O'Hara's office were put in the same storage unit, and he and his team were leaving the area. Twenty minutes after his call they were in the Red Carpet Lounge waiting for their flight to

Jacksonville to be called.

Terry said, "This anti-terrorist stuff is picking up. First-class travel, luxury hotels, great food, and moments of action to escape the boredom of peaceful living."

"Terry, God bless you, but I'm ready for a big chunk of peaceful living. It's good to see you back. I was worried about you going up to Boston," said Peter.

"So was I. I had lost my confidence in tight situations over my stupidity in getting shot and damn near killed. I'm over that now and feel good."

"Amen. I was also more than worried. I wanted my Uncle Terry back. You know, the one who walked without fear."

As their flight descended into Jacksonville Airport, Bernadette put her head on Peter's shoulder and said, "Maybe the IRA threat can be put behind us now. What do you think?"

"Maybe so but let's keep our guard up for a while longer. My enemies will never give up looking for me. But I think I have lost them for now."

Bernadette pulled the Cadillac up two blocks from Terry's condo. Terry had only light luggage and had drilled her into following a security protocol. "Never be so careless that someone watching this condo, which was also your address of record, could connect you to the Brandon house," Terry had told her multiple times.

It bothered her that while Terry was going in to an empty house, she and Peter were going to a home that was filled with love, noise, and laughter with a few barks thrown in.

October 24, 1977

The next morning Peter and Bernadette slept in. They awoke when Mrs. Nguyen brought in coffee with fresh baked biscuits, bacon, and medium poached eggs. Peter was on his second cup of coffee when he switched on the morning news. He was half following a shooting and a fire in Fernandina Beach when he realized the local anchor was talking about Terry's condo. People had called in a 911 report of gunfire very early in the morning.

When the 911 calls brought the police, they found two dead men in the entrance hall, another one on the staircase and a fire rapidly gaining headway. The fire department couldn't save the house. Arson is suspected. All three men were found with weapons. "No identities as yet, but the condo is owned by a Mr. Terry O'Brien," the TV reporter said.

Peter rushed into the bathroom and got Bernadette out of the shower. When she said, "What?" Peter said, "Come quick, look at the TV! Some people killed Terry last night! His condo has burned to a gutted shell. The reporter said two dead armed men were found in the entranceway."

Bernadette screamed, "The bastards were after me and killed Terry to satisfy their crazy code! I'll find them and kill every last one."

"Yes! But not now! I won't let you throw your life away. Terry died for you and me. Don't let him down by making his sacrifice in vain. He wanted to give you

291

a chance to live. You have that now. Respect him as a great warrior who loved you. He died a warrior's death. He took at least two of them with him."

"Oh, Peter! Will they never let me be? If I had stayed in Ireland with the IRA, Terry would be alive right now." Bernadette, still wrapped in a towel, dropped to the floor with her head in her hands.

"No. It just doesn't work like that," Peter said, rushing to hold her. "First, Terry wouldn't hesitate a second over giving his life for yours. Keep the good and happy memories of your remarkable uncle. What do you think Terry did for a living? He constantly put his life on the line to perform some mission or other. Some worth it, some not.

"Protecting you was the best mission he ever had. I want you to remember your uncle was a true hero and he loved you. His sacrifice caused your enemies to fail. Let's keep it that way. Terry made many serious enemies in his decades of military and security work. I think the IRA was behind this, but we can't be sure now. It is time to wait and let them thrash around looking for someone they now will never find. That is victory. That is a gift Terry gave you."

****

No one from the Brandon house attended Terry's funeral service. Peter knew the IRA could have someone there taking pictures. Bernadette was upset by not being able to get some closure from Terry's military funeral. His remains were interred at Arlington.

Thirty-seven

Early November

Peter made arrangement to close up the Florida house. In early November, Peter, Bernadette, Jack and Rip went to the cabin to rest and recover from Terry's death. Bernadette always felt safer at the cabin. Bernadette and Peter placed a bronze plaque inside the hidden room Terry helped build to honor his life of service. The Nguyens stayed behind to complete the job and take their own brief vacation before joining the family at the Pennsylvania cabin.

Living in the Pennsylvania Allegheny Mountains in the winter left little time for remorse. Peter was in charge of cutting and hauling wood to heat the cabin. Bernadette helped him and did all the cleaning and cooking with Jack's help. Mostly, Jack and Rip romped in the snow and slid down the hill on a small toboggan Peter bought in Somerset. Rip wouldn't get on the toboggan but loved to chase it down the hill and jump on Jack at the bottom. The Nguyens arrived three weeks later, just in front of a big snowstorm. They went right to work.

As soon as the roads opened up and Peter had cleared the driveway with his new John Deere tractor, he decided to leave Jack and Rip with the Nguyens and take Bernadette to visit Terry's gravesite in Arlington. He also made an appointment to see Lee Jensen in McLean. After some serious thought, he and Bernadette had decided maybe McLean would be a good place to settle, so he had asked Lee to keep his eyes open for a house with some land.

It was a four-hour road trip from the cabin to McLean in good weather. In their new Jeep station wagon they made good time over the snow-covered roads. Near Tysons Corner, they checked into a Marriot Hotel. The next day was overcast and threatened additional snow. Arlington Cemetery was a lonely, forlorn place. It fit their mood. They found Terry's grave after a little trouble and Bernadette knelt and talked to her Uncle Terry while quietly sobbing. When she finished, Peter took her arm and they walked back to the Jeep.

After lunch at the McLean Deli, they went to Lee's office. Lee told Bernadette how sorry he was about Terry. "Terry saved my life in Vietnam more than once. He was a great and compassionate warrior and the nation needs more people like him."

Lee told them Peter's seed money had turned into a fortune. A number of technical IPOs they had heavily invested in had paid off far beyond expectations. Lee had managed to convert half of the diamonds into cash through several steps. Peter was now a legitimate businessman with real tax obligations!

Lee also had some houses he wanted to show them.

Both of them loved the second house they saw, which overlooked the McLean Public Library with an acre of fenced land backing up to a local park. Peter told Lee to make it happen.

After making arrangements for a move into the new house in a few months and playing tourist in Washington, Peter and Bernadette drove back to the mountain cabin. The day was sunny and bright. Bernadette was able to smile and laugh again. Both felt the imminent danger they had been living with had faded into the background.

Jack, Rip, Peter, and Bernadette thrived that long winter in the cabin. The Nguyens soon had the cabin running like a resort. All were excited to move into the McLean house. Peter told Jack he would now have other kids to play with and a good school to go to. Jack asked, "What about Rip?"

Bernadette said, "Rip will have a big place to run and he will guard us just like he does now. There will be a swimming pool next summer and you can help build it. And I'll be going to school at American University where I'll learn about people and things in South Asia. A long way from here. On the other side of the world. Someday we will all make a trip to India and Nepal."

Peter knew he was committed to helping his new country. The haul from O'Hara's office led to the CIA identification of the traitor congressman who was now doing time. O'Hara had been deported and the bomb plot stopped. A sharp note to the Soviets destroyed Yuri's career, and he was recalled to Moscow.

Peter and Bernadette had talked over many issues, all of them related to their future together. Bernadette, with the wisdom of the Irish said, "When the time comes, the way will be clear. For now, let's enjoy what we have. It has never been better for me." Peter quietly and gently took her into his arms, held her tightly, and said, "Amen."

The prologue to Barry Kelly's first novel, "Justice Beyond Law"

December

Arthur Cohen, Congressman from New York's 10th District, was anxious to begin his usual morning run. Everyone else in the Cohen house was still sleeping, at least in the case of his wife, Shara, who liked waking up softly, especially since their third child was expected late next month. Without his workout he had trouble concentrating on the minutiae of constituent problems. They invaded his time to work on new legislation. At 7:15 a.m. the world looked good. The weather forecast was for a bright sunny early winter day. The first rays of light made the forecast look good. The coolness of the night still prevailed and wafted around him like a cocoon as his ten-minute-a-mile stride carried him down the slope to the C&O Canal. The dirt path along the canal was the best place he had ever found to run. It was good for his over-forty knees. He often felt he could run forever along the canal. This morning he would run for exactly another twelve minutes and ten seconds, and his life would end.

Just before first light Jason settled himself into his shooting position and waited for his target to come striding down the canal path. It wouldn't be long now. In the distance Jason could see a few runners approaching. Runners all have distinctive styles. Jason saw the blue and white warm-up suit come in view. The second runner was his mark, but to be sure Jason used his binoculars to compare the runner to the photo his Control had given him. It was a match. For the last two mornings from his carefully chosen shooting position, he had watched the congressman run along the tow path. Jason liked punctual targets. He had one here. Right on time. The light was good. At one hundred meters he would fire one round into Cohen's chest. Then he planned to hit two more people among the cyclists, runners, and dog walkers to confuse the police and worry the local population.

Jason was concealed near the top of a steep bank. He had a clear view of the canal path. His getaway car was parked just off MacArthur Boulevard, a short walk from his ambush site. The weapon, a Steyr-Mannlicher SSG-69, when broken down could be concealed under his long dark coat. Although Jason was over sixty, he was a born hunter with steady hands and a keen eye. Jason's spare frame carried the same weight it had decades ago when he came across the Canadian border. Nothing about him stood out.

The perfect kill was always easier than the perfect escape. The target neared the stone he had placed to mark the distance. Cohen's left foot landed beside the hundred meter marking stone at the same instant Jason fired his first round. He hit Arthur Cohen in the middle of the chest. Cohen took one more half-step and fell on his face. No one paid any attention to the partially silenced first shot.

Jason held his position and selected the next target, a tall blond ponytailed runner with a near perfect stride, who had been gaining steadily on the blue and white warm up suit. Ponytail saw Cohen fall and broke her stride. Sighting on her upper right thigh, Jason's second shot knocked her down within three feet of his kill. As other runners and bikers seeing the blood and the downed figures scrambled for cover, Jason, secure behind a screen of dead wild grapevines, selected a young male cyclist on a silver racing bike and shot him high on the right shoulder. The bike swerved and plunged into the shallow canal, causing more chaos.

Jason picked up the three brass casings, smoothed out the impressions made in his ambush position, and then worked his way back up the slope, wiping out all traces of his movements.

Jason didn't mind killing. These people were all enemies, and the mission came straight from Moscow. He would just as soon have killed everyone on the canal trail, but he always followed orders. Jason did not hurry. It would be ten minutes before the first District of Columbia police car and an emergency medical unit arrived on the scene and by then he would be part of the morning traffic headed north around the beltway. In two hours Jason would be back on Tilghman Island on the eastern shore of the Chesapeake Bay, secure in his job as an owner-operator of a small marina. He would call his Control as soon as he turned off 495. This job was worth a nice sized bonus.

About the Author

Barry Kelly is no stranger to the world of espionage, counter-terrorism, weapons, martial arts, clandestine tradecraft, deep cover, black operations, para-military operations and the inner workings of the governmental security apparatus. Twenty-seven years of government service provided hands-on experience in all these areas. His immersion in the Cold War began with enlistment in the U.S. Navy during the Korean War. A magna cum laude BA from The University of Pittsburgh and a master's degree from Duke University, through the James B. Duke Fellowship Program, followed his discharge from the Navy.

Kelly's experience at CIA included deep cover operations, a wide spectrum of agent operations, overseas experience, primarily in South and Southeast Asia, a tour as the Station Chief in Moscow, TDY excursions to the Middle East and the Far East. A volunteer assignment in Vietnam resulted in the award of two medals by the Government of South Vietnam for service in the five northern provinces, one of which is The Cross of Gallantry with Silver Star. The author held command positions in three Directorates of the CIA. He was awarded the Certificate of Merit with Distinction, the Intelligence Medal of Merit, the Distinguished Intelligence Medal and the first Intelligence Officer of the Year Award.

After retirement from CIA, Kelly responded to a call from the White House to fill a position on the National Security Staff as Special Assistant to President Reagan in the last two years of his administration. He was responsible for all intelligence activities and operations, including counter-terrorism and covert action. In this position, he chaired the weekly meetings of the top counter-terrorism committee in the government.

Barry Kelly has had a lifelong interest in martial arts. He holds a first Dan Black Belt in Hap-ki-do. Born in Western Pennsylvania, he now lives with his wife, Joan, in South Carolina, a true warrior state where service in the CIA is honored.

PROSE PRESS

The origin of the word prose is Latin, prosa oratio, meaning straightforward discourse.

Prose Press is looking for stories with strong plots.

We offer an affordable, quality publishing option with guaranteed worldwide distribution.

Queries: E-mail only.

prose-cons@outlook.com

CPSIA information can be obtained at www.ICGtesting.com
Printed in the USA
LVOW13s1311160114

369685LV00003B/22/P